Chief Inspector Mary Sweet and The Great Scottish Land Grab

By Tom Richards

First published in 2024 by Storylines Entertainment Ltd
Beara, Bantry, County Cork, Ireland P75A342

© Copyright Storylines Entertainment Ltd

and Tom Richards, 2024
All Rights Reserved

Cover by Touqeer Shahid.

Find him on fiverr.com at Touqeershahid95
Editing by Rose McSweeney

ISBN: 978-1-915959-40-9

Contents

About Chief Inspector Mary Sweet and the Great Scottish Land Grab

Mary Sweet and her Teams are ordered to go to Scotland. There, they must again stop General Gusto Gatwick from causing Mayhem, including death and destruction, to the Ancient Scottish Clans. Inspired by a true story of Scottish history, Mary and her Teams must learn to go back in time to chase the General and his Spies across Scotland. They must stop them from invading England and killing the ancient English King which rules there.

General Gusto also harnesses a Space Time Machine and plans to destroy England by going back in time by 600 years. Using Radiation Poisoning by placing assorted chemicals in the King's wine, they change his DNA so that he will produce only disfigured Royal Children. By doing this dastardly deed, General Gusto knows that England will be defeated by other nations throughout all history. In contemporary times, General Gusto is certain that the Putin Russian Government and their allies will win the next Global War. With Putin finally dead, General Gusto will become Emperor of a New World Order.

Mary Sweet and her Team's primary Mission is to make certain that General Gusto is stopped before he threatens the present world order. Another Mad Caper from the Author of The Madness of Chief Inspector Mary Sweet, this rollicking historical crime caper will have readers turning pages one after the other after the other until The End.

Dedicated to:

Carol Elizabeth Winkler, and how Overjoyed I was
to see you at the Rolling Meadows High School 50th Reunion

&

My best friend *Elle Rose* also known as:
Michelle Leslie who is an American Detective in this
Fictional Novel

&

Mr Wil Arnold, The Original Grumpy Old Poet
who Also Makes Guest Appearance and *Julie Flynn*, a new friend
who makes a short appearance at the end of the story

And to

Mr Larry Power, finance director extraordinaire
who plays the Finance Minister to the French King

Chapter 1

The Murderous General Gatwick
Tests His Time-Travel Machine Over Loch
Ness,
the Fabled Dragon Nessie,'s Watery Home

On a cold winter night, Royal Air Force Private Sarah Scots hurried toward a Scottish Radar Station that was a critical part of NATO's defence system. Looking up at the star-studded northern skies, she noticed a line of bright white lights moving from south to north which were quickly approaching the white dome that housed the radar installation. One of them, at the end of that glowing line, pulsed red and white and then turned suddenly, now on a different trajectory. Sarah realised that unlike the other bright white lights which were in a stable orbit, this one was behaving like it was being controlled by someone on the ground.

The Private broke into a run and entered the warm confines of the radar station's command centre. As Sarah walked quickly down a quiet hallway and into a large room filled with radar monitors, she saw the Captain of the Squadron standing at the Private's assigned desk.

"Private, I see you're ten minutes early yet again," the Captain barked as she saluted him.

"One second, Sir," she replied as she quickly took her seat and switched on the large Radar Monitor. "I need to check on something urgently." Watching the screen glow white and green, and adjusting the controls, she saw a series of white Blips moving at speed toward their Radar Outpost near Stirling Hill, on the Aberdeenshire coast of North East Scotland.

"Sir, look at those," she yelped as she pointed to the screen. "I saw them just now and they were directly south of us. Now, all of those targets are passing directly overhead. In only seconds, they've travelled more miles than most satellites would."

The Captain crouched down and, when he saw them, his moustached face broke into a grave smile. "Those blips. See how equidistant they are? That's the crazy Elon Musk and his fabled line of Starlink satellites that are part of the Private Company, SpaceX. They provide Internet Communications for people living all over the world. They have a very low orbit around the Earth which is why they seem to be travelling so fast."

"Yes, sir, I understand that. But see that single Blip at the end and how it's starting to pulse much larger, and moves at different trajectories from the other satellites? Something must be wrong with that one or someone on the ground is controlling it. Sir, would you mind if I went outside to observe it with a pair of field glasses?"

"Not at all, Private. On your way back, can you please get me a hot cup of tea?"

The private left her work station and, jogging back the way she had come, borrowed a pair of field glasses from a Sargent who guarded the front door. Going outside, this time without her heavy coat, she again looked up into the nighttime sky. The bright white objects were now passing to the north like a brightly-lit toy train painted in a children's illustrated book. But as she watched, one of them turned bright red and, peeling off from the train like an out-of-control caboose, it left its position at the end of that long line and began dancing high in the sky above her head.

"What the hell is that thing doing?" she whispered to herself and, lifting the glasses to her eyes, focused on that strange object that was now jumping back and forth, with what appeared to be flames shooting from one end. "The damned thing is out of control! Sargent," she yelled back toward the open door, "get the Captain out here!"

"What's the problem, Private?" the Sargent replied as he stepped out the door into the cold night air. "Tis freezing, so it is. Even too cold for the poor deer. If you want the Captain out here, go get him yerself, Private Scots!"

Running to the non-commissioned officer, Sarah thrust the glasses into his hands. "You take a look, Sargent. That crazy thing in the sky is going to fall and when it does, someone could get killed or seriously hurt."

As the Sargent placed the cold field glasses against his eyes, the private ran back into the Radar Station. Jogging into the Radar Room, she grabbed her coat and, half-saluting the Captain who was now sitting in her chair, grabbed him by the arm. "Captain, Sir, please come with me right now! A satellite is out of control right above us and, if it falls, it could obliterate an entire village around here or our Radar Station. Sir, maybe another country is attacking us!"

The Captain ran outside with her and, grabbing the glasses from the Sargent, looked up at the strange object that was still dancing above them. "Sargent, have the Lieutenant on watch call NORAD Command. That's not a SpaceX satellite. That's gotta be some sort of missile. And look at that!" he yelled. "That damned thing is accelerating! Call the rest of our Squadron and I don't care if they're sleeping. We need every soldier here right now!"

The Sargent ran back into the Radar Station to carry out his order just as the red object above them began to streak directly north. The cold, still air filled with a huge BOOM and the Captain and Sarah heard glass shatter in the Radar Station. "That's a sonic boom, Captain," the private shouted. "That thing must be moving at more than Mach Five!"

"It's the Russians for sure, Private! They're testing their hypersonic nuclear missiles. But over Scotland? When the Prime Minister finds out, it could be War again!"

As Sarah and her Captain ran back into the Radar Station, ten miles above them and in the cold of Outer Space, a man and women sat in in two chairs in what Private Scots and her Captain had assumed was either an out-of-control satellite or a Hypersonic Missile. Protected by a Titanium Alloy hull, its shape that of a massive black and red Triangle, on the small command deck the woman jerked back and forth in her cushioned seat as she tested her craft's manoeuvrability.

"My wife, we have done it!" the former British General Gusto Gatwick, who was now a Russian General, said as he looked over to his wife who was sitting next to him. "We've gone well beyond Mach Five and have hit Mach Eight! In moments, we will create our own Black Hole and still accelerating, we will go back in time by approximately four-hundred years!"

"Don't you mean six-hundred years, my Darling?" Russian Captain Tully Gale stated from her commander's seat. "We'll be over Loch Ness in two seconds. When we cross it, people will look up and watch our fast ship disappear like we were never there."

"Wife, you are right," the Russian General said as he strapped himself tighter into his seat. "Can I do anything to help you, my love?"

"Push that Orange button when I give the command. Now. Push it!"

When the General pushed the Orange Button, he looked at the accelerometer. It showed that they were travelling now in excess of Mach Ten. "Wife, in moments we will create our own Black Hole. Hang on, my pretty. We'll begin to vibrate violently and then, all we'll see is the stars around us."

Just as the General had told her, the ship—the USSR Vladimir Putin—began to vibrate violently. The accelerometer's needle was now at its maximum speed of Mach Twenty. As the ship rocked, the two British traitors could hear the secret mechanism housed in a special compartment behind them begin to wail as it wound up to a speed only a few Russian engineers had ever witnessed. Every light on the Command Deck went out. The vibration turned more violent and General Gusto and Captain Gale were pushed forward and back in their specially-designed seats until they thought they would pass out or die. The vibration began to subside and the General tapped the protective plastic covering the accelerator as their ship began to slow significantly.

Looking back through the small window that led to the Specialised Black Hole Compartment, Gusto laughed as he witnessed a small black object begin to grow. Looking at the monitor above him that showed the exterior of the vessel's hull, his face grew white as he saw a whirling black object divided by a bright white line emerge from the rear of the vessel and begin to engulf it.

"Look at the bright line! That's the Event Horizon. Soon, our ship will plunge through it and that's when our onboard clock will show that we're going back in time."

"My General! Look at that!" Captain Gale said with wonder in her voice. As the two watched, they saw an entire Galaxy appear around them as the entire hull that surrounded them became transparent. "According to our advanced calculations and timeline, we have now plunged through the Event Horizon and are in the centre of the Milky Way Galaxy. Soon, according to our scientists and astrophysicists, we will turn one-hundred and eighty degrees within this small Black Hole and accelerate back to Earth in only minutes."

"Look at our onboard clock!" Gusto gasped as he watched the digital instrument's red numbers turn back. "See how the clock is moving back quicker and quicker! We're going back in time so fast we can't even see the individual numbers anymore."

Just as Captain Gale had predicted, the entire vessel began to shake again but this time at a much lower velocity, as their Hypersonic Ship turned around and pointed back at Earth. Through the transparent hull, Gusto and Tully watched the stars turn around them and the two could again feel the force of acceleration on their uniformed bodies.

"Just as you anticipated, my good wife," the General said as, around them, the stars disappeared and the hull was visible again. "In moments, we'll be back over Scotland. Then you'll fire our retro-rockets and we'll land safe and sound."

"That's exactly right, my wonderful husband," Captain Gale said as once again, she scanned the instrument panel. "When I give the command, press the Green Button this time. That will slow us with our nuclear rockets. Our specialised heat shield will protect us and our ship as we descend again to Scotland."

"The accelerometer now reads Mach Eleven, my sweet. Is that the speed you predicted we'd be at now?"

"Yes, precisely," she said and, smiling at him, looked again at the stop watch hanging directly above her. "Four, three, two, one. PUSH the Green Button!"

When the General did, their Command Deck once again started to vibrate just as violently as when they'd left the Earth. Now, looking down on their planet through a windshield that no longer was protected by the titanium special alloy mixture that the Russian engineers had developed, the General's face was one of pure awe. "Look! There are no lights on the planet anywhere!"

"How could there be, husband General? If we've gone back in time, electricity hasn't yet been developed. Now, in three seconds push the Red Button. Those are for the standard retro-rockets that will assist us in our final descent. Two, one. Push!"

The General did as he was instructed. The accelerometer's needle moved down to Mach Two and, as it did, the General and Captain Gale could see a dark land mass emerge from the clouds directly below them. "That's it, my General. We're right on course. There is Scotland as it was hundreds of years ago."

As their craft moved through the atmosphere, the General and his wife could see the cloud around them part as if a wave of pure energy had hit them. "There's the sonic boom again," the General said as the ship's vibration stopped for a final time. "What are those brown specs below us? Cattle?"

"Horses, my love. Scottish horses. With men sitting on them."

"Scottish or English warriors, my dear? We must talk to the English first. We must give them all of our many powers. That is, of course, our single Mission. To let the English take over all of Scotland six-hundred years before Russia lost the War to that bitch Chief Inspector Sweet and her band of fools. By doing that, by helping England's early King, we'll make sure that modern England is a weak nation forever! The English will spend all of their time and resources fighting the Scots and other nations and, by changing modern history, our proud Mother Country, Mother Russia, will defeat not only that Chief Inspector, but also the English, the French, America and the rest of the world!"

"Yes, my dear. That will happen when we give the English our many dangerous and fatal gifts including Radiation Poisoning. By doing that, the English Kings, their sons, daughters, relatives and their many wives will bear nothing but idiots for Royal Children! Which will, of course, destroy all of the British Royal lines and England will be decimated by any nation that wants to conquer it! Or a man like me!"

As the two laughed hysterically at the final outcome of their Mission, below the decelerating ship a troop of English soldiers all on horseback trotted along the green grass that lined Loch Ness.

"Good Gawd in Heaven!" a man shouted as the entire troop of soldiers heard a noise that was louder than the guns they had heard when they were at war with the Spaniards. "Look up, men, and that's an order!"

As they looked up, they all beheld a streak of light. "Tis a Heavenly Angel, so it is," a Scottish captive with long, dark, braided hair said to the English Captain. "We'd best get off the horses now and kneel before something so Infinitely Almighty as what we now see above us."

"Tis no Angel, you Scots captive," the Captain roared at the man who he would soon sell as a slave. "Get off that horse, anyway! You're a slave now, and ye can walk all the way back to Londontown."

The captive did as he was bid. Looking up again, he saw the streak of light growing brighter and brighter. "Captain, that be no Angel. 'Tis a fair comet, me-thinks, come to turn you and your troops into dust for me and my Scots Clan to walk on."

Jumping down from the horse, the captive, William Wallace MacSquat, picked up a sharp stone as the Captain and his troops still looked up at the bright object descending toward them. Taking careful aim at the English Officer's head, William threw it with all his might. Hitting his target, the Captain fell from his horse and, as the troops pulled their swords, Wallace began to run toward the lake of Loch Ness as fast as he could.

It's coming down at us!" an English soldier roared. "The Heavenly thing must be angry because it is throwing it's hot breath at us."

As William stopped and looked back, a black and red object shaped like a triangle fell toward the ground and the fire roaring out of its orange mouth enveloped the ground below it in flames. The soldiers and their horses began to burn and, as Wallace dived into the cold waters of Loch Ness, he could feel the heat all around him as the lake began to boil.

Surfacing after minutes holding his breath, he waded to the closest shore and, watching intently, saw a door open on the strangely-shaped thing. When two people dressed in black and red came out, he blessed himself and, looking to Heaven, began laughing.

"Now, that must be two English rotters from Hell come to starve us with a new kind of flying dragon that eats men and its own kind!" Wallace said as he tread water in the large Scottish lake. "I surely to God wish the Loch Ness Monster was here with her entire family. Oh, that my great friend Nessie would help me fight these English Divils. She could feast on the flesh of those strangely-dressed bastards while I would swim off in search of my father and my Clan."

Pulling himself into a standing position, now knee-deep in water, Wallace watched as the two Evil English soldiers came down a silver ladder and stood on Scottish soil. "Bastards they be!" Wallace whispered through clenched teeth. "Oh, that I'd a sword in my hand! I'd skewer them and feed 'em either to Nessie or the Loch Ness fish! Now it's time for me to escape from here because this unarmed Scotsman has no weapon to hand. I'll leave those Englishmen for now but soon, they'll be dead men just like that Captain who captured me and his soldiers are."

Swimming out into the great Lake, he dived beneath the surface and found what looked like a large fish swimming toward him. When they came face-to-face, Wallace smiled at his Loch Ness friend. "Why if it isn't Nessie," the man burbled under the water to the legendary sea monster. "You must have heard me. There be a meal or two for you on the shore just behind me."

As Wallace swam on, the Monster called Nessie swam toward the shore. Raising it small head on a long, thin neck, it saw two creatures moving toward it on small legs.

Standing near their Hypersonic craft, Tully Gale pointed to the nearby lake. "Gusto, look at that! What is it?"

Gusto Gatwick turned around and looked toward the immense Scottish Loch. When he saw a green monster looking down on him and his flabbergasted wife, he thought he'd never seen anything so terrifying in all his life. "Run, Tully, run before it eats us!"

Far below the head of the famous Scottish Sea Monster, Nessie watched as the two creatures began to climb back up into a strange looking object that, to the Loch Ness Monster, looked something like a large fish. As they disappeared into a dark hole in the object, the Monster from Scotland waded onto shore and, bending its neck, placed its teeth against the dark side of the black fish to taste it. "Not anything I want to eat," Nessie said to one of its children who had climbed onto shore in to be with her mother. "Not anything I'd want you to eat, either, Gloria."

Having tasted the horrible thing that she'd thought would serve as supper for her large family who were also hungry, Nessie pushed her daughter back into the waters of the lake and, swimming beside her, moved swiftly into deeper waters. When the Monster finally found Wallace swimming for the far shore, she stopped and, raising her head, smiled down on him.

"Climb onto my big back, kind Wallace, my Scottish warrior," Nessie said to her friend. "Gloria and I will take you to the far shore where, from what my other children have told me, your father and the rest of your family wait in hiding. And do not worry about the tall Black Fish. I tasted it once and know now that it will cause us no harm at least for now."

When Wallace climbed up on the back of the ancient dinosaur, he stood up and from that great height, saw his father and the rest of the male members of the Clan walking toward the shore. All of them raised their hands in greeting and began shouting in welcome.

"Well, Nessie, my friend," Wallace said, "before I go to shore I have a simple question to ask. While you say that the tall Black Fish tasted no good and will not harm us for now, did you have your supper from the guts and hides of those English bastards that climbed back into it??"

"Wallace, they had already climbed into the Fish before I could eat them," Nessie said, looking very disappointed. "No Englishmen for me or my family today. We'll have Lake fish for dinner again."

Patting the Monster's head, Wallace dived off her back and, swimming as fast as he could, reached the shore as his family started shouting in welcome. Climbing from the water, his father was the first to take him by the forearm.

"Cuir fàilte air mo mhac, and welcome home, my brave son Wallace," James Larkin MacSquat said to him in a low voice. "I bring news from the ghosts of the far future, which Our Lord has let me visit. Soon, we will have help to defeat the English and drive them from our lands. But the strange thing is, the person who will help us is not only a woman but English, too."

"English and she'll help us to defeat her own country?" Wallace replied to James. "But the English stick together much like we do."

"Not this time it seems. Come. Let us all eat together and when we're finished, I'll tell you what I know of this woman they call Mary Sweet and what she plans to do to help Scotland thrive again!"

James Larkin threw an arm over his son and, together with their Clan behind them, they began the short march to their village hidden in the forests near the great Lake of Loch Ness.

Chapter 2

The Royal Letter and the Scottish Mission

"This is Senior Detective Tom-Jon McMouse, now dictating on my Private Scrambled Mouse Phone," McMouse said into the small device that he held in his brown and white furry paw. "This is a message especially for our Team Members who have not yet heard that we've been ordered by our King Charles and the Prime Minister to fly immediately to Edinburgh, the capital of Scotland. That's a tall order for most of us who had to go to Paris and Russia on our last successful mission. No one is rested and it's only been a few weeks since we all came home to England."

Detective McMouse sat in a tiny stuffed chair, smoking a briar pipe that was given to him by Sherlock Holmes as his good wife, Mrs McMouse, placed a small measure of MacDragon Scottish Whiskey on the table beside him. Taking the glass in his paw, he put the Mouse satellite phone on the floor as he hoisted the nutshell that held the Scottish short to his nose. As he sniffed it, his whiskers quivered and when he took a small sip of that peat-flavoured whiskey made of Loch Ness lake water, he let out a long sigh.

"Good wife Betty, this is a wonderful Scottish Whiskey," he said as his wife pulled knitted slippers onto his tiny feet that she'd given to him last Christmas. "I wish we could just sit and relax for six months or more. I was away from you and our family for far too long when we had to go to Paris and then to Moscow."

"Don't fret, Tom-Jon," she whispered back to him. "At least we've had over a week together. With any luck, you'll make it home in time for Easter."

"Easter? That's months from now! It's just past Christmas. See, our tree is still up and lit in our comfortable nest beneath the streets of London."

One of the McMouse children came out of the next room and, running to her father, gazed up at the Christmas Tree that still twinkled with lights. "Daddy, is it Christmas again?" she asked as her two round eyes opened wide. "Santa was so very kind to all of us mice and cats this year. My stocking was full of cheese and a tiny set of wooden dolls. But Santa didn't bring them. You and Mum did. You brought them back from your last job, didn't you?"

Lifting Little Sally McMouse up onto his lap, the detective stroked the red curly fur on her head as he bounced his youngest child on his knee. "Sally, what you say is very, very true. Santa can't bring all of you the presents you ask for each year. Mum and Dad have to help him out sometimes. As to that gift you mentioned, that's a nesting set of Russian Mice. You take them to bed with you and your sisters every night, don't you?"

"Sure I do, Dad," Sally said as she yawned. "Can I have a glass of milk? Then I'll fall asleep again."

As Betty heated up a glass of milk for her daughter, McMouse picked up his satellite phone again and hit the recording button with a long nail of a single claw. "So Teams, here's the thing. I know we've all had Christmas at home and I hope you enjoyed it. Chief Inspector Mary Sweet is in the United States with her husband Inspector Bernie Bridgestone. They've been asked by His Royal Highness and our Prime Minister to represent England at the United

Nations regarding our country's defence strategy following the death of President Vladimir Putin. They are also discussing with the United States President how to catch that murderous traitor, General Gusto Gatwick, who managed to slip away following our attempt to capture him in Moskva. Mrs Sweet instructs me to tell all of you that unfortunately, and in all probability, we won't be able to celebrate this New Year's at home. Instead, I'll soon receive a letter from his Royal Highness with our latest, most secret instructions which involves a trip to Scotland for the next three to six months. I'll be back to you on this secure phone as soon as I receive that letter. Signing off for now and a late Happy Christmas. This is Senior Detective Tom-Jon McMouse signing off."

When the Mouse Detective had finished the long recording, he pressed a button on the side of the phone. At once, the room was filled with the Phhiissshhhh as his voice was fully encoded and broadcast via the secure satellite link that the United States had made available to the Team Members who were now spread all over the world.

"There, Mrs McMouse, that's enough work for today," he said as he took another sip of Whiskey. "What I want to do now is go to bed. Did Sally have her milk?"

"She did, Tom-Jon. She had a sip then went right to bed with her other mouse sisters."

"Good." The Mouse stood up from his easy chair placed by the small fire and stretched tall. Looking at his wife, he smiled. "We've a few more days, I think, before we'll have to fly up to Scotland. I'll have to ask the Chief Inspector but this time, because we'll be so close to London, I'll be able to come home every two weeks."

"Wouldn't that be lovely, Tom," she said as she put her furry arms around him. "It's time that I put on my nightdress. If you can come home on every other weekend at least you'll be able to have a home-cooked meal occasionally."

"I hate living out of suitcases," the Detective complained as his ears folded back to cover the hair on his neck. "We all hate it but it has to be done. That damned General! I wish we'd caught him in Moscow. That man should already be in prison. Instead, who knows where he is."

"Why do you have to go to Scotland, Senior Detective," his good wife said as she touched the white hair on his cheek. "If that General could be anywhere in the world, why there?"

"Right before Christmas, the Chief Inspector and I received a lead from a huge Scottish Wolfhound we met not too far from here. His name is MacWoof MacSquat and his owner's name is James Larkin MacSquat. That dumb dog didn't tell us very much but what it did bark and woof made Mary and I believe that the General is now somewhere in Scotland in a new disguise."

"Wonderful. So you'll traipse all the way up to that freezing country and probably find that the lead takes you nowhere at all."

"Probably, my wife. But that's all for tomorrow. Tonight? All I want to do is get into our great big bed and make love to you."

Betty smiled as wide as she could and, as she started toward their bedroom, they both heard something growl at the tiny front door of their home. "Tom-Jon, what was that! Is there a dog at the front door? If it gets in, a beast like that could kill our children."

"Let me check, Betty McMouse. If it's a dog, I'll scare it off with my Mouse Army revolver then come join you in bed."

When Betty went into their bedroom, the Senior Detective walked up to his front door and opened it just a crack. Peeping out, all he could see was a gigantic wet black nose that puffed steam from both large nostrils as it breathed.

"Are you Detective McMouse?" he heard a human voice ask. "I have an urgent letter from King Charles. It's been signed both by him and the Prime Minister. Sir, we've taken the liberty of photocopying that human-sized letter onto something much smaller so you can bring it into your home."

Stepping out into the dark night, the Senior Detective stood in the wet slush that was piled on the path next to his family's mouse house nest. Seeing a black cab drive down the main street in London, the tiny mouse stamped his feet to make them a bit warmer. He looked up to see a Royal Delivery Officer wearing an official black and red uniform and a large grey dog standing next to him. When McMouse, the Human and the dog breathed out, whisps of condensation drifted over their heads.

"My Lord but it's cold!" the Royal Delivery Officer stated as he, too, stamped his feet in a dry patch of the path. He drew out a small valise from his coat pocket as well as a very small pad and pen. "Sign here, Detective McMouse. Proof of Receipt is always required for a Royal letter as important as this one."

McMouse took the pen and pad in his ice-cold paw and scrawled his signature onto the Receipt. Giving it back to the Delivery Officer, the Human used two polished nails on his left hand to rip the tiny paper copy off the pad and gave it back to the Detective. "Many thanks, Detective, and have a good night." Reaching again into the deep pocket of his uniform, the Man took out a tiny white envelope and handed it down to him.

"Thank-you, Officer, for this very important letter," the mouse said as he took the envelope in a paw. "I hope you can go home and get some sleep, now, too."

"Not likely, Senior Detective. It's been a real day of it. One blasted thing after another, ya know?"

As the Royal Delivery Officer turned to leave the McMouse residence, the grey dog pulled back on her leash and started to bark.

"Quiet, Corporal MacSquat," the Officer ordered. "Your infernal barking will wake up every sleeping person on this street!"

The dog stopped barking but refused to follow her master. Instead, she face Detective McMouse and started to woof quietly in a way that the Human Officer couldn't understand.

"Detective Tom-Jon McMouse, my name is Dolores MacSquat," the Great Dane said in Mouse Language. "I have been given a message by King Charles to be delivered directly to you and in secret. For that reason, I've learned some Mouse Language."

"Dolores, what's the Royal Secret Message?" McMouse asked through his chattering teeth. "Try to say it clearly. If you can't say it in Mouse Language, I know some Dog Language."

"I am the direct descendent of MacWoof MacSquat. His ghost has been in touch with me. He is now with his master, James Larkin MacSquat and his Human son, William. My Dog Ancestor told me that the Traitor General Gatwick and his wife Tully Gale are now on a shore near Loch Ness. They worked with Russian Engineers to invent a new type of Hypersonic Vehicle that can go back in time. You must somehow find that vehicle. It's buried in a deep hole near that lake. When you do, you and your Chief Inspector Mary Sweet must go back in time to capture the General and thwart his Horrible Mission. If you choose not to take on this Mission, then in only a few days we'll all be talking in Russian."

"Great Scott! A Time Machine Vehicle!" the mouse shrieked, almost falling over. "Dolores, thank you for that message and please convey my best wishes to our King."

As the Great Dane left with her Master, Detective McMouse staggered back into his small nest and helped himself to another glass of Scottish Whiskey. Finishing it in a single gulp, he pushed the

Royal Envelope into his pocket, then crept into the Master Mouse Bedroom and lay down beside his wife.

"Was that the letter from the King and Prime Minister you were expecting?" Betty asked him from the darkness. "Do you really have to go so soon, husband?"

"I'm afraid so," the Mouse Senior Detective said to his wife. "I've not even read it yet and I'll explain it all in the morning. Good night, darling."

"But I thought we were going to make love again?"

Tom-Jon smiled to her and kissed her tender lips. "Are the children sleeping?"

"What do you think. It's almost midnight."

"Good. Oh, just a moment. I forgot to make sure that no one can read the Royal Letter!"

Getting out of bed again, Tom-Jon took the white envelop from his pocket. Placing it in a small safe near their bed, he closed and locked it. "There, my wife. The Royal letter is in the safe. I'll read it tomorrow. Bad news can wait. But what we'll do now is all good, isn't it?"

"And so it is. But what happens if we have more mice children?"

"Then we'll have to buy a bigger mouse house nest!"

Following their love making, Tom-Jon kissed the cheek of his sleeping wife. Rolling over, he stared down at the safe that was bolted to the floor of their bedroom. "If that's the order I know it is, we won't be gone for three or six months. Our Teams will be gone for hundreds and hundreds of years in a Time Machine!" Then, opening his eyes wide, he realized what a Time Machine really meant. "If we must really ride in a Time Machine, then we can bounce back and forth at will, into any time and place in the whole wide world! I can come home to Betty as often as I want to. I'll have to ask the Chief for permission after we find the damned thing and figure out how to make it work."

Closing his eyes, he tried to sleep and when he couldn't, Detective McMouse got up and, opening the safe in the darkness, went into the living room and read the Royal Letter. By the light of the dying embers in the fireplace, he could barely make out the handwritten order even with his glasses on.

"Damned my eyesight!" the mouse whispered as he threw the glasses, the envelope and the letter on the table. "I need new glasses and I'd best buy them before we go on this Mission. I know what I'll do. I'll make up the fire again and read the Letter in better light."

But then the weariness of a long day came down on him like two weights hitting his eyelids. Sitting in his easy chair, the Detective yawned then scratched his thick belly. "I'll light the fire again soon. I'll just close my eyes for a moment then carry on with my duty."

The next morning, that's where Betty McMouse found her husband. Asleep and snoring in his easy chair by the cold fire. As she walked by him on her way to the kitchen, she saw a white envelope on the table by the fire and a white letter on the floor. Sitting beside her sleeping husband on the arm of his easy chair, she read the letter.

"Oh my Lord, no! Not again!" she whispered as her eyes reread the Royal Message. "My dear Senior Detective McMouse. This handwritten note by your Royal King Charles hereby orders you, Your Royal Teams and Chief Inspector Mary Sweet to immediately go to Edinburgh, Scotland. There, you will meet up with additional teams of Interpol Police who are also looking for General Gusto Gatwick. Use any resources that you may require to find him and arrest him. If you are not able to locate this traitor, as well as his traitorous wife, Tully Gale, we will have War again but this time only between England and all of its many Allies and Russia and its Allies who have been identified as some members of the Chinese Government, members of the North Korean Government, traitors in the Israeli Government and traitors in the US and Ukrainian Governments. Please use your discretion as to who you trust with the unwelcome contents of this handwritten Royal Message. I have also instructed Dolores MacSquat to convey a secret message to you that you must share immediately with Mary Sweet.

"I remain, faithfully and your Royal Servant, and sign this also on behalf of our Prime Minister." *Charles III Rex*

Betty McMouse let the letter fall from her hand. She looked at the dead, cold fireplace and considered using that terrible paper as tinder for a new fire. Instead, she gently took her husband's cold paw.

"Tom-Jon? Wake up, my dear. You need to read this and read it right now."

Opening his two red eyes, her husband looked up at her. "Can't it wait, my mouse wife? I'm so very tired."

"No, it can't wait. You need to read this then call the Chief Inspector immediately!"

Sighing then stretching, the Mouse Detective took the letter from his wife and scanned it. Then, he read it again and again. "Good Lord! This is worse than the last mission. Sweetheart McMouse, please pack my small suitcase. I'll be gone in twenty minutes but," he said, smiling at her, "I'll be back home before you know it."

"You will, Tom-Jon? But how?"

"It's a real Royal secret," he said to her as he stood up. "Soon, I'll be able to tell you all about it. Now, I must get this Royal Letter encoded and send it to the Chief Inspector immediately. Right now, she's speaking before the United Nations. I'll Transmit this as 'urgent' so Mary Sweet will receive this critical Message as soon as possible."

Chapter 3

Mary Sweet Orders the Capture of the Time Machine

"Thank you very much, Madame Secretary, and first may I bring all of you who are attending this special assembly of the United Nations greetings from King Charles, Queen Camilla and our government's Prime Minister."

Chief Inspector Mary Sweet looked down on the half-empty auditorium and sighed to herself. Standing at the tall rostrum on a stage above the Assembly Hall, she put a hand over the microphone and turned to the newly elected United Nations Secretary General, Harsha Ganatra. "Madame Secretary, is the Assembly Hall always this empty?"

The small woman from Mumbai, India, looked back at her special VIP guest. Frowning with displeasure, the first Secretary General of the United Nations looked to Mary Sweet like she wanted to spit a stomach full of fire.

"No, Chief Inspector, this is very unlike any Special Assembly I've ever been to," the woman said in an angry voice. "Since I was appointed as the United Nations representative from India two years ago at the behest of our President, Mister Mondi, we have all tried to work together in the event of a world catastrophe. But this time and now that I'm the Secretary General?" stated as she gazed down at the Assembly Hall. "Less than half of our UN representatives have bothered to attend. Not even the United States, France, Germany, Israel, China or Russia have shown up to vote against the horrors that are happening today in Scotland, the Ukraine and the Gaza Strip at its border with Israel! As I say, it is an outrage!"

"I'm sure my Prime Minister and King Charles would agree with your assessment of the situation," Mary replied. "At least our English representative is here. He is as livid as you and many people are about the murderous intentions of that British traitor, General Gusto Gatwick, as well as Russia and some of its allies."

"Which is good, Mary Sweet. But we need a Quorum to pass a resolution condemning the violence, and possibility of more violence, in the world. It is my intention, as the Secretary General, to ask the United Nations to become directly involved in searching for the traitor General you mention. I fully believe that he intends to start yet another War not only against all of the countries in the free world, but also against any country that will not accept his hatred of democracy. As I've said again and again, we have enough wars in the world already."

The Chief Inspector looked back over her shoulder and saw her husband, Bernie Bridgestone, the newly appointed Co-Chief Inspector of all of Great Britian. As he smiled up at her, Mary again turned to face the half-empty Assembly Hall.

"Ladies and gentlemen that have chosen to attend this highly necessary special Assemblage. My Prime Minister asks all of you to pass a Special Resolution condemning those individuals who are working with General Gusto Gatwick, the Russian Spy, as well as the man himself, who are attempting to invade Scotland and establish it as a separate country. While Scotland has the democratic right to create a separate country based on the opinion of its citizens, nowhere in international law does anyone have the right to overthrow a democratically elected government by a bloody revolution which is that Traitor's intention. No one!"

When she heard a smattering of applause echo high into the immense Hall, Mary Sweet stepped off the rostrum. As the General Secretary took her place, the Chief Inspector sat in a chair next to her husband.

"My dear, that went very well," Bernie said as he leaned over to kiss his wife on the cheek and then handed her a handkerchief. "I'm sure that when it comes to a vote, the Assembly will pass the Special Resolution that our country has put forward."

"Not likely," Mary muttered as she wiped her hands with Bernie's red, white and blue cotton cloth. "Secretary General Ganatra says they don't have a Quorum here today which means that the General Assembly can't pass any resolution at all!"

Bernie smiled as Mary tucked the handkerchief back into his jacket's breast pocket.

"Perhaps, Mary," he replied, "but new United Nations rules state that any Resolution of this nature, one as critical to the world as this, needs only one half of those attending plus one more vote to pass the Special Resolution."

"Ladies and gentlemen, may I again have your attention please!" Secretary General Ganatra spoke clearly into the rostrum microphone. "You have all read the Special Resolution put forward by the British Government. We will now have a vote of hands and the United Nations staff will count those who say 'Aye' and those who say 'Nay.' Now, who says 'Aye' to approve the Special Resolution?"

Hands raised all over the Assembly Hall.

"See, Mary?" Bernie whispered to his wife as he made a quick count of the raised hands. "Over half have voted 'Yes'."

"But see the Representative from Ireland? Bernie, she's raising both hands. That idiot could nullify any vote!"

"They won't be counted by the UN staff. You'll see."

"Now, who says 'Nay'?" the Secretary General continued. "That is, voting against the approval of the Special Resolution?"

What appeared to be *more* than half of those in attendance raised their hands.

"What a worry now!" Mary Sweet stated as her face turned red. "Representatives from Africa and South America are all voting no? And even Mexico and Canada are saying no? What's wrong with them? Do they want to see global War this time, not just War in Europe?"

A voice at the back of the Hall began to shout. "Attention, everyone! My name is Jason Espeagnoe. I am a reporter from Mexico City. I have just heard on the Associated Press that bombs are falling on Edinburgh, the capitol of Scotland!"

"That's a lie!" the Representative from Mexico also shouted as he stood up. "I have just talked to my President in Mexico City. This so-called reporter is a liar! He works as no journaliste! Bombs are not falling anywhere in Scotland. It's a fraud meant to sway our No vote against the Special Resolution."

Across the Assembly Hall, voices rose as Representatives from all parts of the world began to argue among themselves. At the back of the Hall, the main door opened as a tall woman strode in. Mary watched her with interest as she took a microphone from a UN staff member.

"Excuse me. Excuse me, my friends! Excuse me!" the tall woman shouted into the microphone.

"Good God above us. Bernie, isn't that…"

"Your humble Jennifer Markova, our Interpol Heroine who helped us in England, France and Russia? Yes, that's her all right. Who could mistake that voice?"

"Bernie, you know that she's been promoted to the rank of General at Interpol, don't you?"

"No, Mary. I never heard that.."

"I said attention! Внимание мои друзья! Attention, my friends!" Jennifer stated angrily into the microphone.

As the Assembly Hall at last began to grow quiet, General Jennifer Markova marched down the steps and looked up at the General Secretary who still stood at the rostrum. "Madame Secretary, I am General Jennifer Markova from Interpol and I bring you all important news. May I please speak to the General Assembly?"

"If it is important then by all means," the General Secretary replied. "But please, General, make your words brief. We are almost finished taking an important vote."

"I will, Madame Secretary," the General responded as she turned back to the Representatives. "What that reporter from Mexico, Jason Espeagnoe, told you is true! I have Interpol staff working in Edinburgh. One of them phoned me minutes ago. The hotel in which ten of my staff are located was bombed resulting in another catastrophe caused by Gusto Gatwick. Some of my staff lie dead where they fell inside the hotel. Many civilians lie dead all over the hotel and outside of it. Television pictures will be available very soon transmitted on most global TV stations and on the Internet. Believe what you see with your own eyes! This horrendous crime is the work of a genius who makes bombs! We are still not sure if the explosive device came by a missile or if it was planted in the hotel. But I have an idea who is responsible for the many deaths and injuries in addition to that horrible General Gatwick and, as I look across this Hall, I see that the country likely to be mutually responsible has not, I repeat, not attended this Special Assembly!"

More shouting broke out as Mary Sweet and Bernie Bridgestone stood up to watch.

"Oh, Lord! Those two representatives are attacking each other!" Mary said as she watched two men begin to swing their fists at each other. Mary reached for her handbag and, grabbing it, began running toward the edge of the stage. "Look, Bernie. One of them has a revolver!"

Shots rang out and a woman fell over. "Someone call an ambulance!" a UN staff member shouted, showing the audience her hands and face that were covered in the Ambassador's blood and grey and white brain matter. "The Representative from Ireland is dead! She's been assassinated just like John F. Kennedy was! Grab that man before he kills someone else!"

The journalist from Mexico, who stood next to General Markova, looked across the Hall. He saw a large man with his back to him begin to run up the steps to a door. Following him, the journalist began to shout as the man turned and raised his black sidearm.

"It's the Mexican Ambassador, Juan Solvedore!" the journalist cried as the murderer began to shoot his revolver again. "Grab him before he fires again!"

"Bernie, if you don't have a sidearm, stay here!" Mary Sweet ordered as she ran off the stage and into the vast auditorium. Her eyes narrowed as she saw the man, now identified as the United Nations Ambassador from Mexico, point his weapon at the Rostrum behind her. "Harsha Ganatra, get down!" Mary shouted as the perpetrator fired his weapon again and again. As the Secretary fell to the floor and a crowd of assistants covered her with their bodies, Mary looked back toward the Mexican Ambassador. When she saw him hold up the revolver to reload it, the Chief Inspector leaped over one row of auditorium seats and then another. Pulling her police sidearm from her bag, she took aim at the murderer then fired her revolver four times. The man fell onto a seat, blood spilling red from his grey suit coat. As Mary Sweet made her way over more rows of seats and to the side of the Mexican Ambassador, she looked down at him.

"Ambassador, because we're in the United States, I must read you your Miranda rights. You have the right to remain silent. Any words you say may be used…"

"Shut up, you beetch!" the man said through clenched teeth. "I am not who you think I am. The Mexican Ambassador is dead in his hotel room, killed by me this morning. I was given this assignment by a General you know very well because I look like Ambassador Juan Solvedore. Now let me die in peace, you female filth."

"Before you go to Hell, Mister Murderer, I want to know your real name and also want you to answer one simple question," Mary stated as she knelt beside him. "The question is 'Why'? Why did you do it."

"You are an animal pig," the dying man said through his bloody lips. "Let me die, didn't I tell you that?"

"Someone get an ambulance for this man!" she shouted to a UN staff member that stood near her. "We must save this man's life to find out why he was assigned to kill the Irish Representative. Don't just stand there. Hurry!"

As the young man jumped to carry out her command, the so-called Mexican Representative smiled up at her. "It is true what they say, Mary Sweet. You are a very, very good shot with that sidearm you carry. But any ambulance will be too late. You see? I always carry a conccaled weapon."

The murderer pulled a small Russian revolver from the left sleeve of his jacket. Pointing the weapon first at Mary's head, he smiled up at her though his hands shook in spasms of pain.

"It would be so easy to shoot you, Chief Inspector Sweet. But if I did that, you would not be able to stop Vladimir Putin's surviving army personnel from taking control of the entire Earth. That's General Gatwick's only job to complete."

The man she would later find out was a retired KGB operative put his finger on the trigger of the Russian-made Baretta. Still smiling, he pulled the trigger but the gun refused to fire. He pulled the trigger again and again but nothing happened.

"Seems you forgot to fill the chambers with bullets," Mary said to her adversary. "We'll save your life then we'll interrogate you. Officer!" she shouted at a New York Police Officer that had answered the United Nations call for assistance and was now running down the steps toward her. "Put this bastard in an ambulance but frisk him thoroughly first. For all we know, this scum has other concealed weapons on him."

"Will do, Ma'am," the cop replied to the Chief Inspector. As two EMT specialists came up to the critically wounded suspect with an Ambulance gurney, Mary smiled down at the Russian operative one more time.

"I'll call you Vlad for now, my dear Russian. And before you're through talking, you'll reveal the exact location of General Gusto Gatwick and the details of his plan or you'll spend the rest of your life in prison."

"How do you they say it in Ireland?" the bleeding man said with a smile on his face. "No nay, never! Well, no nay never for me. And my name is not Vlad. It is Peotr. You can discover my last name after I die. I will never be jailed for the death of that Irish beetch

Ambassador. She is a relative of the Kennedy Clan and they can all rot in hell for what they did to my Cuba!"

As the Russian suspect was loaded onto the gurney and hurried out of the General Assembly Hall, Mary's husband Bernie came running up to her together with Jennifer Markova.

"Are you all right, my dear?" he asked as he took her in his two strong arms. "You've always been much better than me with a revolver. It's a good thing that man didn't die. Now he can tell us everything he knows and why he shot the Ambassador from Ireland down in cold blood."

"He shot the Ambassador because he is a Russian murderer and an old-fashioned communist sympathiser," General Markova stated clearly. "I know that man. I used to work for him when I was hired as a Russian Spy. His name is Peotr Varkova, a real thug and a man I never trusted."

"Varkova?" Bernie asked. "That name is familiar. But I still don't understand why he shot the Irish Ambassador."

"The Irish Ambassador has always been a supporter of Scotland and their desire for independence from Great Britain," Mary said as she put the sidearm in her jacket pocket. "Bernie, please call Senior Detective McMouse immediately. Order him to assemble our Team Members in London then fly immediately to Edinburgh. Tell him that we'll meet him at their hotel as soon as we can join them."

"Why the sudden rush, my dear? I know we're expecting new orders from the King and Prime Minister but we've not received them yet."

A Captain with Interpol rushed up to General Markova. He carried a black valise and, saluting, opened the locked case and withdrew a white envelope.

"Mon Generale! This is marked Urgent and for the eyes only of you, Inspector Bridgestone and Chief Inspector Sweet," the Captain said as he saluted.

Handing his General the envelope, Jennifer gave it to Mary. When Mary opened it, they all gathered around her as she read their new orders out loud.

"That's it then," she said when she was finished. "I was right all along. The General is already in Scotland and just as that Mexican reporter stated, and as you, General, also reported, the Scottish capitol is being bombed as I speak! It is urgent that we leave right now!"

Mary ran back onto the Assembly Hall stage to find the Secretary General helping one of her staff who had been hit by the Russian assassin.

"Madame Secretary General, I am in urgent need of your assistance," Mary said as she handed Miss Ganatra the letter from the King and Prime Minister. "In short, this states that I must get to Edinburgh, Scotland as soon as possible. Can you tell me how I can arrange quick transport?"

"That is not a problem, Chief Inspector," the Secretary General said as she wiped blood off her hands with an antiseptic cloth. "In that you are a British subject, we can phone the British Embassy for help. But it is easier if you and anyone who needs to go with you, take the Supersonic Aircraft that the Indian Government has just developed. It is sitting on the tarmac at the JFK International Airport. I will call the Indian President and tell him that I am taking control of that aircraft until you safely reach your final destination."

"Thank you, Madame Secretary General," Mary said. "The passengers are only me, my husband Bernie, General Markova and perhaps her aide-de-camp."

"Good!" Harsha Ganatra replied as she smiled broadly. "Chief Inspector, thank you for shooting that deep fake Mexican Ambassador when you did. There could have been many, many more casualties."

"That's what I'm trained to do," Mary said with a smile. "If you ever get to London, Madame Secretary General, it would be an honour if you would stay in our house."

"No more Madame, okay Mary Sweet? From now on, it is simply Harsha."

"And I'm simply Mary."

The two women hugged as General Markova's aid-de-camp stepped onto the stage.

"Chief Inspector, when you are ready, we are, too."

"Then we must fly!" Mary said as she let go of the Secretary General. "Harsha, thank you so much for your hospitality. I'll keep you and the United Nations posted with developments in Scotland."

"Do that. And Mary? When you get to Scotland please phone me. Here's my private number. If you need anything, please let me know."

After the two women exchanged phone numbers, Mary stepped off the Assembly Hall stage and joined her husband. "Where's the Interpol General?"

"She's gone ahead of us to arrange a Police Escort to the airport."

"Bernie, that's good. Let's get the hell out of here. There's blood all over my skirt from when I kneeled beside that Russian jerk. And God, I'm hungry! We've had nothing to eat today."

"We'll get something on the plane."

Following the ride to JFK Airport, Mary and her Team Members were escorted onto the waiting Indian Supersonic Aircraft by a Special Envoy from Scotland. At the top of the stairs and right near the front door of the airplane, the Special Envoy took a small envelope from her pocket.

"Mary Sweet, this envelope contains a letter from our Scottish Prime Minister," the tall Scotsman said in his thick accent. "He says that Edinburgh is still experiencing vast destruction from an assortment of explosive devices. We still have not located the source of where they are fired from. He asks you to land in northern England because it's much safer. He will have many military vehicles waiting at the airport where you and your entire Team will be transported to a safe haven in Edinburgh."

Taking the envelope, Mary shook hands with the Special Envoy then boarded the airplane. Taking off her jacket, she stepped into a large Ladies Room where, using a wet towel, she cleaned the caked dried blood off her skirt.

"That's done, anyway," Mary said to the mirror as she combed her thick blonde hair. "Now, we'll get something to eat and then I'll sleep. I'm told that the flight will take just over two hours. That will be some fast trip, thank God. Then down to business again."

Finished, she stepped out of the toilet and joined her husband. Seeing that Bernie was already asleep, Mary sat down beside him. "Ah, there's the flight attendant now!" Mary said to General Markova who sat in the seat behind her and next to her aide-de-camp. "See? She's already serving lunch."

"Good thing too," Jennifer whispered. "I'm starved and I hope that the Indian food will be excellent as usual."

In moments, Mary felt the aircraft being taxied away from the small VIP terminal that it was parked next to. In moments, they were at the end of a runway. Then, she felt her body lean heavily into her seat as the plane accelerated to take-off speed. "Isn't this amazing!" Mary said to Bernie who was now awake. "See, my dear? We're already climbing high over the City of New York. And see how dark the sky is already? Why, it's as if we're almost in outer space!"

"Maybe we are, my wife," Bernie said as he relaxed in the plush seat. "It's as dark as midnight out there. I really wonder: is the General still here in this current time of ours in the twenty-first century? Is he the one who is organising the bombing of Edinburgh? Or has he gone back in time, like we both suspect, and is now embroiled in mayhem to kill all of his enemies like he usually does?"

"Back in time, Bernie, at least that's my guess," Mary replied. "The bombs that the General is using are coming from the past, not the current time. You wait and see if I'm right or not."

The silver supersonic aircraft flew high above the Polar Ice Cap on its Great Circle Route to Europe. Looking out her window, Mary could see the glint of the sun on the ice-covered northern ocean.

'Already over the Ice Cap?' Mary thought to herself. 'I'd better cat quickly if I'm going to get any sleep at all!"

In his Mouse High Altitude Nest, especially prepared by Air India and built right near Mary Sweet's seat, Senior Detective McMouse was woken by a phone call coming from his Mouse phone. Picking it up, he listened intently then hung up and climbed out of his plush first-class bed. When he crawled out of the Nest he looked up at Mary and saw her frown again.

"Chief, what's wrong now?" McMouse asked his boss. "Are you even more worried than you were before?"

"We're running ahead of schedule," Mary replied to her Senior Detective. "Look at the silver clock on the forward bulkhead and the Estimated Time of Arrival for our aircraft. We'll be in England at least an hour early and are landing at Midlands Airport, close to Nottingham. I'm never going to get any sleep now."

"Boss, don't you worry. When we're on the bus heading for Loch Ness, you can catch at least forty winks while the rest of our Team plans what to do when we get to the Hotel beside that giant Lake."

"No, no sleep for me," Mary replied as she yawned and stretched. "I'll sleep when we finally get to our beds in the Hotel."

The PA crackled as the Captain stated in his smooth Indian accent that their Supersonic aircraft would soon be decreasing its airspeed to sub-sonic speeds. Due to the critical nature of this flight, he would be extending the planes large flaps so that they would land as soon as possible and, due to the turbulence that they would all feel, asked everyone to take their seats and fasten their seatbelts.

"See, my mouse friend?" Mary said as the aircraft began to buffet due to the decrease in airspeed and altitude. "We'll be on the ground in no time at all. Climb back into your nest and fasten your seatbelts. While we're preparing to land, I really promise to try to take a short nap.

When the aircraft touched the ground at Midlands Airport McMouse, still tucked into his fancy Nest, heard his Mouse Phone ring. Answering it, he heard the squeaky voice of his wife, Betty.

"Tom-Jon, are you there?" she asked over the encoded phone. "Scotland Yard let me borrow this Mouse Phone so I could call you. Where are you now?"

"Sweet Mrs Mouse, we just landed in Northern England," her husband replied. "We'll be at the terminal in only five minutes or so."

"Tom-Jon, there's a woman standing right outside the door. Her name is Sally Orchid and she'd like to talk to you."

"By all means. Please put her on."

His phone squealed as he heard his wife open their small front door. Then, he heard her voice offer her tiny phone to Sally Orchid.

"Senior Detective McMouse?" a Human woman's voice asked. "My name is Sally Orchid and I'm to be your assistant on this Mission. I'm sending you my photograph over this phone right now so that when I meet you for this Mission, you'll recognise me."

Pulling the phone away from his ear, McMouse studied a photograph on the screen of a very nice-looking Human Woman with sweeping long blonde hair dressed in an official Scotland Yard uniform. "Nice to meet you, Ms Orchid. Can I ask who assigned you to me?"

"King Charles himself, upon the advice of Chief Inspector Mary Sweet."

"Well I'll be cheese," the mouse replied and started to chuckle. "What a wonderful surprise. Ms Orchid, I've never had an assistant, not even a Mouse Assistant except my wife Betty."

"She and I met just yesterday, when I was assigned to you," the English voice replied. "She's a fine mouse woman, isn't she? When I told her I would be working for you, she was so relieved. She made me promise that I'd have to insist that you don't over-work yourself, and try to sleep and eat."

"Will I see you soon, Ms Orchid?"

"As soon as possible, Senior Detective. I'm being picked up in only moments to go to a nearby Airbase. The King has ordered an RAF Tornado to fly me to Nottingham Airport in a supersonic fighter so I'll be with you very soon. And Sir? Do please call me Sally."

"Okay, but you have to call me Tom-Jon. How's that? Your name will be easy to remember. As you probably know, I have a daughter named Sally."

"Yes Sir, Mister Tom-Jon, your wife told me. Sir, I should tell you one important thing. A year ago, I had something of a nervous breakdown because I was working too hard. I spent about six months in a London Insane Asylum. I was released just before Mary Sweet had to join that Insane Community."

"Really? You had a breakdown? Well, Sally, join the club. All of the members of the Human Team have had a breakdown in one way or another. So don't be embarrassed at all. It goes with the territory when you're trying to crack-down on thieves, murderers, Spies and traitors."

"That's what my psychiatrist told me. And I agree, Sir. We must continue to crack-down on all of those thugs."

"Cracked," McMouse replied. "That's what we all are. Cracked. Okay, I'm going to sign off now. I'll see you soon, Assistant Sally."

"I'll hand you back to your wife, Sir."

Tom-Jon and Betty talked for a few minutes then, when the plane came to a stop, McMouse told her that he had to hang up. "Betty, I'll see you in, I hope, about three days. I still have to ask Mary if I can come to see you because you're so close to us in London."

"I hope so too, Darling Mouse. Goodbye for now!"

When he'd rung-off, the furry mouse yawned and stretched. "A Human Assistant? What will Mary and the King think of next?"

Chapter 4

The Psychiatric Unit Investigation Team Prepares to Take Action by Travelling to Loch Ness, a Lake Filled with History and Monsters

When the Supersonic Aircraft had touched down on the long runway at Midlands Airport, the Captain came on the PA again.

"Ladies and Gentlemen and any Animal Teams we may have onboard. I have to inform you that we've been told to hold on a taxiway for about twenty minutes. An entire formation of RAF Tornadoes is on approach to the Airport and Midlands Ground Control asked us to hold until they all land due to the strong turbulence that they may cause if they have to go around. You see, should they have to abort a landing the pilot immediately lights the fighter's afterburners. If we're caught in that hot stream of gas coming from its two engines, it might not only damage our aircraft but could injure you and our crew. We'll inform you when we're cleared to taxi to the terminal."

'Great!' Mary thought to herself as she tried to go back to sleep. 'One more delay and what else is new! The sooner we get to that Scottish lake to find that damned Time Machine, the sooner we can capture the General!"

Leaning back again in her seat, then closing her eyes, Mary felt the aircraft's brakes let go and heard the loud whine of the immense turbine engines as the Supersonic Aircraft began to taxi again.

"My, that was quick!" Mary said when she saw McMouse climb out of his Nest again. "I must have fallen asleep again. And look at the time! We've been sitting on the taxiway for well over a half an hour!"

"Don't worry, Chief," the mouse replied. "We'll be at Loch Ness in to time at all."

When the aircraft parked at the terminal, the mouse detective made sure that he was first to climb down the steep ramp to a waiting bus. As other Humans came aboard with him, he climbed up onto a red strap and looked for Mary but couldn't see her.

"There'll be another bus along soon," a Human woman said as she smiled. "Senior Detective McMouse? I'm Sally Orchid. I never told you but I'm a Detective with Scotland Yard."

"Sally! So nice to finally get to meet you!" the mouse squealed as the bus pulled away from the Supersonic jet. "I'm so bloody cold right now and half asleep due to all that happened in New York City. So forgive me if I don't say much to you right now."

"The King and Prime Minister told me exactly what happened at the UN Building," Sally replied. "Sir, why not climb into my pocket? The King said that you often go to sleep in the Chief Inspector's pocket, so why not use mine?"

"I think I'll just do that," the mouse said as his tiny mouth broke into a huge big yawn. "If I can sleep for another five minutes, that's all I'll need until we all sleep tonight."

Sally watched through the bus window as they made their way first toward a small VIP terminal but then turned toward a large military hanger. Looking back behind the bus she was riding in, she saw another one loaded with passengers from the Supersonic flight. When both buses entered the hanger, Sally climbed down just as Mary Sweet bounded down the steps of her bus.

"Chief Inspector Sweet, I'm Detective Sally Orchid," she said as she saluted. "I have the Senior Detective in my pocket where I hope he's fast asleep."

"Sally Orchid, the King and Prime Minister have told me all about you including your time in the Asylum," Mary replied. "Welcome to our Human Team of Psychiatric Patients, the PIU!"

As they shook hands, McMouse climbed out of his new Assistant's pocket.

"Chief, it's so good to be on the ground again!" the little mouse squeaked as he climbed up her arm. "I wish we could have gone back to London but the order from His Majesty and the Prime Minister means that was not to be. At least not yet."

"Not yet, that seems to be the name of the game," Mary replied. "I've already met your new Mouse Assistant who happens to be human and she's very, very qualified for that position."

"Thank you, Chief Inspector," Sally replied. "As I explained to my new boss, the King Himself assigned me to protect Senior Detective McMouse while we are all on this uncertain Mission."

"The King Himself?" Mary asked. "He really is an amazing Royal human, isn't he? It seems to me that he cares more about McMouse than anyone else on the Team!" Mary watched as her Senior Detective climbed down her arm and tucked himself into her uniform jacket pocket. "Now, take another nap, McMouse, until we make it safe to Edinburgh and then on to Loch Ness."

"I can't, Chief!" the mouse replied as he looked up at her. "We have the Team to meet. They're flying in on the next Royal Air Force Jet Transport."

Just then they heard the roar of engines and, looking out of the hanger, saw a giant C-17 Globemaster land on the runway. As it taxied toward them they all watched as the aircraft's Captain opened his window and stuck out the Royal Flag.

"His Majesty is on board, and I bet you so is Queen Camilla!" Sally yelled above the roar of the aircraft's four giant engines. As they all covered their ears to protect them against the scream of the turbines, Mary watched as a procession of Royal Marines rolled out a red carpet. When the passenger door opened, a set of stairs on wheels was rolled up to the side of the Royal transport and then out stepped the King and Queen, waving to them.

"Hello, your Majesties!" Mary shouted and hurried toward the bottom of the steps. The King walked down to greet her and, taking his hand, Mary started to bow.

"No more bowing ever, remember Mary Sweet, since the day you were made a Queen when you demonstrated courage and bravery in Russia and France?" the King said to her. "We are on our way to the United States on a very important engagement with that country's President. In that we were headed this way, it was no problem to give your entire Team a lift from London to join you."

"Thank you, Sir," Mary said as she shook his hand. "I'm honoured and am sure my Teams feel the same way. Sir, we received your letter about this new Mission and realise the importance of it. We'll be leaving for Scotland as soon as our military aircraft arrives."

"My Chief Inspector, I have an additional Royal Order for you and your Team Members."

"Yes, Your Majesty, er, I mean, Royal Sir?" Mary said as she stumbled with a way to properly address him. "What order is that and we'll carry it out to the letter."

"Don't bring back that traitorous General alive," the King of Great Britain uttered to her. "When you catch him, have him executed. I'm known as a merciful King but this time? He shall receive no new trial because the man has already been tried and found guilty of murder and many more crimes. Should that man escape from us, he will haunt Great Britain and all of the Royal Families for centuries to come due to the new Time Machine technology he took from the Russian government."

"Sir, do you know where he is?"

"Our engineers and astro-physicists have pondered that very question. We have analysed the last transmission from his Hypersonic Vehicle and fully believe that he travelled back in time as much as four to six hundred years ago. That vehicle is definitely still somewhere in Scotland, or so the analyses indicate, and in all probability is somewhere in Loch Ness. We have Royal Navy Destroyers working with local experts on examining the bottom of the lake. They've picked up signals and radar reflections that are shaped just like that Hypersonic Space Plane."

"Then it's still there despite all of the Time Travel it's done," Mary whispered. "It's amazing. The hull must be made of very strong and resilient metal."

"And so it is," the King said. "The best of British Engineering went into the design of a new type of metal that's stronger and more durable than ever before. The chemical engineering was stolen years ago from our country by a number of Russian Spies."

"Is that so, Sir? If we catch any of those suspects, we'll bring them in. But not General Gusto Gatwick. That, Sir, is a Royal Promise."

"Good. Life is precious but this man's actions have cost too many lives to ever be forgiven by anyone, even God."

"Chief! Look up there!" the mouse shouted as he pointed up past the King's head.

Mary looked up the stairs and saw her Team Members begin to emerge from the transport aircraft. First out were Edith Penrose and her husband Jeremy. Then, George Smith and his wife, Maud. They were followed by Tony and Maria Enwenopa.

"My Human Team! The fellow members of the Psychiatric Investigation Unit! My PIU, how are you all!"

As the Humans began to descend the tall stairs, Mary heard the barks and meows of cats and dogs from just inside the aircraft. "And here come my Animal Teams. Why, look at the kittens and puppies! They've all grown so tall!"

As the Teams of cats, kittens, dogs and grown puppies bounded down the stairs, Mary saw Bluebell, one of her Senior Animal Team Members, and a new litter of white and brown pups bounding up and down the portable stairs as they played in the fresh English air.

"Bluebell!" Mary shouted. "Blue! Get your little puppies down here right now!"

A large black cat leapt down the stairs, past the pups, and he was followed by a black and white female cat and ten kittens of different colours. "Detective Catnip," Mary called, "I see you've found yourself a bride! And look at all the kittens. Seems to me you've found your one true love at last."

"And so I have, my Human Chief," the Cat Detective purred. "I'm proud to introduce you to Mrs Catnip and my gaggle of new kittens."

As Mr and Mrs Catnip began to cry with pleasure, they walked off the stairs and headed toward the nearby hanger with the other dogs and cats.

"Okay, that's part of the animal team," Mary stated to the King. "Where are the others I wonder?"

Then the Mouse Team scampered out of the aircraft with Betty McMouse in the lead. "Senior Detective McMouse, where are you? I'm here with all of our mouse children!" she shrieked with happiness. "Come help me with them and our food and luggage, my dear."

"He's over here, asleep again!" Mary yelled as she pointed toward her jacket pocket and then to her Senior Detective's new Personal Assistant. "Betty, this is Sally Orchid. She's your husband's Personal Assistant while we're in Scotland."

"We've already met," Sally said in her Mouse Language as Mary Sweet looked at her in amazement. "Don't be surprised, Chief Inspector, that I am very proficient in Mouse Language. I studied that in University as well as some Russian and French. I always wanted to join the Scottish Royal Army and, someday, to be a detective like you are."

"Pleased to see you again, Sally," Betty McMouse said in plain English to make sure she could be understood by the tall blonde-haired woman. "Mary I ask where did you say my husband is?"

Mary again pointed a long finger at her jacket pocket. "In here sleeping."

"Ah. My poor mouse man is all tuckered out again."

The Senior Detective, warm and snug in the thick coat pocket, woke at the sound of his wife's pleasant voice. Pushing himself up, he leaned against Mary's stomach for a moment then leaped down to the concrete surrounding the aircraft and gave his wife a huge hug as she came scampering down the stairs.

"What are you doing here, Betty?" the mouse squeaked in Mouse Language. "I haven't had time to talk to Mary Sweet about coming home every other weekend."

"And now, my darling Mouse Husband, you don't have to," Betty squeaked back. "Our King phoned me just after I made the acquaintance of Sally Orchid. He told me to come up here to live while you're based in Scotland. It's only an hour or so plane's ride from where you'll live with the Teams so I'm hoping we can see each other once a week or even more!"

Their Mouse Children, now surrounding their parents, jumped with joy at the prosect. "Please, Daddy, lift me high over your head," Sally McMouse yelped as she jumped up and down on her tiny paws. "That Human woman has the same first name as I do, doesn't she, Dad?"

"Dad now, is it, not Daddy?" her Mouse Father said in plain English as he picked her up and placed her on his shoulder. "I don't think there's going to be any confusion. If I call 'Sally' in Mouse Language that means you. If I say 'Sally' in English then that means my new Human Assistant. And if I say 'Sally! Sally!' in both the Mouse and English Languages that means both of you."

When the mouse had finished talking to his daughter, Mary Sweet picked up the Senior Detective by his coat and let him crawl up her arm to sit on her left shoulder. "So, Senior Detective. I have what I think is great news for you. The King told me that we don't need to capture that General Gusto. All we have to do is find him and then kill that Russian clown. If you'll remember, he's already been tried and found guilty *in abstentia*."

"That's all we have to do, Chief? Then let's get started. The sooner this is over with, the sooner we can all get back to London."

Mary, the Human Sally, and all the McMouse Family hurried across a taxi strip to join the Human Team members. As they started to hurry from the military hanger and into Midlands Airport VIP terminal, McMouse heard a distinctive noise in the sky. "There! Mary, look up there! That has to be the plane sent by the Scottish Government."

When the Boeing 737 landed, it taxied immediately toward them. As the two turbine engines wound down, the front door opened and the internal stairs came out of the aircraft and descended to the concrete below. Mary and her mouse senior detective heard a huge Bark and watched a familiar looked Scottish Wolfhound bound down the steps.

"There's no time to talk or even bark now," MacWoof MacSquat growled to his two London friends. "Get everyone in the aircraft! Edinburgh is now in flames and my master, the great James Larkin MacSquat, says that you must capture that Time Machine right now or that enemy whom you call a General will change history! Our great Scotland is going to hell in a handbasket, and may soon be captured by King Edward the First, and it's all because of that bloody feckin' moron, that General Gatwick Bark-his-name."

The King, who had followed Mary and toward the military 737, looked first from the Wolfhound and then back to Mary. "Did you hear what that ancient Royal dog growled?" the King said as his face turned red. "Yes, Mary Sweet, I've also studied Animal Languages for years! You and many of my subjects know that I love nature and all sorts of beasts in this world. Royal Canine!" the King said to MacWoof. "I know your lineage! I have a number of hand painted pictures on the walls of my palaces that depict your kin going into battle with their Royal owners! If you are MacWoof MacSquat, then I hereby give you this message which Mary Sweet can take back by Time Machine to James MacSquat. Tell him that we will and we must not let the General change history! If we do that, it will be the end of everything we know that is good about not only our country but the world! Tell James that we've managed to see into the past as well as the present using a small version of a Time Machine. Should that General win the battles ahead of us, he will, and I repeat, will become the Emperor of all the Earth and billions of people will die needlessly."

As the Royal dog saluted with one paw, he growled back to the King: "My liege and Master, I shall do whatever you tell me to do. You are related, somehow, to my Royal Master. Therefore, let my good friend Mary Sweet take back your message to James Larkin MacSquat and we will all do everything in our power to end all battles now and forever."

"Good, now all we have to do is deliver your message, Sir," Mary said as she turned to the Royal Wolfhound. "MacWoof, we'll be on-board the aircraft in two shakes. Get back onto the aircraft yourself and ask a Human to radio the Scottish Government. Tell them we're heading first to Loch Ness to find the Hypersonic Vehicle. When we do, we'll send some of my Team Members to join you all back in Edinburgh."

As MacWoof bounded back inside the Boeing 737, MacMouse said goodbye to his entire family. "Betty, trust this good King of ours. I'll be so safe that I don't even need my MacMouse sidearm."

"Oh, yes you do, Senior Detective," Mary laughed. "Get out of my pocket and say goodbye properly to your family. Betty, he'll be back here before you know it."

"I know that's true, Mary Sweet," the mouse wife said in English. "I'll have supper waiting for him and you when you come back here to Nottingham."

It only took a few minutes for all of the Team Members to board the aircraft. When the front door shut and the twin engines were started, with Mary sitting next to Sally and McMouse once again in his Chief's pocket, the plane rolled out to the end of the runway in only seconds.

"McMouse, don't go to sleep this time," Mary told her mouse friend who still sat in her pocket. "I want you to send two messages on your encoded phone. The first is just as our King commanded: get a message to James Larkin MacSquat via our Special Delivery Time Machine satellite. That message must go back in time for at least one thousand years and must be repeated every year for the next three hundred years. Tell James Larkin what the King has ordered. Should he see the General he is to kill him instantly! The General cannot survive or he will change World History and become the only Emperor to ever rule the entire Earth! Do you understand me, Senior Detective?"

"I do," McMouse squealed gravely then he looked to Sally. "Assistant Sally, can you make this secret phone call? In my other jacket pocket, I have a new Time Machine Satellite Phone that the Mouse Time Machine Military Engineers have just now invented with the assistance of our Detective Ghosts, Sherlock Holmes and Doctor Watson. I'll dial the Secret Phone Number then you can speak into it. Use your best Scots accent but make sure you use language that James Larkin can understand."

After McMouse had dialled the number, he handed the very tiny phone up to Mary who, taking the delicate device between two fingers, handed it on to Sally.

"Yes, Sir, Tom-Jon," Sally replied, "I understand exactly what you want me to say. Do you have any further instructions for me?"

"Just make sure you keep that long Antenna on the phone pointed directly up. That way, the Time Machine Satellite will receive its signal."

"That's very good again, my mouse friend, and thank you for getting Sally to make the call. Now onto the next critical phone call. I had a

Sargent in the London Police Station purchase that Ghost of a Detective, Sherlock Holmes, a brand-new phone from the Encrypted Army Mouse Factory right before we left London. Tell him where we're going and to float up here as soon as possible. As I understand it, Mister Holmes and Doctor Watson have chosen to become Ghosts again and this time forever."

"That's correct and will do, Chief. I'll do that right now."

As Senior Detective McMouse began to dial his Army Mouse Encrypted Phone, Mary looked out the window as the aircraft revved up its engines and took off. In only a few seconds, they were flying over long River that snaked back and forth through forests and green fields. 'I was there only two years ago,' she thought to herself as she sat back in her seat. 'I wonder how my friend Edith and the children are? Remember how we all went to Sherwood Forest and stood by the big tree that Robin Hood and his Merry Men used to hide in so many years ago?"

Then she sat bolt upright in her aircraft seat. "McMouse! What a perfect idea. When we go back in time I'll recruit Robin Hood and his band of Merry Men and Women! They'll know what's going on in whatever time the General is in right now. What a great addition to a plan that's now forming in my head!"

"Robinhood and his band of Merry Men and Women?" McMouse replied as he continued to dial on his Encoded phone. "But Mary, Robinhood is nothing but fantasy."

"Nonsense, Mouse. Robinhood is the stuff of legend. He and his band of followers are perfect to help the Scots defeat the English four or five hundred years ago. What about Sherlock Holmes? He's nothing but fiction but he's as real as any Ghost can get."

"Right, Chief," the Mouse muttered as he held the phone to his fuzzy ear. "And dragons can talk too, right?"

"Right! I'll recruit dragons too! What a crazy plan that's forming in this mad head of mine!"

"Here we go again," the mouse said as he rolled his eyes. "Robinhood and talking dragons. What else will we have on our Teams? A pink elephant?"

McMouse pulled out his Encrypted McMouse Army Phone and dialled a Top-Secret number for Sherlock Holmes. After the Phhssss of the encoding, McMouse spoke in a low voice to the Great Detective Ghost.

"Mister Holmes, are you there?" the mouse asked into the phone. "I'm recording this message to make certain it gets to you and Doctor Watson. In a few days, we will have located the General's Hypersonic Vehicle. We will also determine how to fly it and how to make it go back in Time again. Our Chief Inspector Mary Sweet asks if you and the Doctor can join us in Loch Ness at some point in the near future. Sir, when you receive this important message, please phone me straight back."

Having finished the encoded recording, the mouse looked up at his Chief.

"Chief Inspector, that's completed as ordered."

"Good, Mouse Senior Detective. Very good indeed! The plan is starting to come together even though I'm so tired I can't think straight."

Assistant Sally Orchid also finished her phone call and, handing the tiny phone back to Mary who gave the instrument to the mouse, smiled in satisfaction. "There. All the important phone calls are done."

As the two Humans and the mouse sat back and relaxed, they could all hear the yips and meows of the puppies and cats going to sleep on the floor toward the rear of the aircraft.   "Tom-

Jon, when we get to cruising altitude on this short trip to Scotland, let's brief the Teams together, okay?" Mary said quietly. "Sally can help us and that way she'll be able to brief our Teams and other Military Humans if we're not here. I've got a new plan up my sleeve that will surprise that crazy Russian General. And we must figure out how to find that Hypersonic Space Machine in Loch Ness before someone else does."

"Chief, how will we find it?" the mouse asked. "From what you've told me, it's been buried for almost four or five hundred years."

Mary yawned then winked down to her Mouse friend who was now snuggled up on an armrest between the two Humans in an aircraft blanket that the flight attendant had given to them. "It's easy when you know how, McMouse. I had a dream last night about the new MacSquat friends, MacWoof and James Larkin, who we met in London. That dream said that all we had to do to find that elusive Machine is to locate a dragon that's living somewhere in depths of that Murky Loch."

"Now she wants to find a dragon in Loch Ness?" the mouse said to himself as he rolled over to go to sleep. "My poor Chief is suffering from delusions again. And when she re-experiences psychosis? Then, our Teams will be up the creek with nothing but a flying dragon and Robinhood to save us."

Location: Loch Ness, Scotland   Altitude: 500 ft above Sea Level

As the Boeing 737 made its approach to fly at low speed over the long, narrow lake of Loch Ness in the Scottish Highlands, the cockpit door opened and a Military Officer walked out. When she came abreast of the seats Mary and the mouse were sleeping in, she gently shook the Chief Inspector's shoulder.

"Mrs Sweet, I've been asked by our Captain to invite you and your Senior Detective up to the cockpit. She says that you'll have a better view and you can also hear the radio chatter when we talk to the United States Navy Orion Search aircraft that's flying a thousand feet above us."

Mary didn't even blink. She picked up her mouse from off the blanket and, following the pilot, made her way into the cockpit. Sitting down on the small leather covered jump seat, she put on a headset and watched as the pilot, sitting in the left seat, adjusted an instrument.

"Mrs Sweet, I'm now tuning our radio to the same frequency as the Orion aircraft. It's orbiting above the lake now and is using its various radar equipment to scan the lake's bed and the shores on both sides of it."

"Captain, thank you for allowing us to come up front," Mary said as McMouse once again sat on her shoulder. "According to our scientists and archaeologists, that Hypersonic Vehicle should be buried about fifty feet beneath the surface, either on the bottom of the lake or on-shore."

"I'll let the pilots of the Orion know just that, Chief Inspector," the Captain said as she keyed her mic. "Orion one-two-one this is Alpha Chandra Five-five. We have the Chief Inspector on our aircraft and she's sitting right behind me. Stand by one to talk to the Chief."

The Captain handed Mary a black microphone attached to the radio by a long chord. "It's just like you use in the Police Force," the co-pilot who had taken her place in the right seat stated as she looked back at Mary Sweet. "Key the mic to talk and release when you want a response. You'll hear their words through this speaker up here."

Mary and the mouse looked at the small silver grill above both pilots' heads which the co-pilot had pointed to and, when the Chief Inspector keyed the mic, she told the Orion Captain exactly what she'd just said to the Captain flying her aircraft. After a few seconds, Mary heard the Orion come back to her. "Roger that, Chief Inspector. This is Captain Darling flying the Orion. We'll increase the capacity of our radar with new technologies we now use to find Russian subs at great depths. It'll take us an hour or so to ping the entire area and, when we land, we'll share our results with you and the United Kingdom Government."

Mary looked at her mouse as she shook her head. "It's going to be impossible for them to find anything in that great long lake, McMouse. We'll have to find my dragon instead. That great beast will help us or so my dream said."

The Captain banked the Boeing 737 and in only moments they all felt the entire aircraft shudder as the landing gear was extended. When they touched down at a top-secret airbase just south of Edinburgh, Mary went back into the cabin.

"Attention, my Teams!" she shouted. "Don't get up yet. Let's have a very brief meeting before we disembark. Two buses are meeting us at this British Airforce airbase and will drive us to Loch Ness. There, we can start the hunt for the Hypersonic Vehicle and that notorious General."

"But how will we find it if it's been buried for so long?" Edith Penrose, one of the Team's EMT specialists, said from her seat. "Chief, George, the love of my life and one of the best Marine Sargents the world has ever known, has decided to retire due to ongoing problems with his memory. I decided to come along for this first part of the new Mission. But if you don't mind, when you all disembark at Loch Ness, I'm going to stay on the plane and go back to dear George."

"Please give all of our best to George, will you Edith?" Mary replied. "As to your question, I know how to find that terrifying vehicle but I have to do that when we all get to Loch Ness. Edith, you were so instrumental in our First Mission to France and in England that I know someday soon you and George will be awarded the Cross of Saint George. In fact, I have them right here. See?" Mary said as she pulled two boxes from her Chief Inspector's jacket as well as two certificates. "Give one of these to George and let me pin one on you now. The certificates have been signed and dated by King Charles, of course."

As all the Teams broke into applause, meows and barks, Mary walked down the aisle and pinned the Medal of Saint George onto Edith's jacket.

"Good. Now it's done! I'm so happy for the two of you," she said to Edith. "Teams, now that we're done congratulating Edith and George for their heroism when they tried to help us all capture the General and kill that rat President Vladimir Putin, which we did, are there any other questions?"

When no Team member said anything, Mary turned around and began to walk back to her seat. Then the aircraft cabin filled with bright white light. They all heard a BOOM and saw a flash of lightning outside the aircraft.

"We're under attack by the Russian Airforce!" Colonel Francis McOuvre shouted as he climbed out of his seat at the back of the plane. "Mary Sweet, take your seat and you, too, Sally Orchid! I'm going up to the cockpit to help the crew with all of their defensive measures."

As Francis ran down the aisle, he pushed past the Chief Inspector then, when another BOOM roared through the cabin he threw himself on top of Sally just as they all felt the incredible pull of explosive decompression.

"Use your oxygen masks!" Mary shouted to the Team members as she donned a mask that had dropped from above all the passenger seats. "Breathe, Humans and animals. Ghosts don't have to. But breathe!"

Sally put her arms around the strong torso of Francis and, beneath her, he could feel her shaking. "Don't worry, Sally. I've got ya'," he yelled so he could be heard above the roar of wind.

"I know you do, Francis," she yelled back and she looked up at him with her big blue eyes. "I'm glad your hear. Francis, can I call you Frank from now on? We've never really met but Mary has told me all about you. Besides, I have an Uncle named Frank."

"Fine!" Frank replied. "Call me whatever you want. People call me the strangest things."

The roar of the decompression stopped as suddenly as it had started. Then lights came on throughout the cabin. A mist of brilliant white and gold came through a window near Mary Sweet and took a seat right across the aisle from where she was still standing.

"Madame, I have no questions but only one important observation," the voice of Sherlock Holmes stated. "As you well know, myself and my good friend Doctor Watson have been seeking out the hiding places of criminals for well over three-hundred years. I have read all there is to read about this advanced modern aircraft and a time machine it is, certainly! In that you and your living Teams have not been able to find it, might I suggest that it has gone back in time so you will not find that until it appears again in this time, not the old one."

Mary couldn't help but laugh at her old Ghost friend. "My, Mister Holmes, but how you love to make an entrance."

"I do, Madame. Now, if you will please comment on my suggestion?"

"First, I must thank-you, Mister Sherlock Holmes," Mary said as she moved across the aisle toward the seat he was now sitting in. "I have come to the same conclusion but, and here's one thing I've only just learned about: the shore on the western side of Loch Ness was blanketed in radiation not too long ago. My hypothesis, based on this recent scientific evidence, is this: the Hypersonic Vehicle had some sort of mechanical failure. It could well be that they went back in time but I'm fairly certain that the Space Vehicle is now here in this time again. It's been buried there for well over five hundred years, or so says the radio carbon dating."

"Ah-so!" Sherlock said as he rose from his seat. "My dear women, then all we need to do is to trace the radioactive footprint to the point of some sort of deadly explosion. Watson, my friend, do you have such equipment?"

A BOOM again shook the cabin and a Flash of Light half-blinded everyone. Then, a stout man with greying hair rose from the seat next to Sherlock Holmes. "Ladies and gentlemen, Human and Animal Teams. Because there are some new faces with us, may I introduce myself but first my great friend sitting next to me. The gentleman beside me in the dark green deer stalker hat and the matching cape is England's most famous detective, Sherlock Holmes. And I, poor man that I am, and after considerable pressure from our King and Queen, have found that I must again leave my good wife in London for this highly important mission!"

As Doctor Watson stepped into the aircraft aisle, all the Teams could see that this famous man was wearing a tuxedo and a red bow tie. "Forgive my clothing in that I was just on my way to a special engagement of the London Symphony Orchestra in eighteen hundred and twenty something, when I was asked to join you. My name is Doctor Watson and I must say that I'm so happy to meet all of you, particularly those that I've never had the opportunity to work with before."

As Doctor Watson bowed a voice from the front of the aircraft squeaked, "Doctor Watson, it's Senior Detective McMouse way up here. See? You can see me waving at you." When Watson looked, he could see the tiny mouse standing up on top of an aircraft seat, waving one small arm in the air. "Sir, if you don't have the equipment to track that old radioactive cloud, I'm sure I can get one or two new ones for you."

"Thank you, my friend McMouse," the doctor replied. "I would appreciate that. I have one that I invented not too long ago, but your modern technology will be, I'm sure, better than my nineteenth century idea. As soon as we get it and I learn how to use all of the modern equipment, we'll be able to find that Vehicle in no time at all."

The PA crackled and the RAF Captain told everyone to take their seats and buckle their seat belts. As the Boeing 737 changed course and began its steep descent toward a secret military base near the Scottish Lake, a bell chimed three times and Mary and her teams knew that they were on a very short final approach to the short runway. When they landed, the Military Aircraft made its way down the single runway to a waiting bus.

"Right, Teams," Mary said, "we must board our ground transport now. I'll brief you further as we make our way to Loch Ness."

When the Teams were comfortable on the single bus sent by the local representative of the Ministry of Defence, Mary handed out a single piece of paper to each Team Member. "The brief is simple," she said to everyone as the driver started the engine. "We must find the Hypersonic Vehicle and then go back in time to stop the General. If we don't, the consequences will be greater than anyone will ever be able to anticipate. The General plans to beat both the English and

Scottish armies during King Edward the First's invasion of Scotland in the year 1296. If that happens, that Russian bastard will come back to the present and take over the Earth as its first and only Emperor. Now, as I call out your name, Human Team, please raise your hand and shout, 'Here!'"

As Mary shouted their names, each of the Human Team raised a hand high. First there was Tom Enwenopa and his wife Maria who both worked as EMT specialists. They were followed by Francis Assisi also known as Frank to a few close friends, who would be soon promoted to Major. Mary then called out the names of the new Human Team Members.

"Humans, Animal Team and Ghost Team, I'm pleased to introduce you to the new members of our Human Team." As Mary ran through the small list, each new Human Team member stood up and briefly introduced themselves and their specialty.

"My name is Private Sarah Scots. I was the only one to see the Hypersonic Vehicle speed over our radar station. The Ministry of Defence ordered me to join together with a portable radar unit that's on wheels. With this technology, I'll be able to track that Vehicle when, not if, you find it and launch it."

When she sat down, two more women stood up. "Mon amie, my name is Josephine Millet and I am the great-granddaughter of the famous French singer, Edith Piaf. As you may know she was a Spy in the French Underground during World War Two. I am also a Spy but work for the French section of Interpol. It will be my job to attempt to infiltrate the General's spies in whatever time he may travel to, and by doing so, I will destroy all of the weapons he and his various armies may have. Now, may I introduce you to one of my best friends. Her name is simple and though she is not French, she sounds and acts like I do much of the time."

When the thin, tall brown-haired woman stepped aside, a woman with short dark hair and a radiant smile moved into the bus aisle. "Hello, everyone! My name is Elle Rose. I work for a woman named Bridget Wainwright as a Detective based in Denver, Colorado. Before that, I was a social worker based in the south of France. That's why sometimes I speak with a French accent, too. My job for the Human Team is also simple. I will help all of my friends in Interpol to track down and arrest General Gusto Gatwick wherever he may go or in whatever time he may be in. That is, if our Group of Team Members doesn't kill the General first."

Then Sally Orchid stood up and raised her hand. "Hi, my new friends. My name is Sally Orchid and I'm now on special assignment from Scotland Yard, at the bequest of our King, and have been made the new Assistant to Senior Detective McMouse. My job is to do whatever the Senior Detective or the Chief Inspector tells me to do.

"Thank you Sally, Elle Rose and Josephine," Mary said as the other Team Members in the bus politely applauded. "In only a few minutes we will arrive at our destination. There, we will be joined by all of the members of Team Ghost. For those who have not been on a Mission with us before, these deadly people will include Sherlock Holmes and Doctor Watson, and they will be supported in their difficult task to find that Russian General by any number of Royal Ghosts who have passed on many years ago. These Ghosts will include the ancestors of Edward the First, the King who wanted to make Scotland one country with England, as well as other Ghosts who will at time to time appear to help us. That's the end of this quick briefing. Try to rest, particularly you dogs, pups, cats and kittens. You'll soon need all of the energy that you've ever had."

The bus began to move and it quickly made its way past the security gate of the airfield. Outside, it turned left and began to descend down a long straight road that took it through a wonderful Scottish village. Through the windows, the various Team Members saw a large, grey Court House. Lawyers and their clients stood outside in the bright afternoon sunlight, presumably talking about the cases that were scheduled for that afternoon. Further down the street, a publican was opening his old-fashioned bar as a number of older gentlemen and women walked in to have a pint of bitter with a late lunch. One man who had a costume that made him look somewhat like Shakespeare, turned toward Mary as the bus passed him.

"Mary Sweet! I'm Wil Arnold. We went to Secondary School together, remember?" the man shouted in an American accent. "I'm giving a poetry reading here in this famous Scottish Pub this evening. It's based on the Sonnets of the Great Bard of England but also incorporates the poetry I'm writing in my latest book. If you're not busy, maybe you could come along and, after the reading, I'll buy ye a pint of Scottish Ale."

Mary smiled at the man which she did not yet recognise and, waving back at him, turned her head as, across the street, a school principal rang her bell and children walked in from the playground to attend classes again.

The bus passed a park and Mary and her Teams marvelled at the early spring flowers that grew from the damp long grass including Heathers with bright yellow flowers and Bluebells with long green leaves and bluc flowers. "Oh look at those lovely blue flowers, Mama Bluebell!" Mary said to the young mother sitting on the floor near her. "Those flowers are blue but they're as beautiful as you are, and your many new pups!" Blue's pups began to yip as they crawled out of a large bag that a Human had placed on the floor beside the Mama dog. Blue hopped over to her brood and began to feed them. As the half-dozen pups lapped at her nipples, Chief Inspector Claws Catnip, now one of the most famous Black Cats in all of the United Kingdom, crawled in through an open bus window.

"Chief Inspector Mary Sweet," the cat growled as he saluted with his right paw, "I'm sorry my part of the Team is late. We were attempting to catch rats in a local park and the time simply escaped me."

"That's perfectly all right, Chief Inspector Catnip," Mary Sweet replied as she saluted him back. "I know you've been very busy since you and your new Wife Cat were married only a few months ago. And, Sir, congratulations for the reward you and your Team received from the Royal Family's Cats and Dogs. I read about you in the London Times and know you were looking forward to your Honeymoon when you also received orders to go on this Mission."

"Ma'am, I'm proud to serve, and we'll catch that Rat-faced coward, that Russian General Gatwick," the cat hissed back. "Now if you'll excuse me, I'll order my Cat Team to eat their late lunch of mice and cheese that we managed to catch."

Upon hearing that the Cat Team was eating mice for lunch, Senior Detective McMouse crawled back out of Mary's pocket then up her sleeve to sit high on her head. "Chief Inspector Catnip, did you say you were having mice for lunch? I thought you'd promised that you'd never eat mice while you were on duty with my Mouse Team."

Catnip began to laugh and his whiskers quivered. "McMouse, when I say Mice I mean cheese balls shaped as Mice!" the cat lied and Mary knew it. "You have nothing to worry about as long as I'm the Cat Team Chief Inspector."

Inspector Catnip ordered the other members of his Team of Cats into the bus and as they jumped in through the open window, Mary saw that their vehicle was passing an enormous clock tower made of brown marble that was part of the local Church of Scotland Cathedral. The church bells clanged two times and, looking down at her watch, Mary realized that they were running late and would have to make up the time. Striding up the aisle of the bus she stepped to the driver and leaned over his shoulder.

"Sir, we're running well over an hour late and we have a great deal to do before sundown. In that it's still winter, the sun will set in less than three hours. Can you do anything at all to speed up the bus?"

The Private in the British Army looked back at her and smiled, his grin full of tobacco-stained teeth. "Well, Chief, t'would be a real pleasure to speed this pig of a bus up. But see?" he said, pointing at his foot. "I have the pedal to the metal and all this old barn will do is forty miles an hour."

"I know you'll do your best, Private. Can you call ahead and ask the hotel at Loch Ness to have a boat standing by for me and a few others? And also tell them that we'll need a huge meal for all the Team Members before we go to bed. We've not eaten a thing today."

"Will do, Chief Inspector. I'll call the hotel from my mobile phone and tell them exactly what you said to me."

As the driver dialled a phone number with one hand, Mary went back to her seat. Sitting down, she looked up at an overhead shelf and saw Senior Detective McMouse gnawing on a large ripe acorn. "McMouse, you're having lunch at last," Mary squealed up to him in Mouse Language. "If you find a large packet of nuts up there or anything else to eat, can you hand it down and I'll give it to the other Team Members."

"Mary, I'm sorry but this is the only nut up here," McMouse said with his cheeks full of acorn. "But I'll take a look around this shelf in just a minute."

As the mouse finished his small meal, the bus braked then came to a stop. Mary looked out on a dark lake surrounded by tall hills and mountains. "Loch Ness! Already?"

"Yes, Ma'am," the driver said as he opened the front door. "I found a short cut that took off over twenty minutes from the trip."

"Team Members, let's go! Off the bus, right now!"

When Mary stepped out onto the gravel parking lot, she looked first to the hotel bathed in the winter sunlight. Turning around, she saw a boat tied up to a nearby dock. A man standing on the stern waved at her.

"Sorry, darlin', but do you be Mary Sweet, the Chief Inspector?" the man shouted to her.

"That's me, sir. Give me a minute and I'll get aboard."

Watching the various members of her Team march into the grand-looking Scottish hotel, Mary took a moment to study the tall structure made famous by people searching for the Loch Ness Monster. The Loch Ness Lodge Hotel looked to Mary like a large, cozy cottage. When she saw a young man come out the front door to greet the new guests, Mary walked up to him.

"Young man, I'm Chief Inspector Mary Sweet and these are the guests that were booked into your lovely hotel by the Department of Defence."

"Me name is Chistian MacSquat and I'm the grandson of the original owner, Chief Inspector Sweet," the young man replied. "I'm working here over the Christmas Holidays before I have to go back to college in Edinburgh."

Mary studied the young man intently, noting the curling long hair and his sparkling blue eyes. "Christian, I'm delighted to meet you. Did you say your surname is MacSquat? I believe I met the ghost of your Grandfather MacSquat in London a few months back."

"If he do look like me, then yes Ma'am, that was my Grandfather," the young man replied, laughing so hard he almost fell to the ground. "Me Granddad is a very funny man and he's visited me any number of times. He loves to play jokes on living people. Sure, but he's played jokes many times on the tourists who come to the hotel. He'll wait 'til the midnight bells ring from the nearby Church, then roar like a dragon. The guests all wake up and end up out here in the rain, white as a sheet from fear of the living dead."

"Do your guests ever see your Grandpa MacSquat?"

"Why sure they do," Christian said as he took out an old briar pipe and lit it. "Me Granddad loves to frighten the guests half to death. He'll stand outside every room in the hotel and roar all of their names in a voice that's also as loud as ten Nessie Dragons, not just one."

"Nessie the Loch Ness Monster? Christian, that's exactly who I'm looking for. Do you know where she is, by any chance? She's waiting for me or so she told me in a dream I had."

"A dream? Then yes, she's waiting for you. It's that way! Over the hill and down by the lake that looks like the sea. That's where the Great Dragon Nessie do be."

"So, you talk in riddles, do you?"

"Surely I do. Just like me Grandpa MacSquat who is not really my grandfather but a dearly departed ancestor."

"Christian, I know where Nessie do be," the Chief Inspector said with a coy smile on her face. "Come along, dear Christian MacSquat. Yer exactly the young man I needs to have if I'll find my darling Nessie again."

Christian looked at her, his mouth wide open. "You've seen the Great Dragon before, Chief Inspector? Is that why you talk the way you do, now?"

"I have, young man. In my dreams on many occasions. Now come along. Tell your employer that you'll be gone the rest of the day. You have a much more important task to do, and a very large role to play, it seems to me."

"Aye, Ma'am. I'll tell the owner that I'll be gone the rest of the day. But give me a few minutes while I get all these new guests settled and feed them a late lunch which is waiting for them in our dining hall."

Chapter 5

Mary Sweet and her Teams Capture the Hypersonic Space Vehicle (With the Help of Nessie, The Ancient Loch Ness Monster)

It took only ten minutes for Christian to complete his tasks. Then, with the young man by her side, they walked to the nearby dock where the Skipper still waited.

"Here we are, Sir," Mary said as she climbed aboard with her new friend. "Sir, what's your name and the name of your lovely vessel?"

The middle-aged man tamped out his pipe on a palm and smiled at her. "Chief Inspector, please step aboard and you, too, Christian MacSquat. I have the pleasure to introduce you to the *Miss Nessie Rose*, the boat that I use to take passengers out onto the Lake. She's the rosiest boat in the Loch and has worked hard all of her long life to find the Loch Ness Monster. And as to me name? Why, it's Joseph P MacSquat, an Uncle to that lad you have with you."

"Pleased to meet you, Joseph," Mary replied as she stepped off the dock and onto the deck of the *Nessie Rose*. "Please call me Mary. I take it that you're also an ancestor of James Larkin MacSquat?"

"I am, and very proud of it," Joseph said in his thick Scots accent. "The man is a rogue but a wonderful rogue, if you ask me. He took it upon himself to defeat that ol' bastard of a King, King Edward the First of England, time and time again. And yet, he died and then his son died and well, and Scotland is now part of Great Britain which is a true sin and will always be."

As Mary placed her large black bag on a seat near the aft of the vessel, Senior Detective McMouse put out his small furry head from the bag's green interior and looked up at the imposing figure of Joseph MacSquat.

"Joseph, be thee?" the tiny mouse squeaked in Scots-English. "If ye are who I think you are, and if that nephew standing next to you is who I think he is, then finding that Royal Monster Nessie will be as easy as catching a brown trout in these tranquil winter waters."

Both men began to laugh so hard that they almost dropped their briar pipes. "And Mary, ye have a talking Scots mouse too? Ach, but James Larkin MacSquat would love him!"

When the two men stopped laughing, Christian cast off the ropes as Joseph walked into the small wheelhouse and started the engine. "We're underway! Now, it's only a matter of time before we find that Royal Monster Nessie."

The boat made its way out of the small harbour and, turning north, wandered up the length of Loch Ness. Mary, with McMouse on her shoulder so he could also scan the windswept waters of the lake, walked up to the bow. Taking out a pair of special Army Mouse binoculars, the mouse looked carefully in all directions. "Does that be a log, Captain, or a wave or Nessie herself?" the little mouse asked the Skipper through the open wheelhouse window. "Tis Nessie, I think, or I'm a cat not a mouse!" McMouse yelled as he pointed at a few brown humps in the nearby water.

As the small vessel rolled side to side in the gentle wake of a hump-backed series of waves, Skipper Joseph stepped out of the wheelhouse and joined them.

"Well Glory be to the Almighty. If I'm not mistaken that's the real Royal Monster together with one of her small dragon children."

As waves approached through a fine mist that had gathered above the murky waters of the lake, a strange voice sounded out. "Beware all ye who go here! There be dragons in this lake. Now be gone before we two strange Scots creatures breath fire at you!"

"Fire? The dragon will breath fire at us?" Christian yelled from his position at the aft of the boat. "If she does that, we'll be nothing but cinders in a moment!"

"Naw, she's just testing the waters, wanting to know if we're a friend or foe," Joseph explained to his frightened nephew. "Let me get out me microphone and I'll calm the silly creature and let her know who we are."

Joseph walked back into the wheelhouse. There, he killed the engine. As Mary and McMouse watched, he placed a silver microphone to his lips and began to speak. His voice, which sounded like a Scottish General, sounded through the mist.

"Nessie, me Royal Queen of Loch Ness, this be Joseph P MacSquat and a few close friends. We're not here to harm you. Aboard the Nessie Rose, which ye know well, I have a very special person who needs to talk to you."

Out of the mist, the long neck of a dragon appeared. At the Monster's side, a short neck and head swam next to the larger one. Both beasts moved toward the small vessel.

"Ah, but it is you!" Nessie exclaimed as she lowered her head toward the wheelhouse below her. "Joseph MacSquat! It's been a long time since we've met anywhere on this wonderful lake."

"Ah, and isn't it fine, my lovely Nessie," Joseph replied as he stepped out of the wheelhouse. Placing a hand on the dragon's head, he began to scratch her ear. "But don't you look lovely, my darling girl. And who's this with you? Is this a new daughter?"

"And so it is, if truth be told," Nessie replied and Mary, standing nearby, could smell sulphur mixed with fish on the dragon's breath. "Her name is Gloria MacDuff," the dragon continued in Scots-English, "and she was once human. When she died hundreds of years ago, I picked her up out of the depths of the lake and breathed my everlasting breath into her lungs. When she came alive again, I was gobsmacked because she'd been transformed into a small dragon daughter, one that looks just like me."

"And ain't ye beautiful!" Joseph said as Gloria lowered her head toward the deck of the vessel. "And ye do look just like Nessie, don't ye girl!"

As Gloria smiled down at the Skipper, Mary stepped up to the boat's gunwale and looked at both dragon heads that swayed in the breeze above her. "Gloria Macduff, long ago you were the daughter of the Royal Thane of Fife. Your father's strong character was used by William Shakespeare in his play, Macbeth. Am I correct?"

The child dragon lowered her head toward Mary and said in a whisper that smelled of rose petals, "Yes, that is right, my Mary Sweet. In all the dreams I've had since I was cast into this lonely lake by those who murdered me and who were enemies of my father, I have dreamed of thee. Today, all those dreams come true because I know that soon, Scotland will be an independent nation once again."

"Too true, Gloria Macduff. Truer words were never spoken by a dragon or murdered Princess of Scotland."

Mary then looked toward the swaying head of Nessie. "Miss Nessie, if I can be so bold to ask of thee, can ye now take us to the place where that Triangular and peculiar ship is buried? In the dreams I've had of you for many weeks now, you told me it will be easy to find."

"And so it is, my darling Mary," the monster of the lake replied to her. "Follow me and we'll soon be there and you can retrieve what is rightfully ours."

The two great dragons swam through the mist toward a nearby shore as Joseph stepped back into the wheelhouse and started the engine. Slowly, without a sound made by anyone, they motored behind the two dragons.

"That Triangular monstrosity is buried right here!" Nessie roared as she crawled up onto a muddy bank. "My daughter and I will dig a small hole above that thing that can kill both people, horses and even dragons."

As Mary watched from the bow of the boat, Nessie and Gloria used both front flippers to dig three great trenches into the muddy soil. "It be here, not far below the surface of this unholy earth," Nessie grunted as she dug harder. "Dig down far enough and ye'll find what ye are looking for."

"Right!" Mary shouted. "McMouse, did you bring along that radioactive detector that we discussed?"

"Mary, Sherlock Holmes and Doctor Watson have it now and they should be here in seconds."

Above them, a great white cloud began to descend toward the shore of the lake. A bright light flashed and out of the cloud stepped the Ghosts of Holmes and Watson. "I believe you're looking for this, are you not?" Doctor Watson said to Senior Detective

McMouse. "It's my invention that I mentioned but I transformed that with the new one you organised for me and Holmes. I have combined the best of British technologies, using modern twenty-first century science with the science of the nineteenth century which were also extraordinary!"

"Good!" Mary said as she climbed off the boat and stood knee deep in the cold waters of Loch Ness. "Let's find the damned thing. Then, McMouse, call the local teams of Army engineers and they can dig it up."

"That won't be necessary, dear woman," Holmes said as he stepped toward the three trenches that the dragons had dug. "Watson, please hand me that instrument." When Watson handed the famous English detective the radioactivity detector, Holmes switched it on. Swinging it over the triangular trench made by the two dragons, the entire instrument began to glow red and vibrate in his hands. "You see, Madame Chief Inspector? This indicates radioactive materials buried only forty-nine feet, seven inches below the surface."

"But how are you going to get the Hypersonic Vehicle out of there, my friend?" Mary asked the Detective as she waded to shore and walked over to him. "All I need to do is have the Senior Detective McMouse ring…"

"Nonsense!" huffed Holmes as he floated over to Watson. "Madame, remember, Watson and I have been Ghost Detectives for many, many years now. What you propose will take far too long. But what we need to do… now that is Elementary! Do you not agree, my dear Watson?"

"Certainly, I do, Mister Holmes," Watson replied as he floated back into the white cloud. "Give me two shakes and I'll be back out again with the amazingly brilliant machine we've both just invented."

As Mary stood waiting, she was joined by Joseph and Christian. "Why, they're both ghosts just like my ancestor MacSquat is!" Christian exclaimed as he looked to his uncle. "Uncle Joseph, do you know who these two Ghosts are?"

"Of course, I do," the Skipper replied as he lit his pipe again. "It's the famous detective duo! Sherlock Holmes and Doctor Watson. I've read those short-stories time and time again."

As they all watched, the two dragons flew into the cloud. They heard a hammering and some saws working. Then there was a final flash of brilliant white light and the two dragons flew out of the cloud carrying a long wooden scaffold that was fashioned much like an oil rig. A bright golden instrument hung from its centre and swung in the breeze just like the dragon's heads did.

"Careful, Royal Ladies," Sherlock said as he floated up to stand on one of Nessie's wings. "That instrument is very fragile. See? Now we're right over the triangle that you both made. Lower it now. Lower. Lower. There! It's grounded flat on the mud."

Mary, McMouse and the men watched as the feet of the scaffold were planted on the ground. Then the two dragons landed beside it as Watson floated up to stand with Holmes at the top of the long piece of engineering. "Royal Queen Nessie, my great friend!" Watson called down. "We need some fire from both of you to start up the instrument. Could you please use the fire in your belly and point it at the very tip of this golden machine?"

As the two dragons nodded their heads, they both breathed in a long, long breath. Holding it for a moment, they turned their heads to look at the tip of the golden instrument. Breathing out again, a fire emerged that was so hot that the wooden rigging began to smoke.

"Enough, please, at least for now!" Watson commanded through his thick white moustache. "Mister Holmes, the tip of the instrument glows red, not white, so it's time to start up the machine."

"Step back, everyone!" Sherlock Holmes commanded. "I'll press this green button right here," he explained as he pointed to the end of the machine that he and Watson were floating above. "You'll hear an almighty sound like a thunderclap. Then the entire area will begin to vibrate as the machine uses the Earth's magnetic field to form a giant electro-magnetic current. With that, we'll lift this blasted vehicle from where it lies and return it to the rightful owners."

When the Ghost Detective pressed the button, the dragons, mouse and humans heard the sound of a great thunderclap as if they were being attacked by a hundred canons. When the earth beneath their feet began to vibrate, they all fell to the ground except the dragons who looked so frightened they spread their great wings and were ready to fly away. The ground around the triangle began to shake and roll, and then turned transparent.

"More power!" Holmes shouted to Watson. The Doctor reached down, adjusting the instrument. When he did, the ground shook even more violently.

"Look, Sherlock! It's coming up!" Watson exclaimed. As Mary and McMouse looked on, the red and black tip of the Hypersonic Space Vehicle emerged from where it had lain for hundreds of years. Slowly, ever so slowly, the rest of the vehicle began to rise from the fantastically large hole that had been made.

"Almost there! Dragons, lift the rigging so the vehicle has more room to come out!" Sherlock Holmes screamed. The dragons again flew over the tall rigging and slowly lifted it. As the golden instrument continued to glow red hot, the murderous Space Vehicle rose out of the dark hole and, for a moment, hovered over the shaking ground. Then it descended to touch softly against the muddy grass, close to where it had first attacked William Wallace MacSquat and killed soldiers and their horses a thousand years ago.

"Done, and I'm so proud of you again, Misters Holmes and Watson!" Mary yelled as she stepped through the muddy grass to the Hypersonic Vehicle. "McMouse, call the Space Ministry! Tell them we have the secret Vehicle back in our possession. Tonight, after dinner, we'll bring the entire team here, as well as Sarah Scots, who will know how to start the Black Hole Device and can take us back into time to find the General and stop him."

As the sun began to set over Mary and her friends, she looked down at the deep dark hole that was once again filled with nothing but water. "Here lies the bones of those who fought against King Edward the First as well as some English soldiers and their horses," Mary whispered in prayer. "Bless you all, those of you who were murdered by the notorious General Gatwick. Don't fret, for someday soon I'll kill that Russian bastard or put him in a fiery prison for as long as he and that skunk wife of his live."

As Mary stepped back aboard the *Nellie Rose*, she gazed at the silver and black Vehicle that had kept its secrets from its rightful owners for so many, many years. "Tonight, after dinner, I'll bring only a few members of my Teams here," she said to McMouse who was still standing on her shoulder. "Then the real fun begins."

"You know it, Chief," the sleepy mouse whispered to her. "All I want to do now is eat! That's what I want. I'm famished again."

"Eat you will when we get to the hotel, my mouse friend. Then we can all have a short nap and come back here before midnight. With any luck, Sarah Scots will come here too and then, when she learns all there is to know about the secrets of the vehicle, we can take a short hop in it and dance by the light of the silvery moon."

As the boat pulled away from the shore and moved back down the narrow lake, a sliver of the Moon rose in the east, reflecting off the still waters of Loch Ness. "Bless you, Nessie and Gloria, for all you did today," Mary said to the lake. "Sleep well, and with any luck, I'll see you two tomorrow."

A fine mist rose over the tranquil waters and, as Mary looked through the mist which gathered in a dense fog, she saw two long necks swim through the silvery waters that were now reflecting the light of a quarter Moon.

"And God Bless you, too, sweet Mary," a dragon voice whispered in her head. "We'll be here always in your dreams. And when you need us, we'll be right next to you. Just pray the words and we'll be with our Mary Chief Inspector."

'Good dragons', Mary thought to herself as they approached the small harbour close to the hotel. 'Tomorrow is a great day that must just a few Humans and my friend, McMouse'.

As she stepped onto the dock and walked toward the hotel, Mary looked up at the glistening Moon. "Mouse, isn't that a fine Moon tonight? It's light always makes me happy."

"I agree, Chief," the mouse replied as he stood on her shoulder. "You know what else would make me happy? A big plate of Scottish Cheddar Cheese."

Chapter 6

Sarah Scots Pilots the Hypersonic Space Craft Past the Moon and Beyond

As the clock in the local Church near the Loch Ness hotel tolled eleven minutes to midnight, Mary Sweet, Senior Detective McMouse, Sally Orchid, Tony Enwenopa and Colonel Francis McOuvre boarded the boat Skippered by Joseph P MacSquat. As Christian was preparing to cast off from the pier, an English Airforce Jeep pulled to a stop and turned off its bright lights. A woman that Mary recognised as Private Sarah Scots ran from the military vehicle and jumped into the boat carrying only a heavy duffle bag.

"Chief Inspector, Sarah Scots reporting for duty, Ma'am," the young woman said as she saluted. "Chief, I've read everything there is to read about the engineering of that Hypersonic Space Craft and have spent over fifty hours at the controls of a Training Vehicle that our government built following the theft of the complex plans from the Russians. It's very easy to fly, as easy as flying a light airplane. My father taught me to fly when I was only fifteen and I've been flying ever since. That's why the General who is part of this Mission chose me. Not only do I have vast radar experience, and saw that Space Vehicle in flight, but together with my new training and flying know-how, he thought I was the best and only choice."

"Thank you, Private Scots," Mary replied, saluting back. "May I ask you: have you ever been to Outer Space? I'll be honest, I'm surprised that the General didn't select an astronaut from the European Space Agency or even someone from NASA. But if you've been selected and have trained for this flight, then I'm sure your General is absolutely correct in his choice."

"Ma'am, you'll soon see that I have all the experience we need. In my duffle bag are all the training manuals that I used as well as complete schematics of the Vehicle."

Sarah saluted Mary again and, turning on one foot as military people do, she walked through the door that led below decks.

"The *Nessie Rose* will never be the same," Joseph observed as he sucked on his unlit pipe. "The British Military have never before been on my boat. But she seems a grand woman and I'm sure ye will be safe when you get to board that crazy Vehicle."

"And so we will, Joseph," Mary replied. "It's almost midnight and the Ghost Team is expecting us soon. So get underway as soon as you can."

"Will do, Mary Sweet. I'll get the engines started right now."

As the boat left the small harbour, in the thick darkness that surrounded Loch Ness, Mary could only see the quarter Moon poke through the torn fog just above her. As the boat gathered speed, she took Senior Detective McMouse out of her pocket and handed him to Sally. Now on his Assistant's shoulder, they all watched as the fog thinned and the moonlight grew brighter. This time, no long neck of a dragon came out of the fog. Instead, only the light of the moon glittered on the smooth waters of the lake. Relaxing for a moment, Mary took in a deep breath. Her lungs filled with the smell of peat that floated as small particles deep in the Loch and the fresh scent of early crocus that bloomed in the winter grass near the shoreline. She could smell the cheese her mouse friend had for dinner and the soft fragrance of Sally's perfume, as well as the sound of a nearby mallard as, in the dark night, it called for its lost mate.

"Two minutes until we land, Chief Inspector," Joseph said as he stepped out of the wheelhouse. "You tell me you'll be back in no time at all. Christian and I will have a nap below decks. When you're back climb onto the deck and we'll hear you and wake up."

"That's fine, Joseph," Mary replied as she came out of her reverie. "We'll only be gone in the Vehicle for what will seem to you like a minute or even less. But we have to ready the Hypersonic Vehicle for deep space which will take us well over an hour."

As Joseph went back into the wheelhouse, Mary looked up at the glowing Moon and wondered for the first time in over a week about her husband, Hubert. 'What's my old husband doing right now,' she wondered to herself as she sat on a wooden plank and felt the boat rock in the swell of the lake. 'After he was murdered in London and went to Heaven, is he married again? Is he happy? Will I ever get to see him again?' Then Mary thought about her new husband, Bernie. 'I love him, of course. He's such a wonderful man. But, no, he's not Hubert and he never will be. Ever since Hubert was gunned down by the General Gatwick in London, almost a year ago now, I always wonder what would have happened had Bernie died instead of Hubert. I would have done anything to prevent both of their deaths but, though I love Bernie, Hubert is the love of my life and always will be.'

"Thar be land!" she heard a voice say and, standing up from where she sat next to the gunwale, saw Christian ready a rope on the bow. "Mary Sweet! Call all your people and tell them to come up here fast. I'll jump onto land and hold the boat steady with this rope. But she's a fair weight of a wooden vessel so they all have to jump onto land quick before I have to let go."

"Lad, that's just fine," Mary replied as she stepped to the door that led below decks. "Human Team Members and Sarah, come up here right now! We've made landfall again and it's time to go make ready the Space Vehicle."

The muddy grass had started to dry out as Mary and the few selected by her made their way to the Hypersonic Space Vehicle. When they arrived, their boots soaked as they stepped through the still waters of the lake from the *Nessie Rose*, Sarah took a manual out of the Military bag she was carrying. Opening it to the first two pages, she took a small torch from her pocket and began to examine the lower front section of the Space Vehicle. Wiping water off the cold metal, Sarah pushed a white button and a small hatch opened.

"Chief Inspector, I'm going to open the main door now," Sarah said in a hushed voice. "The radiation detector that you used suggests that nothing in the Craft is a danger to any of us."

"Private Scots, if you think it's safe then it is," Mary replied. "Open up the door and let's get on with this first test flight."

Putting her hand into the rectangular box that the open hatch had exposed, Sarah used her fingers to search for anything that would open the door. "I can't feel anything, nothing that will open the outer door," Sarah whispered to the Human Team and McMouse. "Can someone hold the torch so I can see the back of the box?"

Tony took the torch from Sarah and held it high over her head. "How's that, Private? Can you see anything?"

"Not yet. Bring the light closer and that should be grand."

As Tony brought the torch closer to the box, Sarah looked down and saw the gold and black combination lock. "Just as the manual says," she said with joy in her voice. "Now all I need is the right combination for this year."

Paging through the manual again, Sarah found an entire section on the Vehicle's combination lock. "See? If the Time Machine is in 1297, then the entry code is 1297. If it's in 1668, then the combo is 1668. Because the Time Machine Space Vehicle is now in 2023, then the combination will be…"

"Twenty-twenty three!" Mary shouted with joy. "Spin the numbers on the lock to today's combination and let's get into the ship."

Sarah quickly dialled the small numbers to 2023 and, hearing a hiss as loud as a steam engine starting up, they all stood back and watched as the door swung open high above them. A ladder automatically extended to the bottom of the ship and, when it did, Mary clapped her hands three times.

"We're in! Sarah, you go into the craft first. When you've had a chance to familiarise yourself with the Space Vehicle, use your Military radio and tell us to join you."

"Yes Ma'am, Chief Inspector," Private Scots said. Saluting the Chief, she climbed the ladder as fast as any monkey could.

"Look at that kid go!" Colonel Francis McOuvre said as he watched her climb to the top of the Vehicle and enter through the large front hatch. "That Private will be promoted to Lieutenant once we get back from this short test flight."

"You know it, Colonel. You wait. During this short flight, she'll become crazier than I am," Mary replied to him. "I've been fine since we came back from our first Mission to France and Russia. But now! Going into space for the first time! I feel that old dark magical psychosis coming on again."

"You're still seeing Ghosts, aren't you Chief?" the Colonel asked. "Ghosts and dragons when none of them should be here? I see them too which means that we're both crazier than anyone in any insane asylum that I know of. Now all I need is a drink of black Irish Porter and I'll be so nuts that I'll be able to fly that damned spacecraft as well as Private Sarah Scots."

"No drink for you, Colonel. Not until we come back. There's Scottish Porter at the hotel and I hear that it's as good as the Irish version."

"Frank and I had a drink together last night," Sally said as they waited for Sara, and even in the darkness Mary could see the woman blush. "I'd never had Porter before."

"I agree that it's not Guinness or Murphy's or even Beamish," the Colonel replied solemnly. "Give me the Irish brands all the time. But if we're in Scotland then we'll have to drink like the Scottish people do, isn't that right, Sally?"

A bright light high up on the Space Vehicle came on, so bright in blinded everyone below. The sides of the vehicle were also lit in a light so brilliant it seemed to come directly from the sun.

"Look at that, will you?" Mary hissed as she eyed the side of the Space Vehicle and picked up a crowbar from the ground. "That's the old Soviet Union Hammer and Sickle. I'll sickle you, let me tell you, you bastard Putin and General Gusto!"

Walking up to the glittering surface of the Vehicle, she pried off the Red, Gold and Black plaque and, when she was finished, Mary Sweet threw it into the hole that the Space Vehicle had been buried in.

"Go directly to Hell," Colonel McOuvre said with fire in his voice. "Keep falling into the pit God made for Satan until you're joined by that Pig-President Putin and his Russian General."

"Okay, everyone. You can all board now," the all heard Sarah call.

Mary, Senior Detective McMouse and all of the other Humans looked up the long ladder to see Private Scots standing at the open door. "All right, Team," Mary cried, "let's see what Sarah has discovered in the Vehicle."

When they had all climbed up the ladder and stepped inside the thick metal door, Sarah pushed a large red button and the door swung closed. "Everyone, please follow me inside to the control room. It's a small space but this vehicle was designed to carry a few more people that we have."

As they walked into the Command Deck, Sarah handed each of them a Red and Black helmet. "Put these on and you'll feel then take hold of your clothing, right around your neck. This will supply you with oxygen and also a microphone, a speaker and a heads-up display. If we find that one of us must walk in space, I'll give us all Space Suits that will protect us from the deep cold of Outer Space."

As the mouse took a small helmet from Sarah, he saw a metal label printed in English which stated that a Scottish Engineer named Avril had fashioned a Helmet for McMouse out of a piece of a titanium satellite and she had then added the glass shield to the front of it and, inside, a tiny communications system and a mouse-sized heads-up display. When the mouse put on his helmet, it attached to his Uniform Jacket just as Private Scots had said it would.

"It fits fine!" the mouse said from inside his helmet which he toggled the mic with his hairy chin. "This is McMouse speaking. Does anyone hear me, over?"

Mary put her mouth up to the glass visor of the mouse helmet and mouthed the words, "Turn up the volume! Use your chin again!"

The mouse saw her point to his short chin and laughed. "Roger that," he said into the microphone as he toggled the volume control. "Now, does anyone read, over?"

"That's a Wilco," Private Scots replied into the space craft's communications system. "Push the small green button on the right side of your jaw with your tongue, Senior Detective. That will turn on the heads-up display."

When the mouse did as he was asked, the inside of his helmet came alive with various gauges. "Distance from the ground!" he squeaked. "Directional heading! Speed in miles per hour and the percentage of the speed of light. The Current Earth Time in GMT and any time where we'll be! It's all right here in front of my eyes."

"Okay, Team," Mary said as she placed the helmet over her head. "Put on your helmets and then sit down. Private Scots? Have you learned how to turn on the Black Hole Drive?"

"I sure have, Chief Inspector," the Private said as she put on her helmet and sat behind the Space Vehicle's small control desk. "When we have enough altitude, all I have to do is push this button with a finger. We'll all hear the Black Hole device wind up behind us. Then, we'll accelerate so much we'll eventually go faster than the speed of light, just like the General and his wife did."

"Right," Mary said into her helmet's mic. "Team, this is Mary. Do you all read me, over?"

"Captain Sally here, Mary, and I read you," the mouse Assistant said when she'd put on her helmet. "I'm getting a bit of hissing but that will go away soon, or so Frank told me earlier today."

"Roger that, Sally," Tony said into his helmet's mic. "And that's a five-by-five, Chief. Colonel, do you read us?"

"No!" Colonel Frank Assisi yelped as he pulled off his helmet. "This Russian made thing doesn't fit over my head. I need a larger one."

"Colonel, it's adjustable," Private Scots said from her pilot's seat. "Pull it open an inch or two and the helmet will fit."

"Right, and will do," the Colonel cried as he pulled the helmet apart and placed it gently over his head. "If a mouse and the rest of the Team can do it then so can I." He adjusted the internal microphone with his chin and turned on the heads-up display with his tongue. "This is the Colonel. Does anyone hear me?"

"Say 'over', Francis, when you're finished with a sentence," Mary said patiently. "Then we'll all know you're waiting for a reply."

"Right," Francis stated tersely. "This is Frank! It's hot as hell in this helmet and I want out of this damned Vehicle as soon as possible! Over."

"That's a nice 'over', Francis," McMouse replied. "It's over when it's over, right?"

"That's right, mouse," Francis said, boiling mad. "It's not PC of course, not anymore, but it's all over when the Fat Lady sings and this damned Russian contraption blows up and we all die! Over!"

Everyone was silent for a moment until Mary said: "Francis, take a deep breath. Now Sarah, why don't you get this Vehicle moving?"

"Roger that," Sarah replied. "I'm pushing the Black Hole button to bring it to life. And on my mark. Three, Two, One. Now!"

The entire Vehicle began to vibrate and they all heard a loud wailing as the Black Hole Device behind them began to wind up.

"Preparing for launch!" Sarah barked into her mic. "Two, One. Launch!"

They were all pressed deep into their seats as the Vehicle lifted from the muddy grass near Loch Ness. As it took off, the heat and power of its rocket engine blast flattened everything behind it. The grass burned to cinders and the side of the cold lake began to boil.

Swimming in the middle of the Loch, Nessie and her daughter looked up into the clear skies. "Well, Mum, look! What's that flying over our heads?"

"That's Mary Sweet, the talking mouse and some Humans, darling. They're going back in time to see us again and together, we'll catch that King Edward the First and save the lives of all the Scots Clan Men, especially those with the surname MacSquat!"

"Precisely, dear dragon," a voice said as Sherlock Holmes stepped out of a bank of glowing mist. "We'll follow them soon, dear lady, as soon as we're ready. You see, dragon, Watson and I helped to invent a Time Machine over one hundred years ago. We still have it. It was used by Jules Verne in his bestselling classic novel."

"You have a Time Machine, too?" the dragon replied. "But Sherlock Holmes, why don't you go back in time now? Mary Sweet might already need you."

"Soon, Madame Nessie. Soon. I'm waiting for Watson. When he shows up, he'll have the Time Machine with him."

There was another flash of light and a 'hiss' as if something in the lake was cooking. The surface of the water bubbled next to them and all of a sudden, a man on a sled with a large spinning Wheel bolted to the back of the wooden and metal frame floated to the top of the Loch.

"Mister Holmes, I presume," Doctor Watson said to his best friend. "I tested it again and it works quite well! Even Jules Verne would be impressed, I knew, so I took it back in Time to visit him again."

"Did you now, Watson?" Holmes replied. "How is he?"

"Very, very busy. Just like most novelists, I presume. The poor man struggles to make a living but I told him that when we come back from the centre of the universe or one of its many planets, we'll bring him back a bag filled with diamonds."

"Positively elementary, my dear man!" Holmes replied with a grin on his thin lips. "A bag of diamonds! Wait until we make it to the centre of Saturn. We'll find diamonds as big as this lovely dragon!"

They all heard a loud 'Boom' and, looking up, saw the Space Time Machine Vehicle streak toward the setting Moon. "They're on their way!" both dragons roared. "Sirs Holmes and Watson, you have to go right now! That 'Boom' didn't sound right to either of us."

"That, dear dragons, was a Sonic Boom. They're now travelling faster than the speed of sound."

"Yes, but the 'Boom' was much softer than it was when the General went over our heads so many years ago," Nessie said with tears in her eyes. "Sirs, if you don't help them out soon, I'm sure they'll all be quite dead in only a few hours, by Earth time."

"Then, we're off too!" Holmes shouted as he floated over Watson's head and took a seat next to him. "Watson, make room, Man! Start this machine up and head in the direction of the setting quarter Moon. You do the general direction with that lever, and I'll take control of the Time lever," Holmes stated, pointing at the two silver levers that had been bolted to the frame in front of their seats.

"Right you are, dear friend. Here we go yet again!"

The dragons watched as Watson pushed a small lever forward. The wheel behind the two men began to spin again, faster and faster and faster. The waters around them boiled as the small machine hummed loudly and began to shake. Then, in the flash of a dragon's eye, the Machine and the two men were gone!

"Mama, where did the Humans go? Are they dead right below us?"

"Not at all, my little girl. The men have gone Forward or Back in Time, that's all."

The dragons waited until the sun set. When it did, they swam back toward the harbour where they hoped to meet Joseph and Christian, their good friends. But when they finally arrived, the boat's cabin lights as well as the hotel lights were out.

"They're sleeping, all the humans are sleeping, Gloria," Nessie whispered. "Let's try to nap a bit and then we'll catch some fish for breakfast."

As dawn lit the sky, Nessie woke up from her short nap. Looking up, she could see two bright lights hurtling toward the East.

"Goodbye for now, my human friends," Nessie said to the rising sun. "Bless you, Mary Sweet, and know that we'll be there for you when you travel back in time to find Sir Wallace and the rest of the MacSquat Clan."

Chapter 7

Team Members Go Back in Time

As the Hypersonic Space Vehicle accelerated even more, it sent Mary Sweet's Human Team and Senior Detective McMouse past the Moon and onward toward Mars.

Simultaneously, and in a different time and dimension, General Gusto Gatwick and his wife piloted the same Time Machine that Mary Sweet was travelling in. They went faster than the speed of light to go forward in time. The simultaneous availability of the same Space Time Machine is a matter of *unknown* physics. Using a black hole anti-matter device, the Space Vehicle, if flown fast enough, would seem to split in two. One of the Spaceships could go forward in time and to one place in time and space, while the other could go in a very different time and direction.

As Mary Sweet's Space Vehicle moved closer to Mars, Gale Tully engaged the ship's Black Hole Anti-matter Device to create a small black hole at the rear of the vessel. They used it not to go back in time or forward to the Twenty-first Century but to the early years of World War Two. The General and his wife had decided to persuade the Nazi Government and its Leader Adolph Hitler to join them in the fight to defeat the British.

"My dear," General Gusto Gatwick said to his wife Tully Gale after their Space Time Machine had slowed down and began to enter the Earth's atmosphere, "when we persuade Our Führer to join us, and he will when he sees this Extraordinary Space Vehicle that we have stolen from the Russian engineers, we will defeat England in one single blow! With the energy we have on board this Vehicle, we will reduce the entire United Kingdom and all its Allies including the United States to cinders!"

As he finished speaking, a white light began to blink brightly on the ship's Control Console. "My darling husband, that's a sign of bad news," Tully said through the microphone that she had in her space helmet. "This light is a warning that someone has found this same space Time Machine in is certainly the Twenty-First Century. I would guess that the culprit who has stolen the Time-Replica of our Space Vehicle, the one we're now flying in, is none other than…"

"That Bitch of a Chief Inspector, Mary Sweet and her gang of criminals!" General Gatwick yelled through his microphone as he banged his seat with both fists. "She must be and will be killed at the first opportunity. But darling wife, how can she be flying this machine when we're flying it right now?"

"Sweetheart, she's flying this machine one hundred years from the current time we're in," Tully said as she pointed at the Time Clock on the Console. "Right now, we're in the early 1940's. Mary Sweet is, in all probability, testing this Vehicle's advanced Black Hole Technology right now. We should not be worried at all about her. First, you must win the war against the British. Then, when you become Emperor of the world, we can find and execute that criminal Sweet and the rest of her Teams."

As the Space Time Machine continued its descent toward the Earth, far below in the deep blue skies of a warm Paris summer during World War Two, a waiter was serving a glass of red wine to a local singer.

"Mademoiselle Edith Piaf, ma chanteuse préférée, chantez-vous ce soir pour les Parisiens?" Pierre asked the famous singer as he placed a long-stemmed wine glass on her table and filled it with a good local sauterne. "Or to say it in English, because we must practice that before General Patton comes here with his United States Army to free the French, Miss Edith Piaf, my favourite singer, will you be singing for the people of Paris tonight?"

"Tonight, Pierre?" the famous singer replied in English and French. "Non! S'il vous plait! I am not singing to those German Military Officers who have taken over our theatre. Porquoi? Why would I do that?"

"To entertain the thugs who would rather be out murdering the Jews of Paris," the waiter said. "You either sing for them or they won't be where the French Resistance and Underground wants them to be so we can all kill them!"

Pierre reached under Edith's table and took out a large blue bag. Opening it, he withdrew an automatic machine gun that the British had dropped by parachute in Northern France to help the French Resistance fighters win the war against the Nazis. "See, mon amie, look at this lovely weapon. All I have to do is aim it and pull the trigger and many Nazis will die."

"Bonne, Pierre," the woman said as she sipped her glass of red wine. "I have one just like it in my theatre, which I can get to by simply lifting a small trap door on the stage where I sing."

"Bonne, tres bonne!" Pierre replied. "Together, and joined by a deadly group of French Resistance fighters, we will surprise those German Generals and Officers as you finish the French National Anthem which you sing every night, do you not?"

"I do," Edith replied as she took another sip of wine. Looking up, she was startled to see a bright flash and a white line of smoke in the sky. "Pierre, what is that?" Edith asked as her wine glass almost fell over. "Is that a Nazi bomber come to destroy Paris?"

Pierre also looked up. As he did, the white line in the sky flashed the brightest red they had ever seen. A BOOM that was as loud as a thousand bombs hitting the buildings in their lovely city broke all of the windows in the shop-lined street. As people screamed and fled down the Rue de Paris toward the River Seine, a small black and red object began to descend toward the large square in the German Occupied Capital of France.

"Mon Dieu, look at its black and red colours!" the singer cried with astonishment. "That is not a British or German rocket. That is something that perhaps the Soviet Union has sent to help us!"

Getting up from the table, Edith and Pierre ran toward the triangular object as it settled down on the grass of a nearby park. As they watched, a door above them opened and a silver ladder descended to the ground. Two Nazi Officers put their heads out the door and waved to the crowd that had gathered below them. As General Gusto Gatwick, now wearing a Nazi General's Uniform surveyed the Germans who shouted up at them, he smiled at his wife who was now dressed as a German Colonel.

"The Time Machine worked well again, did it not, my good wife?" said Gatwick as he waved down at the hundreds of people who looked as small as ants. "And these Nazi uniforms?" he smirked as he fingered the fine clothe of his jacket, "they are the best disguise my wife has yet designed!"

"Thank you, mein liebender Nazi-General," she replied to him with a smile on her fat face. "See? I have learned some German, Das Deutche, for when we need it. And yes, the Time Machine worked very well. How well we both remember the first time we used it, when we went back in time to destroy both the Ancient English and the Scottish armies near that monstrous lake. This time, we went forward in time. And we are now…"

"A very unfortunate time during that Second World War which the Germans *lost* and the Russians and their allies *won* which was a horrible thing to happen!" the General stated as his eyes grew misty. "Oh, that I could come back as General Rommel the Tank Master. I would have defeated that scum of a General Patton and his Eighth Army and prevented the Allied Armies from landing in Italy."

"Maybe your wish will come true, my Herr Darling Man. One never knows what the future holds in store. Especially, if you can go forward and back and forward in Time over and over again."

"Very, very true." Looking down at the crowd again, Gatwick saw two German soldiers scream up at him, their rifles pointed at him, saying something that he could not understand. "My woman, what do those German soldiers yell at us?"

"They think we're Russians. They want us to come down or they'll shoot us."

"Shoot us? Are they mad? We'll destroy them all in a blink of an eye if they're not careful." He placed a hand on his hip and thought things over for ten seconds. "Darling Tully, we're both dressed as German Officers. Let's make the most of it and salute the immortal Teutonic God that was, and now is again and forever, Our great Führer!"

"What a gifted idea!" his wife replied. "Let's do it together."

Now standing at attention, the couple looked again down at the German soldiers. Taking his Luger pistol out of its black holster he wore at his side, Gusto Gatwick pointed it into the sky and fired one round to get everyone's attention.

"Heil Hitler!" Gatwick and Tully Gale shouted as they saluted by holding their right arms and hands flat and high. "We demand to speak to Our Führer at once! Time is of the essence. If we do not speak to him, it shall be the ruin of the Fatherland, Our Great Nazi Germany!"

As a platoon of German soldiers surrounded the red and black vehicle, one Army private saluted to the two German Officers that stood high above him in what looked somewhat like a V-1 rocket powered bomb, then turned to an Officer beside him. "Sir, is that a new rocket built by our German engineers near Munich?" he asked the Colonel.

"Nein! It is not one of ours, I do not think, Private," the German officer replied. "It has no Swastika on it. This could be like an old Greek Trojan Horse! It is a Russian rocket bomb. See the red and black colours and the Russian military plaque on the side of that thing, the one with the hammer and sickle?"

"If you think we are, we are not Russians," the male German Officer shouted down at him from the door of the rocket. "We have captured this from a manufacturing plant near Moscow. We are bringing you the newest technologies that the Russian's have created but, using our own German engineering skills, we have completely transformed it into the most powerful weapon ever known to man."

As the large crowd on the ground watched, the red, white and black flag of the New Germany unfurled high above them. In the exact centre was the Black German Swastika that Hitler himself had ordered to be sewn onto every flag not only in German but in all of occupied France.

"Seig Heil!" the German soldiers shouted as they saluted the flag. Two German Officers who had thought the strange rocket was from the Soviet Union looked at each other.

"That General has our Nazi Flag flying from this rocket," one Officer said. "Maybe he *is* German though his German is terrible and he speaks with an English accent."

"Humph!" the other Officer replied. "Those two German Officers? They could well be Russian spies. Perhaps they have been recruited by the French Resistance to help them win back Paris."

"Nonsense, my friend!," the other Officer said as he again saluted the flag above him. "See how the flag floats high even in this small wind? And didn't the man and woman shout 'Seig Heil!' and salute as we have all been taught to when we were much younger and were told to join the Nazi Youth? They are German Officers, and that, my friend, is the truth."

Looking again up at the two Uniformed Germans high above him, the Officer cleared his throat and yelled, "Mein friends! You are very welcome to France. Come down to join us."

"That is good!" the General shouted down from the rocket ship. "We will both climb down this ladder now. And then you must bring us to seen Mein Führer at once! We have important information for him."

As the pair of officers climbed down the ladder, the French singer, Edith, and the waiter Pierre watched the loud shouts of welcome as they both stood at the side of the crowd.

"The male is a German General," Edith Piaf whispered. "The other one is, I think, a Captain or a Colonel female officer. Pierre, tell your friends in the Resistance that we are now facing one of the most powerful weapons we have ever had to deal with since the war started."

"I'll do that, mon amie," Pierre replied. "Tonight, after your show, communicate with the British and Americans by Morse Code on your radio. Tell them what we have seen here, this giant rocket, and what we will do to the German Officers who will come to watch you tonight. After your final Encore, we kill them all. Morte!" he chuckled. "Morte, morte, morte!" he chuckled again as he pointed his finger at the German soldiers and pretended to pull the trigger of his weapon.

"I will do just that, Pierre. Now, you go back to the restaurant and I will soon join you. Let me try to get closer to those fat German Officer pigs so that I can hear them talking. As you know, I'm also fluent in German."

"Yes, and they will also know you as the most famous singer in France. In fact, perhaps you could ask them to come to the theatre to be entertained by you tonight."

Edith smiled that coy smile of hers which is one reason why people always called her 'The Little Sparrow'. "What a wonderful idea! Many birds shot at the same time with the same guns, is that right, Pierre?"

"Exactly, my little one," the Frenchman replied as he began to stroll away from her. "I will see you soon back at my restaurant. There, I will get you a fresh glass of wine.

"Bonne, et À bientôt, and see you soon," she replied. "En heure, one single hour, at the most, I promise."

"Good. See you in an hour or less."

When the waiter disappeared into the crowd, Edith made her way toward the fat German officers. Taking a position next to a French woman she knew well who owned the small café near the theatre, Edith listened to the German's conversation as she translated for her friend.

"I will use English because, then, none of these people will understand," Edith whispered to her friend. "The Fat General from the rocket has been promised by that German Colonel that he'll arrange for him to see Hitler tonight during our show. Ah! Hitler himself will come to see me tonight! What a perfect opportunity to gun down all of these criminals at the same time."

"But you must be careful, my darling Edith," the friend replied. "If Hitler is in the theatre, there will be many soldiers there and they will all be carrying weapons, too."

"There is always the explosive device," Edith explained as she took a pack of Gitane cigarettes out of the small purse she was carrying. "I will use one single match to light the long fuse and, when

I walk off stage and out of the theatre with all of our French visitors, that big bomb will go BOOM! Though I would rather shoot them all myself and watch them scream in pain just as they've done to many of our friends."

Both women laughed quietly as they turned from the group of German officers.

"Edith, I won't be at the theatre tonight," her friend said quietly. "My foot is hurting me again. It's the metal pieces from the explosive that went off under me when the German troops invaded our beloved Paris."

"Then go to bed, mon amie," Edith replied. "Go to sleep and if you're awakened in the night by a loud explosion, you know that Hitler is finally dead and the war is over."

As the two women left the crowd, the disguised couple disguised as German General Gusto Gatwick and Colonel Gale walked between two German officers to a waiting vehicle. "German engineering at its best!" Gusto said to his wife as they both sat into the Mercedes. "I bet that Hitler himself sent this to bring us to our wonderful Parisian hotel room."

"Darling, isn't this a wonderful car," Tully replied as the driver started the engine. "When we finish talking to Hitler, let's take a walk around Paris. I love Paris in the summer."

"And so do I," Gusto replied as he took her hand. "See? I'm even wearing an Iron Cross and will tell Hitler that he personally gave that to me for service during the German battle for Saint Petersburg!"

"You're thinking of the battle of Stalingrad," the woman replied. "Use that term instead."

As the long black car drove down the Rue d'Notre Dame, in another time and millions of miles away from the Earth, the triangular Hypersonic Vehicle hurtled toward the outer regions of the Known Universe.

On the small Control Deck of the Space Vehicle, Private Sarah Scots looked up at her console and saw that their speed was way beyond what she'd anticipated.

"Mary Sweet, we've already gone past the speed of light! I need to slow this ship down before we fly past all the planets and into the centre of the Galaxy!"

Mary, still sitting in her specially designed flight seat, looked up toward the Private then back at her Team. Beside her, McMouse lay flat on his seat and smiled up at his Chief.

"Just think, Mary, we're now going backwards in time."

"Yes, my McMouse friend," Mary replied. "Back in time to catch that General idiot, wherever he may fly to."

"But how can he go back in time without the Hypersonic Vehicle we're now flying in?" Tony asked from a nearby couch. "Isn't that impossible or does he have another Time Machine?"

"No, he does not!" explained McMouse. "He's using this same Vehicle and for all we know, right now! He can do that because we're using this Hypersonic Vehicle in the current time, on today's date, while he's using it at some other time and probably in some other place."

"Like on Earth?" Colonel Francis McOuvre asked from the seat behind them. "If he's there, we need to turn this Time Machine around, accelerate again, and go right back to find that Clown General!"

"I agree, Frank," Sally Orchid said from her seat next to him. "If we let him escape, God alone knows when we'll find him again. At some point, when the two Time Machines become one again, we must destroy them both!"

The entire command deck grew silent as they realized that both Frank and Sally were dead right. "Private Sarah," Mary Sweet commanded. "Turn this space machine around right now! We've no idea what the General is up too and we must track him down!"

Suddenly, the Hypersonic Space Vehicle began to shake and oscillate back and forth. A loud BOOM was heard behind them. On her monitor, Private Scots watched as large pieces of the aft section of the craft flew into space.

"I'm declaring an emergency, Chief," the Private shouted through her microphone. "Make sure you're strapped into your seats as tight as possible. The onboard detectors are all in the Red and indicate that our Black Hole Device has melted down!"

"Private, do what you need to do to save the ship," Mary yelled back over the screeching of metal that filled the command deck. "If you can, stop her right now! We need to do a spacewalk to determine if we can get the Device back in operation."

As Sarah powered down the throttle to their rockets, the vibration began to ease. Lowering the titanium screen that protected all of the command deck's windows, the entire crew could see stars everywhere. A bright white star filled the deck with light.

"That's a neutron star," Tony said as he punched a button on his seat. Above them, fitted to the ceiling of the command deck, a large monitor began to glow with small white lights. "This is the star map that was recently uploaded onto the ship by our American and English astronomers. The way I see it, we're close to the centre of the Milky Way Galaxy."

"Understood, Mister Enwenopa," the Private whispered as they all heard the turbine powered rocket engines wind down. "God alone knows how far we are from the Earth. If I activate our Emergency Beacon aboard our Vehicle, it will take eons to be picked up by Earth's scientists."

"So there's no possibility of a rescue," Mary replied. "Very well. Then it's up to us to fix the problem with the Black Hole Device and the mechanisms that power our Stardrive. Francis and Sally, I'm afraid it's up to you to conduct the spacewalk. We'll monitor every step you take. When you get to what's left of the Device housing, we'll see how damaged it is and try to determine a method to fix it."

"Spacewalk? Me?" Francis yelped into his mic. "Why can't Tony do it. He's more qualified than I am."

"Don't worry, Frank," Sally said as she took his hand. "I'll be right next to you."

As the pair climbed out of their seats, a bright flash of light lit up the command deck, even brighter than the nearby neutron star. A mist appeared at the window filled with glimmering light and, as the glowing mist mysteriously poured through the Vehicle's closed windows, they could all hear two familiar voices.

"Mary Sweet and this Human Team! Look outside the window. We've come to rescue you in our ancient Time Machine."

The entire Team looked past the glimmering mist and saw a craft made of wood and metal. Seated side by side in small seats, two Ghosts that the Humans immediately recognised were both waving at them.

"Do not come out of that newfangled Vehicle!" a ghostly voice ordered as the mist pulsed in red and gold colours. "If anyone comes out here into the frigid vacuum of Outer Space, you'll be killed instantly by the radiation from that pulsating neutron star."

Mary realised instantly that the voice was that of her Ghost friend Sherlock Holmes. Peering out the window, she could see the Ghost of Doctor Watson sitting next to him. "Roger that, Mister Holmes," she stated into her helmet's mic. "We'll forget the spacewalk unless you need some assistance."

Francis, whose face was now white as a sheet, looked at Sally. "Did you hear that Ghost? We both could have been fried to death if we had gone outside!"

"Yes, Frank, but we weren't fried, were we?" Sally replied as she took his hand. "Let's just sit back and see how the Ghosts get on."

"My Human friends, this is Doctor Watson talking to you via my latest invention, The Talking Mist Communications System," Watson's ghostly voice said over a loud speaker. "Give us a moment. We will lasso your strange modern Vehicle with a rope that we've brought from Earth with us."

"Just a rope?" the Private said into her microphone. "Doctor Watson, you'll need much more than a simple length of rope to capture our spacecraft."

"Ah, but this is a very special kind of rope," Watson replied. "It's made of a combination of titanium and star stuff that we encountered when we were searching for you in our Time Machine. Hold on while we capture your Space Vehicle."

Outside the window, the Team watched as Watson stood up in his ancient vehicle. Holding a long piece of silver coloured rope, he fashioned a lasso at the end. Swinging it around over his head, he let go of it and they watched as the circle of steel became larger and larger, large enough to encircle their Vehicle.

"I'm going to pull on the rope now," the ghostly voice uttered. "You'll feel your structure shake a bit as we capture your spacecraft and, when I pull back and attach it to our Time Machine, your entire

Vessel will shudder and wobble even more but for only a few seconds."

When the Team felt their ship begin to shake and wobble, they all knew that Watson had been successful.

"Watson, I'll now start the Time Machine Wheel," the speaker said in Sherlock Holmes's voice. "When I count to One, we'll move back in time and find that blasted General!"

The Team watched as the Time Machine Wheel began to spin faster and faster.

"Holmes and Watson, my speed indicator shows that our Vehicle isn't moving at all yet. Not one bloody inch!" Private Scots shouted into her microphone. "Is there any way you can increase the power enough to achieve escape velocity? We'll need that to move away from the neutron star."

"Elementary, my dear Scots woman," Holmes voice replied. "All Watson and I need is a very long length of standard steel rope which you now call a 'cable'. Or something else that will attract energy from that brilliantly pulsating star."

"A cable to attract energy?" Francis stated with a face that was whiter than any Ghost that Sally had ever seen. "They want to get unlimited power from that neutron star? We'll all be dead if we do what they ask us to do."

"Nonsense, my great friend, Francis," the speaker said this time in Watson's voice. "The titanium steel of your Vessel will protect all of you from the power of that small dense sun. And as to Holmes and I? We'll make certain that we're a far enough distance away that no energy of any kind will hurt us. Besides, we're Ghosts, remember?"

"How could I forget?" Frank said to Sally. "Ghosts. Only Ghosts can save us and with my luck, I'll be a Ghost before I know it."

"Francis, please be quiet," Mary ordered as she unbuckled her seatbelt and floated toward the control console. "Private Scots, let them use the Long Range Antenna. It's useless to us now, anyway. If they attach it to their vehicle and when we command the antenna to extend to its maximum length, that should be enough to attract the power that they require."

"Roger that, Chief," the Private replied as she toggled a switch on the console in front of her. "The right section of the High Gain Antenna is now attaching itself to the Ghost's Time Machine. I've instructed the right and middle section of the antenna to extend to maximum length."

As the Team watched, they saw that part of the antenna had already attached itself to the sled-like Time Machine. The two other part of the antenna, extended to a length of more than five-hundred feet, now pointed directly at the nearby star.

"Thank you, Private," a Ghostly voice said. "Now all we have to do is wait for a solar flare and that should do it!"

Private Scots suddenly looked back to her Chief Inspector. "Chief, my indicator shows that a Solar Flare is beginning to make its way toward the end of the antenna. I'm now in complete control of this spacecraft. Everyone, sit down if you're not and prepare for maximum velocity."

As Mary took her seat again, and with all the other Humans already seated, they all looked out as a bright white tendril of light snaked its way from the nearby star toward the end of the antenna.

"Right, Watson, here we go! When the Flare hits that long white and silver pole, that will be enough energy for almost anything that comes to mind!" they all heard Holmes say to his friend. "Chief Inspector Mary Sweet, in three seconds we'll be able to move your spacecraft. In ten seconds, we'll hit maximum velocity and once again, the Black Hole Device will begin working. Then, a few seconds after that, we'll go back in time as we all streak toward our home, the Earth."

"Finally!" Francis said in a hushed voice as he took Sally's hand again. "There's no place like home and, Sally? I swear I'm never going into Space again."

Out the window, the Team saw a brilliant flash of light as the snaking column of white-hot sunlight hit the High Gain antenna that had been extended from their space vehicle. They watched out the window made of high-technology crystal as the Wheel of the Ghost's Ancient Time Machine began to spin, so fast that it seemed to disappear. Their Hypersonic Space Vehicle began to shudder as, behind them, they once again heard a loud BOOM as the Black Hole Device began to spin up.

"It's working!" Mary yelled into her microphone. "Holmes and Watson? You have unlimited energy from that dense sun. Use it now!"

Both Time Machines began to glow a hot white, almost as bright as the neutron star. Watson, seated next to Holmes, looked back over his shoulder to study the spectacular damage to the Hypersonic Space Vehicle. Pieces of the structure that had protected the Black Hole Device floated all around the area. One piece as large as an elephant floated by the Ancient Time Machine.

"My friend, see the fractured metal surrounding the Human's Black Hole Device?" Watson said to Holmes. "If we power it up any more with that star's energy, that poor broken globe will explode due to an overload on the radioactive materials inside of it, and our friends will all be dead."

"Watson, what you say is true," Sherlock replied as he pulled out a pipe and lit it with a very small flare from the neutron star. "Have no fear! We'll use that vast power to pull our friends' strange vehicle fast than the speed of light and then, even if that Black Hole Device explodes, the explosion will be in a different time and they'll all be safe. Now, it's back to Earth where we all started from. Watson, on my mark, push your Time Accelerator lever forward with all the pressure you can muster!"

When Watson did what his friend suggested, their Time Machine began speeding away from the neutron star. The two vehicles were going so fast that stars whizzed past them like streaks of light.

"That's all the power there is, my friend Holmes," the Ghost of Watson said. "In a few shakes, we'll be home again."

On their Hypersonic Space Time Machine, Private Scots and the entire Team looked up at the monitors to see the neutron star recede behind them.

"What a wonderful pair of Ghosts!" Mary exclaimed to her Team. "If it wasn't for them, we'd be lost in space forever! But now, we go back in time and, having proven that this Vehicle works as specified, we can kill that General Gatwick wherever he is and whatever time he's in. Private! Locate the General's Hypersonic Vehicle in its own time and space. Plug those time and space coordinates into the navigation system. In only a few moments, according to our Ghost Friends, we'll all be home again."

As the Team watched the ship's accelerometer and Mach Speed indicator, they could all see that they were already travelling back in time. On the television monitor, a faint yellow star appeared. Then they saw the planet Jupiter and next, Mars. Finally, they could see Earth.

"Oh, it's a cold day in Hell when someone like that General will become the Emperor of the Earth," Tony said into his helmet's mic. "Look at the Date indicator. We're now in the mid-nineteen hundreds. See how the clock is slowing down? Now it's nineteen forty-one. That's at the very beginning of World War Two, at least to the people of the United States and a number of its Allies."

"A cold day in Hell?" Mary squawked back. "You're right. Where that General is going it'll be hotter than Hell and that's a promise!"

Chapter 8

Mary Sweet and her Team Land in the Streets of Paris

On the streets of Paris, a young girl looked up into the sky. A BOOM like the noise of a heavy bombardment shook the streets of her city. Running through a rainfall of shattered glass and toward a nearby theatre, she bolted up a number of concrete steps and found the famous French singer, Edith Piaf, just as she was about to enter.

"Madame, look up at the sky!" the young girl wailed. "The Nazi's are bombing our city again."

"Non, mon fille, my little girl," Edith said to her young friend. "A rocket from the Soviet Union is now descending to the nearby park, didn't you know that? It must be a supply ship come to help us win this filthy war with the Nazi's."

As the two entered the theatre, high overhead in the Hypersonic Vehicle, Mary Sweet looked at the navigation monitor.

"There! See that large red blip?" Mary shouted. "That has to be General Gusto Gatwick. We've successfully tracked him here. He's at a hotel quite near the centre of Paris." Taking off her helmet, she looked back at her small selection of Team Members and then to Private Scots, who was still flying the spacecraft. "Ladies and gentlemen, prepare to go into battle again. Private, after we embark with any weapons we can find on this Vehicle, go forward in time and tell all our other Teams we need their help. Bring them all back here with all of their weapons as soon as you can."

"Understood, Chief Inspector," the Private replied. "Rather than land this ship, why not use the parachutes to drop into Paris as soon as you can. It's almost dark, so from the ground, you'll be almost invisible."

"Parachutes I can do," Frank said to Sally. "I've jumped a number of times now."

"Well, Frank, I've never jumped," Sally replied and Francis saw the fear in her face.

"Sally, I was taught by one of the best instructors in all of England. When we jump, we'll jump together and I'll show you then how easy it is."

"Okay, Team! Prepare to jump," Mary Sweet ordered. As they all donned their parachute packs, Sally pulled hers on back to front.

"Frank, I have this wrong, don't I?" she asked with a note of fear. "I'm going to die in only minutes?"

"Nonsense, Sally," Frank replied. "Let me help you put this on the right way."

As Frank worked on Sally's parachute, Mary and the rest of her Team felt the Vehicle stop and, looking out the window again, saw that they were high over the city of Paris. "Oh, how I love this City!" Mary said to Tony as she donned her parachute. "It's a city that I always wanted my late husband, Hubert, and I to visit. But we never had the time."

"Chief, you're here now so concentrate on your parachute descent," Tony replied as he put on his own jump equipment. "See you on the ground. By the way, there are a number of high-powered carbines and handguns in the small hold right next to the exit door."

"That's super, Tony! Now let's get down on the ground and grab that General Gatwick piss wort!"

In only minutes, when the entire Team had exited the Hypersonic Vehicle, Mary, swinging from her parachute harness, looked up to see her vehicle already heading back into space. Below her, she found that the twinkling lights of Paris held a special note of magic for her.

"Hubert, if you're here, make yourself known to me, please husband," Mary whispered as she fell softly toward the Parisian streets. "We'll have a wonderful time here. Its' almost spring, you know, and after we both help to defeat the Nazi's and capture the General, you and I can be re-married and start life's circle all over again."

A moment later, the entire Team had landed near a wide river that Mary knew was the River Seine. "Team, this way! First, we must go to a nearby theatre to meet a woman that most of you will recognise. Then, and only then, will we find our way to that culprit General's hotel room and there, we will assassinate him and his murderous wife."

As the streetlights flickered all around them McMouse, who had been asleep in Mary's spacesuit pocket and was then transferred by Tony into her Special Forces Uniform Jacket, finally woke up when Mary's feet hit the grass and she rolled over. Climbing up onto her shoulder and clinging to her Uniform, he looked around at the lights of a strange city.

"Chief, where are we now? Back in London, I hope."

"No, mouse. We're in Paris now. We're going to start fighting in World War Two."

"Another war?" McMouse replied as he yawned. "Not another one. Oh, Dear Lord, this time I'll never get home to my wife."

As the pair ran down the street, a German military vehicle moved by them at speed. In the back of the open topped vehicle, they saw a small man sitting next to a German Officer. Both McMouse and Mary knew who it was because they recognised him immediately.

The Enemy. Adolph Hitler. It was only then that Mary realised that her mission was much more than to kill a simple traitorous General. She must also try to kill the Führer. Otherwise, Germany could well win the War and, upon the death of Hitler, General Gusto Gatwick would become the next Führer which, in German, is the definition of Emperor.

"The Führer is Emperor in the German language!" she whispered to the mouse as Mary followed the back of Hitler's transport with dark eyes. "And now we must kill him, too."

Chapter 9

Mary Sweet is Captured by the Gestapo

Mary and her mouse Senior Detective made their way down a Parisian street toward Edith Piaf's theatre. Just as they were climbing the steps toward the front door, a woman dressed in a German military uniform walked up. Pulling out a Luger sidearm, she smiled as she spoke to them in broken English.

"Do not move, my friend," she stated shortly. "I order you to a hotel room that we have prepared especially for you, you bitch of an English woman."

Mary looked at the woman's hand and saw the black sidearm glinting in a nearby streetlight.

"Yes, I am English but I doubt I'm the woman you're looking for. I am a British Chief Inspector with the London Police who has long supported the German cause I am here as a tourist."

"You lie!" the Nazi woman snarled. "You are a British Spy! I am told to capture you or, if you try to escape, to kill you. Now get in front of me or a shoot you right here!" With the weapon pointed at her stomach, Mary had no choice but to stand with her back to the woman. The Nazi pushed the gun into her spine. "Hands up! Now, march!"

"I need to put my hands into my pockets," Mary said as she felt McMouse climb up her arm. "My hands are cold! I should be inside now to watch Edith Piaf singing to many German officers including our Führer. If I were you, you horror of a woman, I'd let me go into the theatre right now or you'll be arrested by the Gestapo."

The Nazi pushed the tip of her weapon even harder into Mary's spine. "March, I say! Now!"

The tiny mouse had already leaped out of Mary's pocket and down onto the pavement. Scampering up the steps to the theatre's front door, he looked back at his Human Friend and in Mouse Language he squeaked, "Don't worry, my Chief. I'll find Edith and together, we'll come to rescue you.

"Please hurry," Mary replied in Mouse Language squeak. "They'll torture me, I'm sure. They'll want to know the locations of the rest of our Teams."

"Done!" the mouse replied. The last time Mary saw him, the tiny mouse was scampering through the front door and into the warm theatre.

"Why do you make that noise in your mouth and nose, that *squeaking*?" the Nazi woman asked as they began to march down a nearby street. "Stop, do you hear me? No more noise at all until we reach your hotel."

Within minutes, Mary Sweet was taken into a dilapidated hotel. The wooden floor boards were warped and the reception area smelled of something that made her want to vomit. Marching her past a framed photo of Adolph Hitler, the Nazi woman forced her to turn down a hallway then in through an open door. In a dim light, she could see two German Officers, each dressed in Gestapo uniforms with Silver Skulls on their uniform hats, studying some papers spread on the desk that that sat at.

"You are Mary Barkeley Sweet," a German officer stated in English as he held up a single sheet of paper. "This is your photo, is it not?"

Mary moved slowly to the table. Looking at the photo, she shook her head. "Nein. That is not me. Nor is my middle name 'Barkeley'. I was never given a middle name."

"But that is you!" the other Gestapo Agent stated in his thick Berlin accent. "The woman in this photo looks exactly like you except that her hair is black not blonde like you have. You have simply dyed your hair, is true?"

"Nein again," Mary stated. When one of the Gestapo agents motioned for her to take a seat, Mary became determined to stand. "My name is Mary Sweet and only that. I have been given permission by your Government to visit Paris as a tourist. I am on leave from my job as a German Spy who was assigned by Mein Führer to live in London and extract secrets from British politicians and officers."

"You are German Spy? You work for us?" an Agent said as he frowned and banged a fist on the desk. "You are no German Spy! You work for the English government as well as the French Resistance." Standing, he bent toward her, staring at her with his two black eyes. "You are a Chief Inspector based in London. That is what our records show."

"Your records are incorrect. I am a German Spy working directly for Mein Führer and have come here to give him my latest report on the state of the English Airforce, as I was ordered to."

"Nein! I tell you Nien!" the other Agent yelled as he also banged a fist on the desk. "You are no Spy at all! Nor have you ever met our Führer! Now, we know that you have come here to kill all of us, those who are loyal to Adolph Hitler. We also know that you have many Teams of the French Resistance with you. Unless you want to be taken by that woman behind you and be beaten within an inch of your life by her, you will tell us what we want to know."

"But none of what you say is true!" Mary said as she tried her best to smile. "Your information is Nein. False. I'm not sure how to say it in German."

"If you were a Spy for Germany you would know good German," a Gestapo agent stated. "We have received this *Goot* information from a German General you may know. General Gatwick, who is English but has worked for us since before this War started."

The Nazi woman behind Mary put her lips near her ear. "Perhaps you would like a nice cup of English tea and tell these gentlemen what they wish to know before I begin to beat you."

"That Gatwick is a fake and a fraud and always tells lies," Mary stated flatly. "I have been ordered by our Führer to assassinate him and that woman who says she is his wife. I have a great deal of German but I am so stressed that I am unable to remember most of it. So, get on with it. If you want to beat me and torture me, then do so. I will tell you nothing because I have nothing to tell."

"Oh, but you do and you will, Mary," one of the Agents said to her as he smiled. "When this German soldier is done with you, your own son will not recognise your face."

"Oh, shut up and get on with it!" Mary yelled. "I've never been tortured before and I have no son. Stop wasting my time and just do it."

"Thy will be done!" the Agent stated and, snapping his fingers, the woman Nazi soldier led Mary back out of the room.

"You are a tough English woman," the Nazi stated as she led Mary down the hall. "My name is Zelda. I am your tourist guide this evening."

"Tourist guide," Mary said in a stern voice. "You're very lucky I don't have my revolver with me or I'd shoot you in the face."

"No weapon for you tonight," Zelda replied as she took Mary into a small room and switched on a bright overhead light. "Now, sit in that chair. I think you'll find it very comfortable."

"I'm rather tired anyway. By the way, I'd appreciate it if you'd be rather gentle with my hair. I've always been proud of it."

"Courage you have, my friend," Zelda said as she put on a pair of leather gloves. "Let us see if you have courage when I am done beating you."

As Mary sat down, the woman hit her once in the nose. Mary Sweet could feel blood trickle down onto her lips. "Is that all you've got, my Zelda? Even a mouse can hit better than that."

Zelda hit her again and again. When she was finished with the flurry of her fists, she looked down at the small English woman and smiled again. "Now, you will tell me the location of your Resistance Teams. Do it now or I will beat you to death."

"Death, schmesh," Mary stated tasting the blood in her mouth. "Go on. Hit me some more! I rather like being hit. When you hit me, you look like a Pink Elephant, you're that fat."

"A what?" the woman said. "A pink…? Well, let's see if I can make you look like a dead cow."

As Mary felt the woman's fists hit her face over and over again, she thought she could see a giant Lizard staring down at her as it crawled across the ceiling. "Oh, look! What a lovely green Lizard."

"A what? I know what 'lizard' means in English. Where do you see it? Where?"

"There!" Mary said as she pointed up. "It tells me it wants to eat you for dinner."

"Dinner? The Lizard wants to eat me?" Looking down at her English captive, this time the woman shook her head. "You are crazy, no? I should not have to beat you. You will tell me nothing of interest to the Gestapo Agents because you know nothing. You really are a Spy for the Führer, aren't you?"

"Yes," Mary gurgled through her bloody mouth. She spit, and saw her blood on the floor. "I was tortured before by the English and the Scots. They broke my face all up as well as many bones in my body. But I refused to talk."

"Good, that is very good." Zelda sat down on a nearby bench and, flexing her hands, smiled back at Mary Sweet. "You have survived my beating and there are many who have not. So, I know you are a loyal German woman like me. Together, the German woman will help to defeat all of Britain."

"So very true," Mary sighed as she felt her head falling to her shoulder. "I think I'll have a short sleep right now."

"You do that. Then, I will get you a coffee and a cigarette."

The door opened and one of the Gestapo Agents walked in. He looked down at his victim and said to his torturer, "Zelda, has she talked yet?"

"Yes," the German woman replied. "But she has said nothing of interest. Mein friend, she is an English woman because she is born there. But can't you see her face and blonde hair through all that blood? She is German woman! A Spy for Our Führer, just like she said."

The Agent walked over to Mary Sweet. "So, you truly are a Spy working for Hitler? If so, that is quite easy to find out. He's staying in the hotel just next door to this building. You will have a coffee and I will find out if what you say is true very soon."

'*I'm already asleep,*' Mary thought to herself as he head fell onto her chest. 'I taste honey now, not blood. Oh, that I had one small cup of tea and a plate of scones and jam! Maybe I'll hear McMouse squeaking as he rescues me or even Sherlock Holmes'.

In her sleep, Mary Sweet began talking in Mouse Language. The Private and German Agent both looked at each other and frowned.

"The squeaking woman has gone quite mad due to the many blows that you've given to her," the Agent said as he frowned. "Our Führer will not be a happy man. He could have you executed for what you've done."

"It was you who ordered me to strike her many times to get her to tell us something that she had no knowledge of," the woman soldier replied. As Zelda watched from the wooden bench, the female whom she now knew to be a German Spy began to snore. "That woman is one of the most courageous Germans I've ever met," Zelda whispered to the Gestapo Agent. "Sir, do make certain that she works for Hitler. Mad as she is, and as you know better than me, she could be a double agent also working for the British. In the meantime, we'll both have coffee and a cigarette while the woman is sleeping."

"Done, Private Zelda," the Agent stated as he turned away from her. "Do not befriend this mad woman. As you say, Hitler might not know this female at all. Guard her well for, if she escapes, it will be *you* sitting in that chair!"

In the city centre Theatre of Paris, McMouse crawled up onto the small dark stage as Edith Piaf began to sing the French National Anthem, *La Marseillaise*. The Mouse Senior Detective looked out on the audience sitting at small square tables in the shadows. He could see a fat General sitting next to a gorgeous blonde woman sharing a bottle of Champagne. At another table, a group of High-Ranking German Officers were laughing as they played cards and smoking cigarettes. Further back in the crowded restaurant that also served as Edith's theatre, a large part of lower ranking officers drank beer from large steins and sang the German National Anthem in protest to Edith's song. When the Germans sang loud enough to drown out Edith's singing, a number of Frenchmen and Frenchwomen stood up and sang with Edith. Back and forth they sang and the song turned into a chant.

"Viva la France!" a French woman shouted.

"Down with France!" a German officer shouted back. "Long live Germany, our Fatherland!"

As they kept chanting, the front door opened and, as a gust of cold wind entered the room, a small group of soldiers all carrying sub-machine guns, entered.

"It is Mein Führer!" a General shouted as the entire room stood up. "He has come to see the French woman sing, just as he promised he would."

As McMouse and Edith Piaf looked down from the stage, Pierre, the waiter who was also a high-ranking French Resistance officer, leaped up from the floor to stand next to the French singer.

"Look! It is Adolph Hitler who now joins us!" he shouted. "Let us welcome him to Paris in the best way we know!"

As Hitler entered the room many of the French people began to clap slowly as all the Germans shouted, "Heil Hitler!" and gave him the flat-handed salute. Hitler, following his line of soldiers, took a seat at the very front of the house. A French waitress offered him a bottle of wine but all the Führer did was ignore her.

"Bring Our Führer an ashtray! He needs to smoke!" a soldier said. As the waitress ran to do his bidding, on stage Edith continued singing the French National Anthem. As she neared the end of the famous song, a French woman stood up and shouted again, "Viva La France!"

The Germans all shouted back, "Lang lebe Deutschland! Sig Heil! Sig Heil! Sig Heil!"

"Quiet!" Hitler yelled as he stood up at the table. "I have come here to see the famous Edith Piaf sing. She has sung her national anthem which is very understandable given the circumstances."

Adolph Hitler began to slap his hands together in applause as Edith finished the French Anthem. Because Hitler did it, the other Germans began to applaud, too. Looking up at the singer with his small black eyes, he smiled through his strange moustache.

"Mademoiselle Piaf, would you please sing something else for me and my good friends? Choose anything that you'd like to sing. I know all of your songs in both German and French and, if you don't mind, I'll join you on stage and sing with you."

Still on the stage next to Edith and McMouse, Pierre smiled so widely he showed all of his white teeth. "Oh, it is so perfect, is it not!" he whispered to the French singer. "Ten seconds from now, take out your weapon and begin shooting. I will give a signal to the other Resistance fighters here who will also get ready."

As McMouse and Edith watched, the Resistance Officer took out a lighter and a cigarette. Lighting it, he held the flame high over his head. When he did, a dozen men and women stood up. All of them started reaching for black bags beneath their tables and chairs.

"Pierre, my machine gun is hidden beneath the trap door at my feet," Edith said to the waiter. "Stand in front of me and I will get it."

"And I will take out my Mouse Revolver as well as my Mouse Tommy Gun," the tiny Mouse squeaked as he took the weapons from a small green bag that lay on the floor near his small hairy paws. "I have other friends of mine, all of my Human and Animal Teams, who are now at the front door. When we open fire on the Germans, they will also open fire with many different types of weapons including a modern bazooka that they brought with them from our time."

"So, the tiny mouse talks again!" Pierre whispered as he stood in front of Edith. "It is good that you have many more weapons, my good friend. We will start shooting when Edith begins to sing and as Hitler steps toward the stage."

As the French woman opened the trap door and pulled out her machine gun from its hiding place, she stood up and smiled down at the crowd.

"Mister Hitler, sir, while you are not my Führer, I will welcome you to Paris by allowing you up here to sing with me!" she said into her microphone. When the French members of the audience began to clap, Edith started to tap on the microphone. "Testing again. Testing," she said into it. "My dear friends, comrades and German visitors. I now sing something that I so very much love. It is a love song but it is also a song of loss and heartbreak. I give you *Non, Je Ne Regrette Rien*. No Regrets, as they say in English but for Hitler, I will sing it in German, too."

As the Führer stepped toward the stage, the front door opened again. From his standing position on top of Pierre's head, McMouse saw the Teams of Humans and Animals walk into the theatre.

"We're all here, Pierre, mon amie bon," the mouse whispered into Pierre's ear. "Give the word, and we'll all begin shooting." McMouse held up his Tommy Gun. Taking aim on the Fat German General, he pulled off the safety and smiled down at his target. "That fat general is the first one to go. He is the type of German officer who could order the capture of my best friend, Mary Sweet."

"Then do it. And do it when I shout 'Now!'" Pierre replied with a huge wink from one of eye.

Hitler was only five or six steps from the stage when Pierre held up his machine gun and shouted, "NOW! *Maintenant!*"

The room erupted in a firefight as the French Resistance and the Teams led by McMouse began to kill the German officers. The Fat General rose to his feet as the mouse sprayed him with tiny bullets. Looking down at his Uniform jacket, the General saw tiny wounds erupt from his chest as blood spilled down onto the table.

"What are they shooting?" he asked to the woman sitting next to him. "These are mere pebbles. They won't kill anyone. Pour me another glass of Champagne, won't you my darling?"

McMouse took aim at the German General's fat face. The *rat-tat-tat* from his Tommy Gun filled the air as the General was hit in both eyes, his nose, both cheeks and in his forehead.

"Mein Gott! I am morte!" the General cried as he fell onto the woman's shoulders. As blood spilled onto her white dress, she began to scream in German for help.

"Kill them!" Pierre shouted as he sprayed the German soldiers with more bullets. "Kill them all!"

As the entire house erupted in murderous fire, the German soldiers with Hitler began to fire back. Running within the small phalanx of soldiers, Hitler was taken quickly toward a side door that a German soldier blew open with a short blast from his machine gun. As Hitler stormed toward the open door, the Team of Animals appeared. They jumped and hopped through the broken door and into the deadly battle. Colonel Catnip, the Black Cat Leader of the Cat Team, leapt up onto the Führer's back, digging claws into both shoulders and biting the German Leader on the back of the neck.

"Someone get this animal off of me!" Hitler cried as a German Colonel hit Catnip with an open hand. When the Cat Leader fell onto the floor, he turned and began to hiss.

"You will all die!" he hissed as he opened his mouth and showed his long fangs to the German Officer. "Give up now, before you are all dead!"

"Catnip, no!" McMouse screamed from on top of Pierre's head. "You are not big enough to take a bullet anywhere in your thin body!"

The German Colonel smiled as he pulled out a small revolver from the holster on his hip. Taking aim, he fired two times. Colonel Catnip was knocked off his feet, and McMouse could see that he had been shot in the head and the stomach.

"He's dead!" the mouse cried. "My cat friend is dead! And look! See how many mice, dogs and other cats are also dead or wounded."

Looking down, McMouse could see the floor of the theatre littered with the small bodies of the Animal Team. Some of their legs or whiskers twitched, as did the tail of a small dark dog, and McMouse knew that those animals were only wounded and still alive. "But some will be dead by morning, I'm sure of that," he said. "Now it's time to get my own back on those that have killed my Cat best friend."

Leaping off of Pierre's head and onto a nearby table, the mouse took aim at the German Officer who had killed the Cat Colonel. As he did, Pierre ran toward the edge of the stage.

"We are letting Hitler get away!" Pierre shouted as he leaped onto the floor. Edith opened fire with her machine gun, spraying the remaining German officers with a long hail of bullets. Reloading, she opened fire again.

"We will win this night!" she screamed as she shot a German woman Army officer in the neck and head. "Viva La France, I tell you, again and again and again!"

McMouse fired his tiny machine gun at the German Colonel who had killed Catnip but, when he missed, Pierre fired three times and struck the Colonel in the stomach. Running through the crowd that fought each other, he again aimed his weapon at the German Colonel but the Colonel, who was dying from his wound, aimed at Pierre with a Luger and fired one time. McMouse could only watch as his French Resistance Friend fell onto the floor. Turning around, he watched Hitler protected by his phalanx of German soldiers escape out the side door of the Theatre. Hearing a familiar war cry at the front of the Theatre, McMouse spun again. He watched as Tony Enwenopa, dressed in a Green Royal Marine Uniform, held up a bazooka from where he stood by the front door. Already loaded, he took aim at the group of Hitler body guards that had not followed their Leader but had instead been ordered to protect the German Officers.

"Heads down!" Tony shouted as he took aim. "Piaf, tell your friends that I'm shooting now!"

"Tête baissée!" she screamed three times. "Get your heads down, mon amies."

"Fire in the hold!" Tony screamed as he pulled the bazooka trigger. The modern-day rocket left the steel tube and exploded almost immediately. As the smoke cleared, the mouse, now standing on Edith's head, could see that all of the German soldiers and Officers were either dead or severely wounded. He also counted the bodies of a number of French resistance fighters among the dead and wounded.

"We have lost some of our people but their deaths will not go in vain," Edith said to him as she climbed down from the stage. Looking across the room, she saw the body of a French Resistance Fighter lying on the floor next to a German Officer that he had killed. "Oh my God! It is Pierre! He is dead!"

As she hurried through the many bloody corpses to the body of her friend, she could see that he'd been shot one time in the head.

"His death was quick but that is no mercy," she said as she fell to her knees beside him. "Mouse? He is one of the bravest Resistance fighters we have. He will be very hard to replace. But replace him we must though I will always miss him."

"And you will replace him," the mouse said as he leapt off her head and onto the bloody floor. "Just as we will have to replace our courageous Colonel Catnip, the Leader of our Animal Team."

As Resistance fighters ran out of the theatre in pursuit of Adolph Hitler, and others killed some gravely wounded German soldiers with a single shot to the head, the Mouse Senior Detective hopped off of Edith's head and scrambled toward the front door.

"Miss Piaf, I need your help and fast!" the tiny mouse said in plain English. "Mary Sweet is being held prisoner in a nearby hotel. For all I know, they've already killed her. But if we go find her as fast as we can, maybe we can save her life."

"We will do that now, my mouse," the singer said as she wiped the blood from her machine gun. "Wait outside. I will be out in a single minute. Then we will find your Leader, that Mary Sweet, and rescue her."

"Will do, Miss Piaf," the mouse squeaked in English as he bounded out the front door. "I'll wait for you right here!"

As the mouse waited outside, he watched as the wounded Animal Team members and French Resistance fighters were carried to a waiting ambulance.

"The French are always prepared," he said to an exhausted looking female cat who sat on the cold steps beside him. "With a little luck, the French doctors will save many, many lives tonight."

"Don't you mean today, Mister McMouse?" the woman replied. "See? It is already getting light again. Though I don't care if I see another day."

Seeing the tears in her wide eyes, the mouse realised just who he was talking to. They conversed together in a combination of Mouse and Cat Languages. "Oh, I'm so sorry. You're Catnip's wife, aren't you? And you know who I am?"

"My darling Cat Husband told me all about you. He said that you were his only Mouse Friend he ever had."

"And he was the only Cat Friend I ever had. He was the best Cat…"

Crying again for a moment, she used a paw to dry both of her eyes. "Yes, he was. My name is Sasha. Catnip and I have been married for only a few months but I've already had many litters of kittens. They'll remember their father because I'll always remind him of how kind he was to me. A male cat marrying a female as old as I am now, and I am seven years older than he is now."

"When he comes out, ride with him to the hospital. You never know, he might still be…"

"Alive? No, McMouse. My Cat Husband is dead. I felt his stomach and it's as cold as London ice."

"I'm so sorry. I'll always remember him."

"As we all will."

When a Human Ambulance driver came out of the theatre carrying the mortal remains of Colonel Catnip Sasha hopped, unseen, into the ambulance before the back doors were closed.

"She's going to be there if he wakes up," the mouse sighed. "Who knows? Maybe my Cat Friend is still alive somewhere. Maybe up in Cat Heaven."

Edith Piaf rushed out of the theatre with a number of Resistance fighters. Stepping up to her mouse friend, she put her hand down to him. He hopped up her arm and stood on her shoulder. Looking around, he saw his Human Team British Army Officer.

"Tony Enwenopa!" the Mouse Senior Detective yelled. "Get over here and bring your bazooka and more projectiles. We're going to go rescue the Chief Inspector right now!"

"Will do, Senior Detective," Tony stated as a French woman help him reload his long weapon. "Got us a few more projectiles in this bag. See?" he said as he lifted a heavy green military bag off the ground. "Be with you in a minute, Chief!"

"I'm not a chief, not yet anyway!" the mouse squeaked sharply. "But by the time we get out of here and back to Scotland and our own time, we could all be promoted again."

As dawn broke over Paris, a group of Resistance Fighters and their Allies ran down the empty Paris streets. "The hotel is only a few minutes from here," McMouse yelled into Edith's left ear as he clung to the dress that covered her shoulder. "We've still got a good chance of rescuing her."

"Tres bon!" the singer replied as she jogged down the street. "And when we rescue her, I will personally kill anyone who has hurt her."

"As I will, Miss Edith," the mouse replied.

As the small phalanx of fighters approached the hotel where Mary was being held, the sun rose over the blue skies of the city. Keeping to the shadows of the building, Edith held up a hand and all the fighters who were following her stopped. As she crept through the front door with the mouse still on her shoulder, she could hear music playing and two women singing.

McMouse realized that one of the voices was Mary Sweet's. Taking out his Tommy Gun again, the mouse and all of the humans who were with him moved down a long hallway and toward an open door filled with light.

Chapter 10

King Edward the First Invades Scotland
While Hundreds of Years Later
The Chief Inspector Escapes from the Gestapo

In the small Scottish village of MacSquat, in the year of Our Lord 1296 AD, the MacSquat Clan including all the men, women and children—anyone strong enough to stand up to the English Armies—slaved away to make swords, bullets, arrows and bows to defend their country. The farrier who usually shod horse's hooves worked in his open shed at the back of his thatched cottage which was his home. He pumped the leather billows beneath the fire and when the metal that he'd stolen from the English had been completely melted, he poured it into a box filled with wet sand. Within it, he'd fashioned a number of small globes and when the molten lead fell into them, they cooled to form ammunition for the many guns that William Wallace, the son of their Leader James, had stolen when he made his escape from King Edward the First.

As the giant of a man waited for the new bullets to cool, he turned his attention to the sword that he was sharpening. As a small boy beside him spun a large wheel made of granite, the man whose name was James Fraser placed the side of the sword against the spinning round disc of rock and watched as it sparked in bright flames.

"Jack, spin it faster!" he called to his ten-year-old son. "Put yer back into what you're doing. With a sword like this, and when we sharpen it, killing the English Soldiers who will soon invade our village will be easy."

As the boy pulled a long 'L' shaped handle that was attached to the wheel faster, the wheel spun faster too. "Da', look at the bright flames that the sword makes!" Jack shouted to his Da'. "It's bright enough to frighten away those English fools."

"Right you are, son!" James laughed. "Faster, now. Get your shoulder into it!"

As the wheel spun faster and the sparks grew even brighter, William Wallace stepped into the farrier's yard and, seeing him working, picked up a sharpened sword and waved it toward the man's son.

"Jack, that's the sharpest sword I've ever seen in my entire life! Sharpen a dozen of them just like this and we'll be ready for that English King's invasion."

James turned when he heard the familiar voice and, taking the sword that was still red hot from its sharpening, pointed it at his friend's belly.

"Ah, 'tis that lazy fool of a man, William Wallace, my best friend or so my son reminds me all the time. Did you enjoy your stay in the English Army camp when those pigs caught you?"

"Don't you point that sword at me, you fool of the Fraser Clan," Wallace replied as he laughed. Grinning, he parried his friend's sword and placed the edge of his newly sharpened weapon on the man's shoulder. "How about if I cut off a long lock of your red hair, James? Women wear long hair, not male soldiers."

"It's true I have long hair but I keep mine braided so it doesn't get into my eyes when I fight!" the seven-foot-tall Scottish soldier said as he placed his hand carefully around Wallace's sword. "Women like braided hair not the sort of unkept hair that you have on your head. William, your hair blows into your eyes with every blow you give to the English. How in God's name do you see anything?"

"I see with my two eyes!" Wallace said as he laughed again. "Finish sharpening all your weapons and join me and my father in the Village square. We've already planned how we'll defeat the English but that plan depends on other Scots Clans joining us in battle which is what we must discuss."

"Other Clans will join us in battle, including my own, and that's a promise, my friend!" James replied as he chuckled. "I've sent a messenger to tell my Clan Leader that they must meet us here with his entire Army by tonight. I've also asked him to have other Clans who are fast friends of ours join us on the battlefield. And when they all keep their solemn promise, we'll deliver a blow to that miserable King Edward that he'll never recover from."

"God willing, James. Now, I'm going to go see my wife and, after a quick meal, will see you in the square."

"Meal me arse!" the giant soldier laughed as he made a circle with the fingers of one hand and pushed a finger from his other hand through it, the Scots gesture for making sex. "You won't be eating nothin' at all, not with that fine woman. What's her name, anyway?"

"Gloria. I found her in the nearby Loch. She was of Royal Scottish ancestry when she was killed by the English a hundred years ago but she was brought back to life by the great Sea Monster, Nessie."

"So yer wife is still a Sea Monster?"

"Not anymore, my friend," Wallace said as he grinned. "Now she's nothing but a beautiful Human woman. I must go now to join my father, James Larkin MacSquat. See you in an hour and bring every weapon you have."

As Wallace walked back out the gate that led into the farrier's yard, James looked back at his son who was still spinning the wheel. "Now there's one man I'd give my life for. Jack, if you ever have a best friend, make sure he's just like that Leader of a Scots man."

"I'll do that, father," the boy replied. "My arms are getting tired. How many more swords do we have to sharpen?"

"Ten more. I tell you what. I'll spin the wheel for a while and you sharpen the swords. How's that?"

The boys eyes glittered when his father treated him like an adult. "Da', can I go into battle with you and William Wallace?"

"Never!" his father roared. "You're not yet eleven years old. When you get to be fifteen, and after I train you, then you can fight the English and any other group of bastards that decide they want to take our country away from us."

"But Da', I've been practicing my sword play!" the boy said as he reached out and grabbed a sword. "It's fun! Come on, let's practice a bit and after I beat you we can finish sharpening the other swords."

"Later, son," James replied as he stepped up to the handle of the grinding stone. "First, we finish what we started. Then, perhaps tomorrow, I'll teach you a bit about how to use a sword in battle, and maybe show you how to handle an axe, too."

"A real one, just like this?" the boy asked as he picked up his father's axe. "It's so heavy! I'll never be able to lift it to kill an Englishman."

"I'll make you a smaller one when I find some time. Now come on! I'm spinning this damned thing as fast as I can. Start grinding one of those swords from that pile over there!"

As the boy picked up a sword and started to sharpen it, high overhead General Gusto Gatwick sat alone at the controls of the Hypersonic Time Machine. Seeing the lakes of Scotland below him, he looked up at the accelerometer and the glowing red date and realised that he'd gone back in time, not forward as was his intention.

"The fool that I am again!" he yelled at no one. "Oh, that my good wife Tully Gale was still here. She knew how to fly this thing. But she's dead at the hand of my sworn enemy, Mary Sweet. When I make Putin come back to life, I'll see to it that the bitch of a Chief Inspector and all of her Team Members are killed just like my wife was."

Reaching forward, he moved a single lever and saw the Mach Speed again increase. He knew that in only seconds he would be back in the Twenty-First Century. "And then, I will complete my last mission. I will make Putin rise and then I will lie to him like he lied to me! And after that, oblivion for him in a Hellish Prison as I become not only the new Leader of Nazi Germany but also the new Czar of Russia and then the Emperor of the World!"

On a vast plain only a mile from the hills and mountains where the MacSquat Village was located, English King Edward the First cantered his white stallion at the head of a long line of soldiers. Hundreds of men were mounted on stallions. Each wore silver armour and carried a variety of weapons including lances, pikes and swords. When the King put up an arm, the entire battalion came to a stop. Looking back over his shoulder, Edward pulled up his steel visor and grinned at a General who sat on his horse that halted beside the King.

"General Rollens, turn around and look at the amazing line of English soldiers marching toward us," the King said as he swept an arm toward the groups of men that had just moved onto the plain. "I'm so proud of each one of them. Look, man, and count your blessings! With such an Army, we'll easily defeat the Scots and capture this entire filthy country."

When the General did as he was ordered, he also grinned at the three-thousand armed and well-trained soldiers who marched toward them as if they were a single man.

"Look, my King, at how well they've all learned to follow orders!" the General replied. "The Scots don't have a chance. This is the largest Army of any kind to invade Scotland."

"And General, look what's behind the column. See that the enormously long wooden arm upon which a giant cup is suspended? It will blow the traitorous village of MacSquat back into the dark ages."

Peering through the fine mist that was blowing toward them from the nearby long narrow lake of Loch Ness, both Englishmen could see the King's new *trebuchets*, a giant catapult, which the designers had christened Edward's WarWolf. Through the mist which was quickly growing denser, the King and his General could hear the galloping of hooves and a soldier on horseback appeared.

"My King Edward, the Colonel in charge of the WarWolf wants to know where you want him to place it."

"Tell your Colonel to bring it here where we are resting for a moment," the King replied. "We're almost in range of the MacSquat Village. In another few hundred yards, we'll use the enormous boulders that we've brought with us and hurl them across the plain to destroy the Scots houses and kill many of the MacSquat Clan."

The soldier saluted and as the King watched, he cantered back into the mist to carry out the Royal order. "Good!" the King shouted and, putting up his arm, signalled to the soldiers near him to begin marching across the plain again.

"One horse will follow another and our mounted troops will soon find a place of fine weather," he said to his General as the kicked their horses into a gallop and headed toward the waters of Loch Ness. "This infernal lake they call a Loch only gets in our way and brings me nasty weather! If I had my way, I'd fill it with English slurry and let all of the locals die of thirst."

High in the hills above the plain, Willam Wallace looked down on the English troops as they marched out of the white mist that sparkled brightly in the sun. Turning to his friend, James Frasier, Wallace looked back to see a hundred of his men, all well-armed, hidden among the trees.

"I hope the other Clans got the message that the English were coming. Now they're here and there is no sign of any other Scots to help us ward off this piss-tree of an enemy."

James grinned as if his friend's words were a subtle joke. "William, you worry too much," the giant of a man said as he pointed at a tree. "Climb that there fair oak and ye'll see exactly who's come to help us do battle with the English and how many armed soldiers are with him."

When William climbed the tree and looked to the north, he could see masses of Scotsmen on horseback trotting onto the plain and toward the English battalion.

"Are those the colours of Robert the Bruce?" he called down to James. "The flags that a number of horsemen are carrying are all blue and white and, in the middle, I think is the Holy Cross of Scotland."

"Aye, my friend. 'Tis the Bruce who has come to fight. He has convinced some of the other Tribal Elders to follow him in battle."

"The Bruce!" William sang from high in the oak. "A fair thee well to the English is all I can say. The Bruce is the smartest battle tactician in all the land and someday, God willing, he will be made King of Scotland." Turning toward the Scots soldiers who were hiding all around him, William began to laugh as he called down to them: "My friends. Robert the Bruce is here with thousands of soldiers. Surely, it is us who will win this day of battle. Three cheers for The Bruce!"

As the men began to cheer, down on the plain below them the King looked toward the hills that had now come so much closer. Slowing his stallion, the King waited for his General to catch up.

"General, do you hear those Scots cheering in the hills high above us? They're cheering they're own deaths."

"Yes, my Liege. I know they do. Sire, are we close enough to have your catapult hit the village?"

"We are, General. Tell the Colonel in charge of that new fighting machine to position the WarWolf right next to me. When the catapult is moved up here, bring all of our troops into position for a Mighty Attack on the Scots."

A half-mile North of the King and his troops, mighty Robert the Bruce kicked the side of his stallion to urge him into a gallop. He raised his arm and shouted "Attack!" Behind him, his thousand troops which included men on horseback as well as armed footmen, ran toward King Edward's three-thousand strong army. As they moved closer to the enemy, The Bruce looked behind him toward a line of furze, expecting to see the armies of other Clans that had promised to join them.

"Where are the great Clans of Northern Scotland!" he shouted to a soldier riding at his side. "I told them that the English were coming. We have no choice but to attack without the promised reinforcements."

As the legion of Scotsmen charged forward, James Larkin MacSquat with other armed soldiers of his Clan ran down the hills and toward The Bruce and his many soldiers. As the Leader of the MacSquat Clan ran onto the plain, he shouted to The Bruce, "Sire, I would never let you down! My men at arms number only thirty but more are waiting in the hills above us and other friends of ours are expected here at any moment."

"Where are your horses?" The Bruce shouted back. "Are you all on foot?"

"Aye, Sire. Horses we sold to buy more weapons to beat the English bastards."

Nodding to his Scots ally, the great future King of Scotland motioned his soldiers on horseback to go faster. Quickly outdistancing the MacSquat fighters, his entire troop of the Clan The Bruce threw themselves into battle.

"Take no quarter!" The Bruce shouted as he drew his sword and began to kill English soldiers. "When you find that English so-called King, leave his death to me!"

On a nearby hill only a quarter of a mile away, Edward looked down at the battle. English foot soldiers were engaged in a great battle against the Scots. "General! Tell a third of your soldiers on horseback to charge now! As they move forward, have our remaining foot soldiers follow them. And as to that The Bruce, leave him be and let me kill him!"

As the two great armies continued in the violent battle, James Fraser and William Wallace with more MacSquat soldiers ran down their tall hill and onto the plain. Screaming for God's blessing, they entered the fray against the English King and his soldiers.

"James Fraser!" Wallace yelled to his best friend as together they ran toward a group of English soldiers. "Throw me a sword because I've lost mine. It's stuck in the belly of an Englishman that I met a few yards back!"

James did as he was bid and, throwing William Wallace his sword, ran like a stallion into the thick of battle, unarmed. "I'll find a sword after I kill a soldier or two with my bare hands."

As Wallace used his sword and an axe to kill a number of English Officers, he saw in the distance what looked like a giant wooden crane. As he watched, an English soldier lit a torch and began to wave it.

"Oh, Lord God, Edward has brought the monstrous WarWolf!" Wallace shouted to the men behind him. "Clan MacSquat, prepare to take cover because they'll start to throw great balls of fire at us!"

On the small rise near the battle, King Edward looked back over his shoulder and saw that his catapult had been pulled into position. As he watched, one of his soldiers lit a huge boulder that had been covered in pitch with a torch. More soldiers began to pull back on a rope that made the end of the long wooden spar bend down to the ground. At the very end, the dangling boulder burned fiercely. When they were ready, the Commander of the WarWolf looked to his King for the next command.

"Open fire!" Edward shouted and, when the soldiers let go of the rope and the long wooden spar whipped forward, a ball of fire thundered into the air and over the heads of every fighting man on the field.

On the field of battle, William Wallace watched as a streak of fire flew over his fighters. In only moments he realised the King's true target.

"The bastards are going after our village!" William roared to anyone that could hear him. As he killed an English soldier with one thrust of his sword, he saw his good friend running toward him. "James! Get home! Rescue your wife and family and anyone else you can find alive! See what that murderous King is doing?"

When James heard his friend's order, he looked toward the small rise and saw the WarWolf fire again. Filled with new rage, he lifted a pike from a dead English Colonel. Using it as if he was killing cattle, he roared with anger as he swung the pike toward the head of every English soldier's head he could see. Nearby, William watched his friend kill at least a dozen English men. Throwing down the pike, James picked up two swords and stabbed ten Englishmen to death with them.

Wallace, sweating like a pig with blood all over his face and body due to the many Englishmen he had already killed, thrust his sword into the chin of a mounted English soldier that was charging toward him and, grabbing the horse's harness, handed it to James.

"Off with ye' now are there'll be no one left alive in the village!" William shouted to his friend. "Get every living person that you find into hiding in the forests and the lake. Then grab any other men you can find and get back here!"

"Aye, my friend," James shouted as he mounted the horse. As William watched, James galloped right past William's father, James Larkin MacSquat, who was fighting a number of English soldiers at the same time.

"Father, I'm over here!" William shouted as he slayed yet another English man. Wiping the blood off the blade with the red and white flag of England that he'd found on the ground, he looked up at James Larkin and grinned. "They die easy now, don't they, Da'?"

"So they do, boy," James Larkin shouted as he killed one man after another. "See how smooth my sword goes through their armour? That's due to James Fraser and his son's hard work."

"So it is, father," William replied.

When he heard a Scotsman shout, "James Larkin, look out behind you!" he saw his father hit in the side by an English pike and watched as the silver end of it came out his father's back covered in blood. Running toward James, William encountered a group of English soldiers and, stopping only a moment, skewered them all with one thrust of a lance that he'd taken from the belly of a fellow Scotsman. Turning back toward his father, William watched as an English Colonel stabbed James Larkin over and over again in the body and neck with a short sword. Screaming yet again, William ran up to the Colonel and, hitting him with his fists in the head and side a number of times, took the short sword and stabbed him to death. As the man fell to the ground, William turned to see that his father was also on the ground, surrounded by the men of the Clan MacSquat.

"Oh, father. What have they done to you? Are you in pain?"

"Pain, my boy? What's pain?" his father said as he smiled. "I never felt any pain at all in the heat of battle. Soon, when I'm in Heaven, I'll be told that I can go back to our village again to kill an English King. That's the mission given to me by Our Lord. To throw the English King off our land."

"And so you will, father," William said quietly. Kneeling beside James Larkin, William took his father's hand in his own. "Be at peace now and when you see my mother, tell her that I will see her when someday I also leave this Earth."

"Leave? Son, you'll never die! You are now the new Leader of the Clan MacSquat! Leave me, now. Go find that Edward and kill him in return for what he's done to your father."

As James Larkin's eyes closed, all the men surrounding him saw that he'd breathed his last. "James Larkin MacSquat is dead!" a soldier cried out as he pointed his sword to the sky. "Now, we shall take vengeance against him by killing every last English soldier including that King."

In a room at the hotel where she had been tortured, Mary Sweet woke in a huge bed and, looking toward the open window, saw the blue skies filled with sunlight high above Paris. Putting out her right arm, she took a large white pillow and, pulling it toward her, hugged it with all of her might until she saw that the pillow cover was smeared with red blood.

"Oh, I remember now where I am," she said to a nurse who stood at the door. "I'm in my home in London. Or am I still in Berlin? I can't wait until I see my husband Hubert when he comes home from work."

"Nein, Madam, you are not in London at all!" the nurse replied and, when she walked over and stood beside the bed, Mary saw that it was not a nurse but a large female dragon instead. "My Chief Inspector, don't you recognise me?" the dragon asked as it stretched its wings and touched the ceiling. "I'm your best friend from Loch Ness. Its's Nessie! Don't you remember me?"

"Oh, I'm so very sorry," Mary replied as she rose from the bed and sat back on the blood-stained pillows. "I remember now. I do! That terrible Nazi woman beat me to within an inch of my life!"

"Yes, she did," Nessie said quietly. "She stands just outside the door. Why don't I eat her for breakfast and then I'll rescue you from this horrible prison."

"Not yet, my Dragon friend. We must wait until Senior Inspector Mouse comes back to me. Then we can all escape together."

It was only then that Mary woke up. She began to think that the beating she had received was a nightmare. But looking down again at the blood-stained pillow, she realized that what she remembered wasn't a nightmare but instead a horrible reality. The Chief Inspector looked up at Nessie and smiled again.

"When we escape we must re-capture our Hypersonic Time Machine. We must go back in time, back to when Edward the First was King. He's winning on the battlefield right now and is about to dethrone the rightful King of Scotland. But with the help of my Nessie and all of your children and many relatives, as well as a Man of Legendary Bravery named Robin Hood who will side with Scotland, we'll beat that King of England into submission and the Scots will not only rule on its own but will also one day rule all of Great Britain."

Climbing back into the bed, Mary Sweet thought about what she'd just whispered to her giant Dragon friend.

'If we can change history and if Scotland becomes the leading country of Great Britain, it will eventually be more powerful than almost any country in the world. It will surpass England as well as most other Allied powers in the supply of new technologies as well as simple brain-power to overcome not only those countries that would make War in the future but will also help to feed the entirety of the world's population.'

As she finished her thought, Mary pumped a fist into the air and yelled, "Eureka! I've found it! Nessie, forget about our Mouse

Friend for now. We must get to Scotland as fast as possible and go back into time. When the Scots defeat the English, and Edward the First is captured, and as I just said, it will change the course of future history! Putin will never be president of Russia. General Gusto Gatwick might never be born. Or if he is, and helps Putin to become alive again, neither of them will have any friends or allies to help Gusto or Putin to become Emperor of the World!"

Climbing out of bed, Mary tiptoed to the door and peeped out of it. In the hall, she could see the rotund figure of Nazi Private Zelda smoking a cigarette. Winking at her Dragon friend who was peering over Mary's shoulder, she sauntered out the door of her room and walked up to the Private.

"Private, can I steal a smoke from you?" Mary asked her. "The ones you gave me are now all gone.

"Certainly, my new friend," the woman said as she took a cigarette out of a full packet. "I got these from my Gestapo Agent friend after he made love to me last night while you were sleeping."

"Did he now? And Zelda, what was he like in bed?"

"Eh!" the Private whispered as she moved her hand up and down. "In bed he is nothing at all. German men are never good at making love."

"Too true, Private," Mary answered as she put the cigarette between her lips. "Zelda, do you have a light?"

"Nein. I've used up all of my matches. I have another box in my room. I'll be right back."

As the woman started to walk down the hall, Nessie came out of Mary's room.

"Zelda! I found a light!" Mary called. As the Private turned around, Mary held up her unlit cigarette. The Dragon snorted then breathed in. Exhaling with a thin, red-hot tongue of fire, the cigarette that Mary held between two fingers was suddenly lit.

"Why don't you have another cigarette, my Zelda, and let my Dragon Friend light it for you!"

Looking up and focusing on the giant face of the Dragon, the Private began screaming. "What is that enormous green creature beside you? Are you crazy to be just standing there! Run and we'll get my machine gun and kill it before it kills both of us!"

"Oh, that's not necessary," Mary said as she let the Dragon squash her lit cigarette with its large wing. "Nessie won't harm a soul. Not unless I tell her to." Looking up at the Dragon, Mary frowned. "Nessie, give that Nazi Private a taste of things to come for her when she finally dies and goes to Hell."

As the Nazi Private watched, the Dragon breathed in again only this time as deep as she could. Breathing out, a ball of red, green, blue, white and gold fire lit up not only the hallway but, like a flamethrower, completely engulfed the Nazi Private.

"I'm burning to death!" the Private gasped as she fell to the ground with all of her clothes in flames. "I'm…my…my arm is melting. You have killed me. Killed me. Killed…" Then the voice grew quiet as the body was consumed by fire.

"Well done, Dragon Nessie, and that's the last word we'll ever hear from that murderer," Mary said as she stepped back into her room. "In a moment, I suspect that an entire brigade of German troops will be here to see what caused that huge fire. So let me get dressed and we'll make our escape before it's too late."

As the Dragon stood guard by the door, Mary slipped back into an old robe the Nazi Private had given to her. Opening the room's only window, Mary looked down just in time to see Senior Detective McMouse run down the street toward the hotel. "McMouse! Up here!"

Looking up to a hotel window, the tiny mouse began to smile at last. "I thought I'd never find you, Chief!" he squeaked. "Let's get you out of there before they kill you!"

"I already have a way, mouse. Go back to our Hypersonic Space Craft and get Sarah Scots to make it ready for lift off. Nessie the Loch Ness Monster is here and, as soon as we kill as many German troops as we can, I'll fly on its back and meet you in the centre of Berlin."

"Done, Chief Inspector!" the mouse said as he turned and started scampering back down the street. Hearing the clatter of machine gun fire, he stopped and turned around again. The Dragon Monster was flying out the window with Mary Sweet on her back. Turning in mid-air, the Dragon ducked and weaved to avoid German gunfire coming from the hotel windows. Then, Nessie breathed out as much fire as she could, so much that the entire hotel was engulfed in flames. As Mary and Nessie heard German soldiers scream in pain from the open hotel windows, the Dragon turned again and, flapping both wings, flew down the street and out of sight.

"Good thing that Dragon is on our side," McMouse said as he heard more screaming come from the dying German troops trapped inside the hotel. "In there, it must be hot enough to make scrambled German eggs!"

Relieved that he'd found his Chief, and knowing that it would take at least an hour for Sarah Scots to ready their Spacecraft for flight, the mouse sauntered back down the street as he whistled an Edith Piaf song.

"Oh, I love Paris in the springtime and in the summer!" the mouse shouted to anyone who could hear him. "Now, it's back to Scotland and, with any luck, we'll wrap up this mission and I can bring my good wife here, to modern Paris when the weather is warm!"

Chapter 11

How King Edward Overruns the Scottish Village of MacSquat but Is Defeated in Battle by That Scottish Clan

In Scotland, and still back in the Thirteenth Century, King Edward and his Royal Army were winning on the battlefield despite the brave efforts of the Scots. As William Wallace and the MacSquat Clan carried the body of his dead father toward the high hills, James Fraser ran from the trees and into his village. Finding a group of English soldiers standing on the path in front of him, he killed one of them with his bare hands by snapping the soldier's neck, then taking the dead man's sword, and screaming in rage, he killed five more soldiers. Wiping the sword on the back of a dead English soldier, he ran onto a worn path of stone and up a small hill.

Entering the Village MacSquat, James at first saw nothing but bodies of women and children face down in the mud outside their shattered houses.

"Bessie! Bessie Frasier!" James screamed as he ran down the muddy lane that was filled with the smoke of burning wood. "Bessie, where are you!"

Coming to a line of homes that still stood within the Village rubble, he ran to the last house, and then to the front door of his home. As he lay a hand on the wooden latch, the entryway opened and Bessie peered out, her face filled with terror. But when she saw her husband, the look on her face turned to relief.

"James, thank God you're alive!" she said as she started to cry. "Jack's not here! I looked all over your farrier's workshop to see if he was still sharpening swords but he's not there."

Falling to her knees and now sobbing uncontrollably, James put his large arms around her. "He's not dead, woman. That lad will never die. I told him not to follow me into battle but knowing our son, that's exactly what he did."

As Bessie watched from their home's front steps, James ran to his workshop and filled his arms with newly sharpened swords. Holding an axe in his teeth, he ran back into the muddy lane. Then he saw Jack running toward him with blood all over his face.

"Jack where in God's name have you been!" the giant of a man yelled at his son. "You've made me and your mother scared to death. Now get in the house right now and keep your mother safe from the English hoards that are marching this way."

"No father!" the child cried. "You said I'd be a man when I killed an English soldier. I've not done that yet but I've wounded one and made off with his pike."

Holding the weapon high, James could see that the pointed end was coated with blood. "Is that English blood I see, Jack?" James said as he placed the swords and the axe down on the lane. "If it is then you're almost a man but not quite yet."

"Please, father, let me fight in battle. You know I can do it. You trained me, didn't you?"

"One lesson is all you had, boy. Enough of that now. See what that King has done to our village."

As both of them turned around to look back at what remained of their Clan's homes, they could see nothing but smoke, fire, rubble and the horrible odour of burning flesh.

"That King has a great deal to pay for," James said through clenched teeth. "See what his WarWolf did to our Village? When he leads his men here I'll kill the bastard with my bare hands."

"And you will, father. And I'll kill a score of Englishmen."

As they watched children, women and old men carry the bodies of the fallen to a nearby field, James could hear the thin sound of drums echoing across the hills toward them.

"'Tis that King or 'tis William Wallace with The Bruce! Come, lad. Grab up some of these swords then say farewell to your Mam. Despite my better judgement, it's time for you to become a man though I'd rather it weren't so."

"Father, I'll be eleven years old next month. By our Army's standards, I'm already a young man. I've seen many friends my age fighting on the battlefield."

As James and Jack gathered up the swords, Bessie came down the steps and, grabbing her boy in both arms, kissed him. "May Our Lord and the Blessed Virgin watch over you, my son," she whispered to him. "May you come back to me unharmed. May the Angels and the Spirits of War guide you and your father back to me."

Done with her simple blessing, she began crying again as she looked toward the far hills. "James! Look! Is that an English flag I see yonder?"

"It is, Bessie," James replied as he saw a red and white flag marching up a nearby hill. "Don't go back into the house. Instead, take all the people you can find and head for the higher hills or mountains until this battle is over. Jack, do as you will for you are now a man. Could you not go with your mother? She and the other villagers need your protection."

"I will, father, if you insist. But you promised me that I could…"

"I know, I know."

James placed his hands on his wife's waist and, lifting her high, he kissed her. "That will keep both of us until my son and I come home from battle. We won't be gone long and that's a promise."

"If that's your promise, James, then make sure you keep it," she replied. "The Lord Bless and keep you safe, too."

"Of that, I'm also sure. Come, Jack. Into battle we both must go."

As her men walked down the muddy lane of the burning village, and disappeared into the pitch-black smoke, Bessie decided there and then never to cry again until they both came back to her unscathed.

"My two men are all that matter to me," she said as she went back into her home to pack a few things. "If James and Jack won't cry, then neither will I. I'll do what my husband told me to. It's into the hills and mountains those who are still alive must go to protect what's left of the MacSquat race."

Having marched up onto a hill above the Village MacSquat, King Edward sat on his white stallion and smiled in victory. Turning to his General, he smiled so wide that he hurt his mouth.

"General, look at what we've done to this ugly village. We've destroyed it."

"Yes, Sire, you have with your giant weapon. Now William Wallace and Robert the Bruce will have no choice but to come here to protect those still left alive. When that happens, and with this small squadron of soldiers we have behind us, we'll complete this simple task and go back to London. It's the easiest part of our battle. We've whipped the Scots on the battlefield. Now, all we have to do is kill the women and children and that will be the end of the MacSquat resistance."

"Right you are, General. And that's an order. Kill any survivors you find then it's London we'll be bound for in only a few hours. Prepare to sound the attack when you see the flag of The Bruce coming for us. He has but a few soldiers with him. The rest? Why, they're all dead on the battlefield, killed by my Army of brave English soldiers."

"I will do as you say, Sire. We're ready when you give this final order."

"I give that order now. Sound the attack again. Do not kill The Bruce. Instead, capture and torture him to tell us where any other Scots armies might lay in waiting to attack us as we march back to London.

Thirty minutes later, in the treeline only a half-mile from the King and his small group of soldiers, William Wallace called all the members of his surviving Army together. Forming a circle around him, his soldiers saw that their new Leader had tears in his eyes.

"Do you hear that screaming coming from the far fields?" Wallace said in a hushed tone as he pulled his sword from its leather scabbard. "Those are the screams of The Bruce. The King's Army were able to capture him and win this battle because no other Clans would dare fight the English."

"It's treason!" a voice cried and Wallace turned to see his friend James running up the hill. "Look what I found in the hands of the English soldiers I just now killed." James Fraser held up the blue and white flag of Robert the Bruce as high as he could and started to wave it. "We are no longer many, too few to fight the King's Army. But I say we attack them now and, despite the horrible odds, by our Faith in a Living God, we can still win the day."

"The man is insane!" a villager said to Wallace. "If we attack there will be nothing left of our Clan."

"No, there will not," Wallace concurred. "But as James says, if we put our lives in the hands of the Lord then at least we'll give the survivors of our Village time to hide in the high hills. That way, our Clan will survive the dreaded English."

As they all gathered their various weapons, the son of James came running up the hill. "Father, my mother is safe as are many of the Villagers. They are all hiding in the high hills and mountains as you suggested."

"And now he wants to kill an English soldier and become a man, isn't that right James?" Wallace asked.

"Tis folly to be sure," the giant Scotsman replied. "But so many of us have lost sons, wives and daughters, I would be a selfish man to keep him from going into battle with us." James knelt down beside his son and blessed Jack's head with the Sign of the Cross. "Let the Lord's will be done, Jack. With this blessing, let no Englishman touch you. You must survive to become an adult and then you can father your own son and perhaps a daughter."

"Which will be a blessing come true," Wallace whispered as he looked to the skies above him. "Oh, for a mighty storm to come in and bring with it my friendly Dragon from Loch Ness. That Nessie one and her daughter breathe fire."

"I know of the Monster you're talking about," the Village priest said as he walked down the hill toward them. Wallace saw that the priest's face was black from smoke and his white smock was ripped almost in half from where an English sword had tried to kill the good man. "I have blessed all the Villagers after I buried our dead. Should that flying Monster come to us, I will bless her, too."

"Then it's into battle we must go again," Wallace said and frowning at Jack, said to him, "You must mind your father's back. Do not charge lightly into battle. Pick one single soldier and do your very best when fighting him."

"I promise, William Wallace," the boy replied. "I will only make a charge when you or my father tell me to."

"Then we're off!" the new Leader of the MacSquat clan roared. "We will kill as many enemies as we can. But remember, you must leave the English King to me!" Turning to the priest, he finally shouted, "Father, bless us all who remain to defend our Clan. Bless our enemies, too. Bless us three times and, when we attack the English, please pray that we'll win this battle just like David did when he slew Goliath, the Giant man who would have killed every Jew in the Promised Land."

As the brave soldiers ran down the hill toward the battlefield, above them the rays of sunlight glinted off the silver hull of something in the sky. "Father, what is that?" Jack asked breathlessly. "It could be a sign from Heaven that help is on the way."

"If it is help, Jack, let it not tarry or we will all be dead in only minutes."

High above them, Sarah Scots sat at the controls of the new Helios Time Machine that had been given to Mary Sweet. Having flown in her old Space Time Machine into the distant future, she had met a group of Scottish engineers in the Twenty-Second Century.

There, they had presented her with the new technology that, so they said, would change not only history but help Humankind fly to other Galaxies. Now standing behind the Sargent who was sitting in the Left Seat, Mary placed a hand on the pilot's shoulder.

"All you have to do is *think* of what you want to do and this New-Technology Space Vehicle will follow all the details of your orders," Mary said to Sargent Sarah Scots.

"This is so easy to fly, Chief Inspector," the pilot, who had been promoted to Sargeant, replied. "As you just said, I don't even need controls to fly this new vehicle. I just think of where I want to go, and the Helios Time Machine does as I tell it to."

"Nor do we need a spacesuit, Sarah, or microphones," Mary Sweet said in her thoughts. "All we need to do is *think* what needs to be said and our *entire Team hears it*!"

Looking over her shoulder, in the immense Command Room of the Helios, Mary could see all of her many Teams looking at her. The Human Teams either stood or sat on benches while the Animal Teams sat or crouched on the steel deck that had been carpeted in something that looked like felt.

"And we always have gravity, don't we, Sarah?" Mary asked her. "We have plenty of oxygen and enough supplies including food and water to travel in this Time-Sensitive Space Craft for over a year."

"That we do, Chief," a tiny voice squeaked. Looking down at her from where he stood on the ceiling, Senior Inspector McMouse smiled broadly and twitched his whiskers. "See? I can even stand on the ceiling using my Anti-Gravity Boots! What super engineering by those Twenty-Second Century Scots."

"Which means, McMouse?"

"Which means, Mary Sweet, that everything is exactly as it should be."

"Good! Very good! Right, you Teams. Get ready to descend to the ground on our brand-new Space Travel Beams."

As all the Teams stood up and smiled, Sarah Scots thought to the Helios, "Helios, activate the Space Travel Beams and place our Teams at the exact coordinates I gave you a minute earlier."

"I will obey your orders, Sargent," Helios thought back to her in a soft Scots accent. "Activated in three, two, one. Now!"

The entire Spacecraft began to vibrate slightly as all of the Team Members closed their eyes. "Chief Inspector, I'll be waiting right here for you," Sarah thought to Mary Sweet. "If you need me at any time, just send your thought to me and I'll pull you right back to the Helios."

Mary had her eyes tight as did the rest of the Team Members. After a bright flash of light, she opened them again and saw a large field in front of her.

"Right! Teams, get into position. Humans, grab any modern weapon you want from that large container over there!" As Mary pointed to a location right near them, the container that she had mentioned suddenly appeared beneath a ball of light. Then she looked up into the sky and concentrating as hard as she could, thought of a simple phrase and repeated it over and over again.

"*My Dragon friend Nessie, come to me. My Dragon friend Nessie, come to me. My Dragon friend Nessie, come to me.*" When she looked up, she could see a small black dot flying toward them. When it was hovering above the Team, she could hear Nessie in her mind.

"I'm here, my Human friend. And my daughter is right behind me."

"Good, my friend. Wait for a moment. On our way here, we stopped in Nottingham, England. There, I asked Robin Hood and his Merry Men to help us. While he's an Englishman, Robin is of Scots descent. He told me that he'd meet us here and battle that English pig King that wants to take over Scotland. Besides, Robin knows that the King is a traitor. Robin and his Men, as well as his wife Maid Marion, demanded that Sherwood Forest be made into a separate country or a part of Scotland. In reply, the King killed many English citizens in Nottingham."

"I will do as I am bid, Mary Sweet," the dragon this time said in a loud Dragon voice and, looking to the southwest, smiled as wide as she could. "Would those Merry Men be mounted on horseback?"

"They would."

"Well, I can already see them. Oh my! That Robin Hood Human man seems to have brought over a thousand other humans on horseback with him!"

"Good again, Dragon friend. When I can see him, I'll give the order for our Team to charge against the Enemy. With your daughter and any other winged children you might have brought with you, fly over the English Army and use your fire to chase them back to their own country."

"It shall be a pleasure, my Mary Sweet," the Dragon replied and, flapping her wings, flew toward the English Army.

Mary Sweet smiled and looked back at her Teams. "Psychiatric Unit Investigation Team! You are now an Army! Use every weapon we have to destroy that English King's soldiers and save Scotland and our future!"

Turning again to look at the field of battle, she could see a single Clan of Scotsmen charge across the battlefield littered with bodies and on toward the English soldiers. Then she saw Robin and his vast Army of Horseback Soldiers charge against the King's Army.

Hearing the roars of both Armies as they entered battle, she saw the bright flash of silver steel and a lone man astride a white stallion.

"There be the last King of England, at least for a few hundred years," Mary laughed. "Right all my Teams! On my order. Charge the battlefield!"

As the Humans all ran forward and the Animal Teams including Dogs, Cats and Mice leaped, jumped or scampered toward the English King, Mary looked up at a small Dragon that flew toward her. Sitting on its head she saw McMouse looking down at her.

"I've a ring side seat again for the battle! Chief Inspector, come up and join me. From here, you can command our Teams any way you want and act as a look-out for the Scots Clan and Robins Merry Men!"

When the Dragon flew down to her, Mary climbed up onto its large scaled head. Sitting down next to her Mouse friend, Mary looked down into the Dragon's golden eye.

"Why, you're not Gloria, Nessie's daughter. Which Dragon are you?"

"Me name is Dragon MacSweet and I come from a Clan of Dragons located long ago near Auld London."

"The MacSweet Dragons? I didn't know I had any relations who were flying dragons. Do you have a first name?"

"Surely, I do. The name is Hubert. Actually, I'm a distant relative of your husband. I saw him not too long ago fishing in a lake right near where I now live, which is in Twenty-First Century Southeast Scotland, right near the small town of Edinburgh."

"You saw my husband Hubert?" Mary gasped. "How is he?"

"For an English ghost, he looks wonderful, Mary Sweet. He sends his love to you and tells you to be careful."

"Careful we'll all be, Hubert the Dragon MacSweet. Now please fly us over to the battle."

"Will-eye do!" the Dragon roared and, lifting off high into the air, flew as fast as it could toward the raging battle. Looking down from the Dragon's head, McMouse and Mary could see King Edward using his sword to kill one poor attacking Scotsman after another.

"But here comes Robin Hood and our Teams!" Mary roared. "Dragon, attack that King with your big flame. Take a deep breath and if we're all lucky, you'll roast him to death in his armour."

"No can do, me Mary," the Dragon replied. "Fire breathers come from the Loch. Us Dragons from elsewhere do not breathe fire. But we do breathe out water!"

"Then do it, Dragon, and do it now before that bastard of a King kills more men!"

As the Dragon breathed out tonnes of water on the King and his Army, Robin Hood, his men, and Maid Marion flew into battle on top of their horses.

"It's a hunting we will go, just like we did against that Nottingham Sheriff!" Robin Hood yelled to Friar Tuck who rode on a fast donkey next to him. "Maid Marion! Come up alongside me or next to the Frair! When the Friar blows his horn, we'll charge those English brutes and engage them in battle."

Marion, who had long red hair and was of very fair complexion, smiled at him as she came galloping to his side. "Oh, husband to be, though I now call you only 'husband'. I've my sword right here. Lead us into battle anywhere in the world and we'll always follow thee."

"Enough of the old-fashioned English verse," the Dragon roared above them. "You be in Scotland now so learn to talk like the Scots!"

"Why, 'tis a flying dragon!" Friar Tuck said as he took out his horn. "Dragon, I'll blow my horn now. With your water and our many, many men, we'll defeat these nasty Englishman or I'll have nothing for my supper tonight."

"Blow, Friar, blow that trumpet of yours!" Robin ordered as he raised his long sword. "Call in our large hounds, too! See all the dogs and cats ahead of us that Mary Sweet has brought to fight with us? Our hounds can join them in the fray and eat many an English soldier."

As the Friar blew his long horn made from the white tusk of a Whale, Robin with Marion and his Merry Men charged the English troops together with the remnants of the MacSquat Clan Army. As they all engaged in battle, William Wallace with James at his side, and Jack who stood behind them, each killed an English soldier. Seeing the fresh mounted troops and animals locked in battle with the English Army, Wallace called to his men, "Come to me, my Clan! Rest for a moment. I'm not sure who has come to our aid but now is our time. Remember, leave the King to me. James, for now you are the Leader of our men! Find The Bruce and, if he's not dead, bring him to safety. He will be our King, by God, or I'm not William Wallace! As for me, I'll go try to kill that terrible English King."

As James left with Jack and the rest of the Clansmen, Wallace picked up two fresh swords. Looking across the battlefield, he saw an English General and then the King, both still mounted on horseback.

"Hey, Edward! Over here!" Wallace screamed. "Meet thy death and its name is Scotland!"

Charging toward the King, Wallace threw one of the swords at the General. Turning in mid-air, it's point struck the neck of the General in the throat, where his pale skin was exposed between his helmet and his armour. As the man fell from his horse and to the ground, Wallace ran past a number of fighting men and, grabbing the halter of the King's stallion, which had reared up on its hind legs plunged his other sword into the King's thigh. Screaming, King Edward tried to kick his horse into a gallop but the stallion refused to move. Seeing that his time had come, Wallace reached up and grabbed the King's armour. Pulling with all of his might, the Leader of the MacSquat Clan pulled the King off the horse. When he fell to the ground on his back, Wallace walked over to him, standing with both feet on the King's chest.

"Edward, you are no longer King because you have fallen," Wallace yelled over the roar of battle. "Open your visor and look upon your death."

The King used a gloved finger to open his visor. Peering up at the Scotsman who had defeated him in single-handed combat, Edward could only smile. "If it's my death I see, then let me say a prayer. When I'm finished then do it. But give me a clean death."

"Why, you fallen King? You gave no quarter to the many Scots people you slayed using that terrible new weapon of yours. But that weapon is now in our hands and we shall call it the James Larkin Memorial Slingshot. We shall never use it to kill people, not ever! We were never as cruel as you and never will be. Now, King and I'll call you that one final time. Say your prayers and then you'll die but by a slow death. You're already bleeding from your leg and the scent of that Royal Blood will drive the dogs that I see around us quite mad! They'll eat you for dinner and we'll save your bones for tomorrow's animal breakfast."

Taking off his silver helmet with two gloved hands, the fallen King looked across the battlefield. From where he lay, he could see huge dogs and hounds attacking his troops. As he watched, a soldier screamed as five hounds ripped off his armour and, using their sharp teeth, devoured his face.

"If I am to die like that…no, never! I would rather die by my own hand."

"With what weapon, fallen Edward? This one?" Wallace pulled out a short sword hidden beneath Edward's armour. "A sharp little sword, isn't it? No, you'll never use it. Not now. But I'll use that to teach my people the art of fighting at close quarters. A handsome prize from the battlefield for me, isn't it, my would-be Sire?"

As King Edward watched, Wallace began to whistle. "Dogs and hounds! Over here! I have a Royal feast for your grand dinner! Hear me, dogs. Do my bidding and do it now!"

The dogs all heard him. Barking, they started to run toward Wallace. "Edward the First, you'll be the only Edward to ever try to conquer and rule Scotland. Now, be gone forever. I bid you a long farewell."

Wallace began walking toward his men who were still fighting the surviving English soldiers. Hearing Edward scream in horror, he looked back just in time to see a large Black Labrador grab Edward's gloved hand and begin to tug on it. The fingers of the glove turned blood red and, as the dog pulled harder and another dog grabbed Edward's wrist, the Lab found that it had the fallen King's entire hand in its mouth.

"Good dog," Wallace said as he strode back into battle. "Now the pack of dogs will make short work of that man. When they're finished, we'll take all of his armour and any jewellery that we find and give it to those who need it. Now, let's kill the rest of these soldiers or make them surrender. Then, with The Bruce as our King, we'll make Scotland whole again and raise a large army to secure our boarders against the English forever."

When Edward finished screaming, all Wallace could hear was the delighted yips of pups and the meows of kittens as they, too, joined the pack to feast on the dead King. Turning back to the battlefield, his head consumed with finding and freeing The Bruce, Wallace grabbed a sword from one of the remaining Scottish fighters and picked up a pike from the ground. Hearing a familiar voice scream in pain, the two men ran back across the battlefield where they saw, in the near distance, a small group of English soldiers surrounding a The Bruce who had been tied to a tall stake. Below him, a pile of wood had been placed at his feet. As the two Scottish warriors watched, an English soldier threw a bucket of tar onto the wood then, lighting it with a torch that he held, stepped back as the fire took hold.

"The Bruce, we're here!" Wallace shouted. "Hang on, my great Leader. In a moment we'll set you free."

An English soldier looked to his Captain as he stepped toward the Senior Leader of all the Scottish Clans.

"You are The Bruce, the would-be King of Scotland and England, are you not?" the Captain said to the Scot that was watching the fire climb toward his feet. "Tell us where your other Clans are or I'll let the fire consume you. Be afraid, man, very afraid. If you do not tell me what I want to know, you'll go straight to Hell in the brilliant fires of Hell."

"Burn me alive, for I do not care, you English swine," The Bruce replied. He spit on the fire and looked at the English Captain with eyes that held a look of defiance. "You will never defeat the Scottish people. This is our land and our country. Now be quiet. Let me say my prayers that My Dear Lord will save me."

The Captain began to laugh as did his group of men. When he heard a Scottish voice yell to him, he turned to look back at the battlefield. There, he saw two men stand. Both held swords which they waved at him.

"Here, you English swill. Come for your dinner for your King Edward is now cooked enough to feed you as well as your small group of men."

"What! That's impossible! Our King is alive and is now bound for London."

"Wrong again, you pig, you swine, you gutless Englishman. Do you want proof? Then take this!"

As the Captain watched, the Scotsman threw something silver toward him. Landing at his feet, he picked it up and found himself holding nothing but a gloved hand. Taking off the glove, he saw King Edward's ring.

"To arms!" the Captain shouted. "Two of you stay here! If that The Bruce tells you where his Clans are cut him down. Otherwise, let him burn to death."

As the Captain and his men drew their swords and began running toward the Scotsman, Wallace looked to the other Clan member. "Who are you, for I do not know. You wear the mask of a Wolf. Take it off so I might identify you before we kill these few English soldiers."

When the man took off his mask, Wallace immediately recognised his best friend. "But James, I thought you were still in the Village looking for your son, Jack. Where is he, anyway?"

"He is dead, Wallace. The English bastards killed him."

"Did they. Well…" Wallace felt his eyes fill with tears as he put his hand on his friend's arm. "Tis a woeful thing these pigs do. Kill your son, did they? Then they have also killed my son. From this day and from now on, no more Scots people will die at the hand of an Englishman and that is my oath and promise to you. Now, James, let us forget our troubles. Let us kill these men and rescue The Bruce to lead us in a final battle of victory."

The two men raised their swords. As they faced the English soldiers that ran toward them, Wallace could see that the fire had now taken hold and was about to kill their Leader.

"Oh, woe to us and to all of Scotland!" Wallace shouted as he looked to the sky. "My Mary Sweet, we need rain to come to save The Bruce! If you hear me, ask our God to help us right now!"

High above the battlefield, Mary and McMouse still sat on the head of the Dragon.

"Okay, Dragon, it's time now," Mary said into the ear of her new flying friend. "See that smoke down there? Aim well with your mighty stream of water and put out that fire!"

The Dragon MacSweet took careful aim with his tongue then opened his enormous mouth. Breathing out with all of his might, they all watched as a stream of water as long and as wide as the River Thames flew down toward the ground below them. As they all watched, the fire went out and was replaced by a column of white steam.

"Dragon, you've an amazing aim and did exactly what I asked you to do," Mary said. "Hip-hip-hurray for now we have won the day! Dragon, when we all get home to Modern London, I'll ask our King to knight you. You'll be the first flying dragon to receive knighthood, did you know that?"

"I did not know, my new friend Mary Sweet," the Dragon said as it circled over the tall white column of smoke. "Soon, I will make my way back to London. Then, I will have a very long sleep. When I wake up, we'll all be back in a London that we'll all recognise."

"And so we will, Dragon. Now please place us on the ground near that smouldering fire and we'll hop off your head and end this long battle."

When the Dragon did as he was bid, Mary and McMouse found themselves standing before The Bruce. Still tied to a blackened stake, his clothes had been burned but his eyes were filled with laughter.

"Take off these ropes, woman!" The Bruce roared. "You and that Mystical Dragon have saved my life. For that reason, you, the Dragon and anyone else who helped you will be knighted as a Royal Leader of Scotland."

"Thank you, my friend," Mary said as she and McMouse began to untie his hands. "But I am already Royalty. You see, in a time very far from now, another King of England who is a firm friend of Scotland made me a Royal Queen. Soon, when I go forward in time to my home in London again, I shall tell King Charles that you send him greetings for your ancestors will be equal in stature and power to him."

"An English King will be our friend?" The Bruce asked as, now free, he climbed over the smouldering pile of blackened wood. "If that is true, then maybe all of our prayers will soon be answered. Perhaps no English Army will ever try to invade Scotland again."

"What you say is quite true," McMouse answered in a Scots accent. "Sire, ye shall soon be our new King of Scotland and England. When that happens, we will never have War in our country again."

"Why, the tiny mouse sitting on your shoulder talks!" The Bruce said to Mary. "If a mouse from Scotland talks, then anything at all is possible! Now, let me get back to my friend, William Wallace. He is kneeling together with a man that I do not know. Perhaps they are saying prayers for the fallen."

"Yes, they are," Mary said. "See the Englishmen at their feet that they slew while you and I were talking? They are not praying for them, I don't think, but someone that is much closer to them."

"I bid ye farewell, Queen. I hope to see you before you leave for London."

Mary and McMouse watched as The Bruce walked over to William Wallace and James. Seeing the three men talk, The Bruce also got down on his knees.

"They pray for Jack, the son of James," Mary whispered to her mouse friend. "But they need not pray at all! For, as we were flying here on the Dragon's head, I saw Jack run toward the high hills and he's now with his mother. Of that I am certain again."

"But Mary, how could you recognise this Jack from high above him when you've never even met him?" the mouse asked.

"Well, Mouse, I seem to have a new gift. As you know I've always rather enjoyed seeing and hearing things which most other humans can't do. Now, I seem to remember things that I've never really experienced. It's like a dream but it's not because, as you'll also see, these dreams are the truth!"

"Then we'd better get over to the men, Chief. Our Teams need to help them defeat any last English soldiers who have not heard about their King's death. When that's finished, can we please get out of here and go home again?"

"And so we will, McMouse. We will do that in only moments. And then, by the light of the silvery full Moon, we'll find our Space Time Machine and go home for good! But first, I must find Wallace and his best friend James. The father and the young Scots soldier must become aware that his boy is still living. Having protected his mother in the hills above us, he has once again gone to battle and is standing guard on some English soldiers."

"But…but…but Mary, you've not seen that young Scots man, have you? You've never even met him, by my reconning. How can you see him when the poor boy is likely to be already dead."

Mary Sweet winked at her mouse friend and looked to the Heavens.

"I told you, McMouse. I have a new gift that's Heaven sent. Let's face it, I'll always be insane until the day that I die. But now – like many others who are as mad as me – I'm psychic and have the ability to see things and people that are there when others cannot."

Now laying down on her shoulder, the mouse looked up at Mary's eyes. "You mean you can see dead people?"

"Dead, yes. I see my husband Hubert all the time and he's dead. But I can also see living people and locate them when they are so very far away."

"Dead people and living, distant people," the mouse said as he sat up again. "Mary, you really should become a private investigator when we're done with this mission. Just think of all the crimes you could solve! Why, you could talk to those that have been murdered and they could tell you who or what killed them."

"A Private Eye? Me, mouse? No way am I going to chase down ghosts who have been murdered. I'll leave that up to our good friends, Ghosts Watson and Holmes. Now, let's find James and Wallace and give them the good news."

Having climbed back up on the Dragon's head, the mouse and Mary Sweet now looked down again on the battlefield and watched as the surviving Scots did battle with the surviving English soldiers. Seeing how few Scots there were in that final battle, Mary used a compact radio transceiver to call her Human Team. "Human Team! Now's the time. Use your weapons but train them carefully. Destroy all the English soldiers that you find but don't you dare hit our friends and allies."

On the ground below the flying Dragon, and as the battlefield began rocking with explosions and the sound of unfamiliar gunfire, an English soldier turned to his mate. Both had been horribly wounded by the Scottish Clan and the gang of Horsemen led by a man some called Robin Hood.

"Mate, it's a sad day for England," one soldier said. "See that flying Dragon over us? And how it bathed us with water? It's a sign all English soldiers fear. The Dragon of England is now fighting against Edward's soldiers."

"The King be dead anyway, mate," the other soldier replied. "And as for Robin Hood? Why that's the 'hood that lives in Nottingham in that big tree in Sherwood Forest. Don't know about you, ducks, but as for me, I'm gonna surrender."

"To the Scots? Are you crazy? They'll have their dogs eat us for dinner."

"Naw, mate. The King's been a dog's dinner. No, they'll send us over the border to England and tell us never to come back here again."

"Are you sure?"

"Sure I am. I was talking to a man from Scotland the other day when we were marching to the battlefield. He told me that most people from Scotland are peace loving people."

"Peace loving? Well, if you say so. But with all the weapons the Scots have collected from us, I'll bet you five ta' one that it's England that they'll start to march on."

"Maybe you're right, mate. But I'd rather have a Scottish King than King Edward any day of the good auld week. That King was a tyrant by any standard."

Standing nearby and guarding them with a captured sword taken from King Edward's bloody body, young Jack Fraser looked down and smiled. "Ye be some good troops and if ye both ask William Wallace and Robert the Bruce kindly, you can join our new Scottish Army."

"Can we now, youngster?" a soldier asked. "Well, I'd rather be with your Army than with that yon mess of an auld eaten King. Did ya' know he never fed us properly?"

"In our Army, we all eat like Scottish Lords."

"Do ye now? All of ya'."

"All."

"Well, lad, if that's the case, the two of us will join ye' in any battle to come!"

Jack walked to a fire that he had lit earlier and, taking a pan from the heat, walked back to the two captives and offered them a meal.

"Gents, 'tis only a few sausages and some fried bread that me Mam gave to me when last I saw her. I've already had a fine meal with my Mam so eat yer fill."

As the two soldiers grabbed the hot food from the frying pan, Jack looked up to see a Flying Dragon circling over his head. "Why, 'tis my friend that Wonder Beast flying to our rescue," the boy said. "That will be the end of the English Army, by all things that are good."

"Lad, it's not the end of the English Army," one of the soldiers said. "We're here, ain't we? And those that survive who be on our side, why, they'll join the Scots Army, too."

"Ye be sure?"

"Sure as me mudder's Christmas Pudding," the other English soldier said. "Now, who be those two large men that are walking this way? Good God! They both hold swords and now they're running toward us. Lad, tell those Scotsmen what we've said. That we're now loyal to the Scots cause and an independent country of Scotland."

"So I will, Gents," the lad replied as he watched the two men running toward him. When they were nearer, he immediately recognised his father. The giant of a man threw down his sword as he came closer and, holding out both arms, grabbed his son as he began crying.

"Oh, my Jack. My Jack. I thought ye be dead."

"No, father. I did what you told me," Jack replied as he looked into his father's eyes. "I went to find Mam which I did. They had all sorts of Scotsmen there so, when I told her I'd come down here to find you, she agreed and that's what I did."

"Did you now, my grown son. See that Dragon flying overhead? On its head sits a crazy woman, Mary Sweet, and a talking mouse! Did you ever hear of such a thing? A talking mouse and a real flying Dragon."

"Flying it is, father," the lad replied. "Why is not Wallace coming closer?"

"He came with me to find you when that Mary woman told us where you were. He's just giving us some time together. The Giant James waved a hand and William Wallace trotted over too see them both.

"Well, look what we have here!" the Leader of the Clan MacSquat said as he touched Jack's shoulder with a side of his sword. "And two prisoners you have now, do you, man?"

"Why, you called me man!" Jack exclaimed as he stepped out of his father's strong arms. "Sir, these two English soldiers surrendered to me. They have sworn fealty to the new Scots King and have promised that, if the time ever comes, they'll fight with us and any Army we raise."

"Will they now?" Wallace replied as he looked at the two English soldiers who were squatting by a small campfire. "That's a wonderful thing, Jack the Lad who is now a truly grown man. When we have to fight again, I'll make you a Corporal in our new Army."

"Thy will be done, Sir," Jack replied. "Now, if you don't mind I'll clean up here and hand these English lads over to some other Scottish people so that I can help us win this last battle."

"No need, Jack," James replied as he placed an arm around his son's shoulders. "The battle is won! Mary Sweet and that Flying Dragon, together with other men, women and animals, have convinced the remaining English soldiers and their officers to surrender to Robert The Bruce! Now, it's a time of celebration. We'll let these English captives go back to join their mates. As for the three of us, well, my son, we must go home to rebuild our village and live for a time in peace."

"Which is what we all want to do," Wallace said as he put his sword in its sheath. "A time for peace, making children, large meals and praying again. A time to simply be normal."

"And normal we are now," a woman's voice said above them. Looking up, the three of them as well as the English soldiers could see the Dragon hovering just over their heads. "By the Grace of our Gods, it's time to go home! So get you home and we will too. And on the day I see thee again we'll have a wedding for that Jack of yours as well as all those who will become engaged as peace descends again on your lands."

Looking up at the Dragon, all the men could see Mary's blonde hair blowing in the wind made by the Dragon's flapping wings. Waving to her, she waved back and, as they watched, they could see the tiny arm of the talking mouse waving at them, too.

"Well, that's it, then," Wallace said to his friends. "If Mary is leaving this place of horrible carnage, then it's time for us to go home, too. Come, Jack. Come, James. Let us go back to find our families."

As the men walked back toward the battlefield that was still littered with corpses, Mary and McMouse looked toward the Southwest and there saw a star that flew across the clear blue sky.

"That's Captain Sarah Scots, of course," Mary said as she took a communications device out of her pocket. "I'll have her land in five minutes. And Dragon our new friend? You can come with us! That new-fangled Space Vehicle has room for one hundred Dragons as large as you are."

"As big as that?" the Dragon replied as it flapped onward toward the Scottish border. "I'll take you up on that, Mary Sweet. My flapping wings are getting sore and very tired."

"Good! Mouse, make ready for all of us to board the Rocket Ship. In only minutes, we'll all be back in London where we belong!"

As Mary, McMouse and all of the Human and Animal Teams boarded the new Rocket, the satellite phone started to ping in the pocket of the tiny mouse. Answering the phone call, he listened intently then, his eyes as round as two large globes, he hung up. Looking at Mary, who was just sitting down in her Spacecraft seat, he frowned at no one in particular.

"Chief, that was the King. He is reminding us that our Mission isn't quite over. First, we have to find and capture General Gatwick, the traitor and, if he's alive again, capture or kill that would-be Emperor of the World, Vladimir Puttin."

"Good God, yet again, McMouse," Mary responded. "My head is like melting butter! I'd completely forgotten that we had two more large parts of our Mission to accomplish. Then, we can go home as we planned. Mouse, please give the order to Captain Sarah to go first to Edinburgh, Scotland, to see a fine wedding between Prince Edward, the son of the fallen King, and his new Queen, our beloved Dragon who is now again a human being, our dear Gloria. As you know, Mouse, Gloria is also the daughter of Nessie, our great friend from the Loch. Then ask Sarah to alter our flight plan. Go ahead in time and back to World War Two. We may have to stop in Paris, England and Germany. Then it's off to Russia again where we will destroy our sworn enemies."

"Wilco and Roger that, Chief," the mouse said as he unbuckled his seatbelt. But as he rose to carry out Mary's wishes, a voice in his head whispered to him that Mary's wishes had already been turned into a new flight plan by their Space Vehicle.

"Amazing technology, isn't it Mary," the Mouse said as he re-buckled his seatbelt. "Did you hear the thought that our new Spaceship whispered to me?"

"No, my Mouse, I didn't. I was thinking of all that we've accomplished so far and the fact that we will succeed beyond expectations before we head home again."

Chapter 12

Putin Lives Again!

As the Space Vehicle made the short hop to the capital of Scotland and because the English King, Edward the First was dead, in Edinburgh on a table made of marble a Peace Treaty was signed between Scotland's new King Robert The Bruce and Edward's eldest son, Prince Edward the Second. As part of that Treaty, Prince Edward had to give up the throne to England and swear fealty to The Bruce on bended knee. Also, he swore to marry a Scottish Princess who The Bruce named as Gloria The Bruce, the magical daughter of Nessie of Loch Ness. Both men agreed to the wedding knowing that it would permanently cement the relationship between their two countries and provide an heir to the throne to both England and Scotland which, so read the Treaty, would become a single united nation.

At the wedding which took place in Edinburgh, Mary Sweet and McMouse were given seats quite near the altar. From there, they could see the new Royal couple swear allegiance to the Scottish flag as well as to the new combined flag of the new nation which was coloured in blue, white and red but no longer had any cross on it.

"Look how much history has changed already!" McMouse squeaked quietly to Mary in his very small voice. "See the new flag of the new single nation? The colours symbolise both England and Scotland but, with no cross, it also represents a nation of tolerance and lasting peace. Mind you, they may change that someday soon. And that Human woman with the Prince. Is she really Gloria, the daughter of our Dragon friend, Nessie?"

"Quite so, McMouse," Mary whispered back. "Remember how our flying Dragon friend Nessie had told us that her daughter was of Human Royal Lineage? It turns out that she really is the true daughter of Robert The Bruce! Years ago, far away from here, Robert The Bruce was a Flying Dragon. He met Nessie and, well, they married and had a baby girl. Someday, using the magic that Gloria has now, Nessie may come back as a Human woman."

"Wow, and isn't that fantastic! It's all a fairytale come true. Do you think that English Prince and Robert's Scottish daughter will really get along?"

"Absolutely, mouse! Edward the young Prince is nothing at all like his murderous father. I'm told that he's as kind as many English people that we know back in London in modern times. Besides, with his blood and Gloria's bound together, they'll make great children who will one day become our King and Queen of a new Great Britain!"

"But does Scotland really become the ruler of a modern-day Great Britain? What about what is now, in our time, Great Britain and the Commonwealth?"

"They'll all still be there but it will be very different, my senior detective friend. Scotland will become more powerful than almost any country in the world. History will change quite dramatically, I'm sure. We'll see what happens when we get back to the Twenty-First Century!"

As they both looked back to the altar and watched the Scottish Bishop bless the Royal couple, the mouse with his very sensitive ears heard a small noise from the ceiling of the enormous

Church. Looking up, he watched as part of the ceiling was pulled up and back and saw the smiling face of Nessie looking down on them.

"Daughter Gloria!" the mother Dragon cried in a joyful puff of smoke. "I have come to see your wedding because you and your Prince invited me here."

"Mother!" the young Princess cried out as she and her new husband looked up. "Don't stay up there! Come down here so you can join us at our wedding party."

Nessie put her head into the cavernous upper part of the Church and gave a very short snort through both of her large nostrils. "Inside this small Church? Why daughter, I'll never fit. Did you tell your prince that you're part Flying Dragon as well as Royal Human?"

"I did, Mother, the first time we met. He told me that he doesn't mind what I am because he loves me."

"I'm so glad. Your father was Human, as you know, and with that Scottish King The Bruce as your 'Da your offspring will also be half Human and half Dragon which is an outstanding heritage."

Prince Edward put his arm around his new bride and looked up at his new Mother-in-Law Dragon. "Mother Nessie Dragon, you and my new Princess need to also know that I'm also part Dragon. That's why there is a large red dragon on the flag of England!"

"Part Dragon too?" Nessie called down. "Then this marriage is perfect! I'll see you at your wedding party which, I gather, is being held in a large park next to this magnificent Cathedral."

"See you there, Mumsy!" both Gloria and Edward cried as the Dragon disappeared from the top of the Church.

"See, mouse, what did I tell you?" Mary Sweet said to her mouse friend. "With flying dragons as part of our New Scottish

Heritage, is it any wonder that modern Scotland will someday develop a flying Time Machine like the one we flew here in?"

"Not a problem for Flying Dragon Scottish Engineers," the mouse sniffed. "But now what? Chief, what's next? Is it back to England?"

"That's right, mouse. Now, we must go forward in time. Then forward again! When we're done, history will be changed dramatically and total peace will bring a new Dawn to our planet."

A day later, after the Wedding Party was held for the Royal couple, Mary and all her Teams re-boarded the Space Vehicle which was also a Time Machine now named *The Gloria* in honour of the new bride. Repainted in blue and white like the Scottish flag, Sarah Scots blasted off from the park next to the Cathedral. Climbing quickly above the Earth, she thought to the Space Time Machine, "Gloria, my friend and co-pilot, we need to go forward in time to the latter days of World War Two. Our destination is Paris, France."

"Will do, my Captain," *The Gloria* chirped over a loud speaker so that everyone could hear. "We're now at the speed of light and I'll ramp up our single engine so that we'll go forward in time. Time of destination: May, 1944. Place: Paris France."

"Belay that order, Sarah Scots!" Mary yelled. "In May 1944, the Allies were preparing for the huge and deadly invasion of Normandy. Keep the date the same but instead of Paris, make your destination first over the White Cliffs of Dover and then Berlin, Germany. Teams!" she shouted so that everyone could hear her. "Our mission is very simple. We must capture Adolph Hitler alive before that General Gusto Gatwick does. By doing so, we can make Germany surrender! That way, so many soldiers and innocent people will survive World War Two!"

"Destination as commanded by Chief Inspector Mary Sweet, Gloria," Sarah Scots thought to her spaceship. "Chief Inspector, we'll be there in three minutes. That's real time."

"Three minutes it is! When you make your final descent, I'll bail out and land in General Eisenhower's Army camp. I need to talk to him to make him understand that he needs to call off the invasion or delay it significantly."

"Mary Sweet, you're bailing out over England?" the Mouse said from his seat beside hers. "If you're going to meet that famous General Eisenhower, I want to go, too."

"Okay, McMouse. Get your high-altitude gear on as well as your parachute. We have a minute or less before we must bail out of our Space Time Machine."

"Understood, Chief," the mouse said as he reached into his military duffle bag and took out the special high-altitude gear. "Chief, I'll see you on the ground. Then, we can find General Eisenhower and give him all the details of our Special Operation to find and arrest Hitler."

"It would be a good idea if you don't talk," Mary replied. "Mouse, get Edith Piaf on your special radio transmitter. Tell us that, if she can, she is to meet us in England. There, she'll not only be safe but can help us to convince the General that we're telling the truth."

"What a good idea! Why not have *The Gloria* pick her up and bring her over to us? It will only take a few minutes."

"Mouse, why is it you're always smarter than I am? You get yourself to the hatch. I'll tell Sarah Scots that new order. See you on the ground, my mouse."

"Roger that!" the mouse replied with a grin. "I'm going to find some cheese when I get to the U.S. Army Canteen. The Americans make great cheddar cheese, too!"

"And they'll have real silk stockings," Mary said with a sigh. "Mouse, get us two pair. One for me and one for Miss Piaf. She'll be delighted with them."

"That's an easy task, Chief. Okay, see you later."

In moments, the mouse had bailed out of the Space Vehicle high over England. Looking down, he could see the White Cliffs of Dover and then a huge number of ships and boats of all sizes nestled beneath them. He could also see what seemed to be a thousand aircraft lined up next to a few long runways which had been made of tarmacadam. As he popped his parachute and slowed down, he started to look for a tent with a four-star General's flag flying above it. Seeing it, he ordered his parachute in Mouse Language to turn to the right. When the automated voice of his small Mouse Army 'chute confirmed the order, the Mouse looked down again from an altitude of five-hundred feet and saw the four-star flag flying over a dark green tent.

"Mary Sweet, I have the General's tent in sight," the Mouse said into his special radio. "Eisenhower's tent has a four-star flag flying above it."

"I'll be right there, Senior Detective," the mouse heard in his special transceiver. "You find the Army Canteen and get those supplies while I start to talk to the General. See you in his tent, my friend."

"That's a Roger," the mouse replied. "See you there, Chief."

When McMouse landed on his tiny feet, he released the parachute then scampered into the nearby Canteen. There, he saw General Eisenhower dressed in his olive uniform having lunch with his Chief of Staff.

"Good God above, there's the General himself!" the mouse squeaked in Mouse Language. "I'll grab some cheese and two pairs of silk stockings as I'd promised my Chief then find my way to the General's tent where I'll wait for Mary Sweet."

He grabbed two pairs of free silk stockings from a table and a few crumbs of American Cheddar Cheese that he found beneath the General's feet. Stuffing them into a mouse-sized Army duffle bag that an American relative of his given to him, he scampered out of the Canteen and, running as fast as he could, saw the General's tent in the near distance. Looking over his shoulder, the mouse saw his relative running behind him. Both scampered up to the General's tent and hid under the wooden steps.

"That's enough running and jumping for one day," McMouse said to the relative who had followed him. "Did you say your name is Julia? Are you sure that we're related?"

"Yes, we're related, McMouse," the female mouse said as she placed a crumb of cheese on a small seashell for her visitor. "I'm from the Southwest Coast of Ireland. But I immigrated to America by boat with many other Irish mouse relatives and, when I found myself in New York City, I joined the American Mice-Army. Now, I work as a Spy for the American Army. They call me Madam Pink Panther. That's my code name."

"Madam Pink Panther?" the mouse said as he began to eat the cheese. "Julia, I hope that when we all go home you can meet my wife in London."

"I'd love that, cousin," Julia said with her tiny mouth full of cheese. "I'm sure that you have many mice-children in your nest. I'm not married but someday I'd love to cradle some baby mice in my lap."

"Cousins? You're sure we're cousins?"

"Of course I'm sure, McMouse. My full name is Julia McFlynn McMouse. What's your first name?"

"Tom-Jon. That's what my wife Betty calls me."

"Tom-Jon, if you know any single men-mice in London or Ireland, let me know. There are many men-mice in the American Army with me but I'm related to them all."

"I understand, Julia. Yes, mice have way too many relatives." Finished with his morsel of cheese, McMouse looked between the slats of the wooden steps and his small lips broke into a smile. "Oh, look up there in the sky! See that orange and black parachute? That's my boss Mary Sweet."

As Julia finished her cheese, they both saw Mary's brown Army boots land just beside them. Hurrying out from beneath the steps, they both looked up at the tall figure of the Chief Inspector.

"Good day, Mary Sweet," McMouse said as he saluted. "May I introduce you to Julia McFlynn McMouse, my cousin."

"Pleased to meet you, Julia," Mary said as she smiled down on them. "As you can see, I'm wearing my new U.S. Army Officer's Uniform. By order of President Roosevelt, the current president of the United States, who was in touch with Prime Minister Winston Churchill, I am now a U.S. Army Three-Star General!"

"Holy-Moly!" both mice yelled as they snapped to attention and saluted her. "Three-Stars and see how they gleam in the sunlight!"

"Three-stars," Mary stated with a frown on her face. "Now where's that General Eisenhower! By order of President Roosevelt, our Commander-In-Chief, I've been sent here to demote him!"

They all heard the sound of boots marching toward them and, as Mary turned around, she saluted General Eisenhower.

"General, I'm General Mary Sweet. I'm bringing you new orders from the Prime Minister. I suggest you read them right now and then, by order of President Roosevelt, you and I must discuss them."

"I'll read this letter when I'm good and ready," the General said as he took a brown envelope from her. "Don't you know what day it is? It's the fifth of June. Tomorrow, all of my troops are invading Germany."

"Not so fast, General," Mary stated with fire in her eyes. "Read that before you do anything else. Your Commander-In-Chief orders it. If you don't comply with his direct orders, and those from Churchill, I'm authorised to demote you to the rank of a one-star General and take over your Command."

"Demote me? Like I did to Patton? Are you absurd?" General Eisenhower scratched the thin hair on his head then opened the envelope. Scanning it, he looked up at Mary with a broad smile. "You honestly have the capability to travel in time?"

"Yes, sir, we do. It's a Scottish invention. With our Space Time Machine Vehicle, *The Gloria*, we can go faster than the speed of light. With that technology, we can go forward and back in time, and across the known Universe. General, can we talk in your tent alone? There are many things you need to know about what happens when you change history."

Looking down at the letter, the General smiled again. "Yep, like kill Hitler or capture him tomorrow," the pleasant man said to her as he took Mary's arm. "General Sweet, we've a great deal to talk about. With this new invention, Scotland's new machine is going to save a great number of lives."

As Mary and General Eisenhower went into his tent, the two mice scampered across a wide stretch of concrete and sat on the grass beside it.

"See that large glider over there, cousin McMouse?" Julia said as she pointed to an American glider with a tiny finger. "I'm supposed to go up in that tomorrow morning with the rest of my cousins in the U.S. Mouse Army."

"It seems to me, Julia, that you won't have to go now," McMouse replied. "Why don't you come with Mary and me when we leave? We can drop you in Paris, France, then we must go to Germany. France is lovely this time of year and there are many Parisian mouse-men there looking for a girlfriend."

"Can I really go with you in that amazing Spacecraft your Mary Sweet mentioned moments ago?" she asked. "I'd love that. Flying in a glider over Normandy would be very, very dangerous not only to me but to anyone else who had to come with us."

"I don't even have to ask my General, Julia. Mary will be delighted to have you."

And so, on that historic day in a General's tent near the White Cliffs of Dover, history was rewritten. As I, Tom-Jon McMouse, write in my journal by the light of my torch in a nest beneath the tent of General Sweet, I can only count our lucky stars that as dawn breaks tomorrow, no American or English soldier will die in a hail of bullets as they invade the beaches of Normandy. Nor will any Germans. Of course, there will always be Wars but, if what Mary Sweet predicts comes true, this Terrible World War Two will end in only a week or so.

As I look up at the twinkling stars, I think of my wife, Betty McMouse and my children. I know that soon, very soon now, I'll be home with them and when I do, I'll never leave them or England again.

Chapter 13

The Capture of Adolph Hitler
and the Early Ending of World War Two

Now in Germany and working again for the French Resistance, the French singer Edith Piaf walked swiftly down the cold streets of Berlin. Allied bombers had gutted many Nazi Party buildings and a vast majority of German Generals and regular soldiers thought that their Führer was dead. As Edith approached a German restaurant that had its windows covered in blackout curtains, she could hear the wail of a nearby siren which signalled another attack on the city.

"Everyone! Get inside or into your nearest bomb shelter!" a German soldier cried. "Allied enemy bombers will hit our city yet again! *Hurry! Beeil dich!*"

As old men, women and children hurried to carry out the order, Edith walked up to another soldier who was guarding the front door. Presenting her identification papers to him, which had been forged by the French Resistance, the German soldier glanced once at her and stepped aside.

"Your papers say that you are the girlfriend of Hitler," the German corporal said. "Is it true that our Führer has died in the Reichstag when bombs were dropped on it this morning?"

"That is not true, Corporal," Edith replied in her best German accent. "He was injured but is very much alive. As I understand it, he is now in hiding in a large bunker somewhere in Berlin. I have not seen him since yesterday evening."

"Ah so!" the soldier said with a look of satisfaction on his face. "He is in the Bunker just down the street. That's what the Generals in the restaurant were discussing when I took time to have a stein of beer."

"Take heart, Corporal. All is not lost. Soon, the Luftwaffe will re-engage our enemies and, with Hitler leading us, we shall not only get back what has been stolen from us but we will win the War."

"Which is very good," the soldier replied as he opened the front door. "Get in. The bombs will fall soon."

"Nein, my friend. I will take shelter in the Bunker with Mein Führer. Can you show me where the door is hidden?"

"Just down the street," the soldier said as he smiled. "It has our Swastika above the door and can easily be seen due to the light that his hanging just above it."

"That is so good of you, Mein Soldier," Edith replied as she turned away and started to hurry down the street. "Bonne chance, as the French say."

"And Good Luck to you, too!" the soldier called back.

Edith started to run down the empty street and as she did, bombs started to fall on the city. Seeing a man hidden in the shadows, she motioned to him to follow her. As he ran onto the street, a dozen more Resistance fighters all dressed in black came out of hiding and followed him. When Edith saw a large Nazi emblem carved into the cement above a steel door, she took a Luger from her coat and ran toward it. Standing at the door and banging on the steel with two fists, the door opened and a German Army Lieutenant looked out.

"I am looking for Mein Führer," Edith said as more bombs hit the Reichstag just beside the Bunker. "Tell him his new girlfriend is waiting for him."

"Ah, the new *Freundin*! Yes, our Leader is waiting for you together with the woman who is his new wife." The soldier winked at Edith. "Our Führer loves the ladies, doesn't he? He is in his bedroom and asleep right now. Let me take you downstairs and get you a glass of champagne. When the Führer wakes, I'm sure he will see you. Your name please?"

"Edith Piaf," she replied and then swiftly pointed the handgun at him. "Take us inside now, *mon frere* or this will be the last time you will open any door."

When the German Officer saw the men dressed in black standing behind her, he put up his hands.

"The Bunker is filled with an entire Regiment of Army and Air Force officers. You will never escape alive."

"No matter. Now move!"

As Edith and her fighters crept down the stairs behind the Lieutenant, a German General came out of a side door.

"Put up your hands. Both of them!" a Resistance fighter roared. "If you do not comply I will kill you."

The General in the German Luftwaffe only smiled and shook his head. "You do not know who you point your gun at. I am General Herman Goering, the Leader of the Nazi Party. The Führer has just resigned from his office and is getting ready to take his own life as well as the lives of his new wife, Eva Braun, other Nazi Party Leaders as well as their families."

"That is never going to happen," Edith shouted as she moved past General Goering. "If you are now the Leader of the Nazi Party, then you are under arrest for violating the Geneva Convention." Turning from him, she pointed to five of her men. "You five! Come with me. We must save the Führer from committing suicide. When we do, we will change the course of the War!"

"Viva la France!" a Resistance fighter shouted. "May God save France and our Allies."

"But never the Russians," another Frenchman shouted. "They will never get into Berlin. They continue to be trapped on the Russian Front near Stalingrad."

"Good!" Edith added. "June Nineteen-Forty-Four, and the Sixth, Seventh or the Eighth day of this month will go down in history as the day the War ended! A year or more earlier than we thought." Looking up the grey cement stairway, she saw another French Resistance Fighter stepping down them. Shrugging his shoulders, he smiled at Edith and the other fighters.

"*Pardon moi* but I am very late. I only have my pistol with me."

"Your name is Jon?" Edith asked. "My friend, you are very welcome. Guard this fat General while we other three search some of this Bunker.

The Frenchman obeyed the order and placed his weapon against the belly of Goering. Knowing that the Nazi General was being well guarded, Edith and the other French fighters ran down a long hallway lit with bright lights. With her men, Edith opened a number of steel doors. When they saw German soldiers, they shot them. When they saw women and children, Edith left one man to guard them and kept running. When they found a locked door, they banged on it.

"Open in the name of Adolph Hitler!" she shouted. "The Russian Army has entered this Bunker and claim they have won the war."

When she heard the door unlock and then open, Edith and her men found a woman and six children staring back at them.

"I am Magda Goebbels, the wife of the Minister of Propaganda, Joseph Goebbels," a woman said as she stepped toward Edith. "My children are asleep so please keep your voices down."

Edith pushed the woman back into the room and, seeing the children asleep, lowered her voice. "Magda, we all know what you plan to do because our local Clairvoyant, a Spy name Mary Sweet, told me about the future. You were going to kill your children with cyanide then you and your husband, that misfit Minister, were going to commit suicide."

When Edith saw the woman's face turn white, she smiled brightly and walked to the centre of the room. "Children! Wake up! Your other father, Adolph, wants to play football with you outside."

"He does?" a four-year-old girl said as she stretched in her bunkbed. "He's outside? But we've been told by him to stay in our room with Mama."

"No, he was only joking," Edith replied. "Now wake up your brothers and sisters. I see that you're already dressed so get on your coats and then follow the man dressed in black outside."

"My children are not going anywhere without me!" Mrs Goebbels stated as tears filled her eyes. "If the Russians have really captured this Bunker as you say, then we are all doomed. All of my girls and any woman in this Bunker will be raped."

"There are no Russians only German soldiers," Edith said to the children in her best German. "Your Mama is just upset. Now hurry up. You don't want to keep Adolph waiting, do you?"

When the children were dressed, they all followed one of Edith's French Resistance fighters back down the long hallway.

"Good, that's done," she whispered to one of her soldiers.

"But what about her?" he asked as he nodded his head toward Magda Goebbels. "*Morte*?"

"No. No death to her. That's far too easy. Put a man in here to guard her. When we find her husband, we'll lock them back in this room and then hand them over to General Patton when he arrives in this fallen city."

Having saved the lives of the Goebbel children from the murderous hands of their mother, and with another Resistance Fighter on guard, Edith and three French fighters ran further down the hallway and came at last to a large steel door. When she tried the steel lock, the door opened. A waiter dressed in a white suite coat and black bow tie was coming out of a door at the back of the long room which Edith assumed was the entryway to Hitler's bedroom.

"Get on your knees!" she shouted as she pointed the Lugar at the head of the waiter. Placing a tray filled with wine glasses on a large desk, the man slid down on his knees.

"I am only a poor waiter," the man said with a frightened voice. "I am French and have been forced to wait on Hitler since the invasion of Paris. If I did not do what I was told, the pig General Goering told me that my wife and three children would be shot."

"What is your name, Frenchman?" Edith asked. "Say it clearly or I well may shoot you right here."

"My name is Francois Leibermann. I am French but also a Jew."

"Leibermann? Francois Leibermann? The famous French musician? Why, you've composed some of the best classical music

I've ever heard. I saw you conduct an orchestra as they played your best symphony when I was learning to sing."

"Yes, Madam. And you are Edith Piaf, the Little Bird. I've heard you sing many times in our French theatres."

"Get up, Francois. Come with us. You no longer need to be a waiter. You are now a French Resistance Fighter." As the man stood up again, Edith walked across the long room to a large black door. "This is his bedroom?"

"Oui," Francois replied. "He is in there with Eva Braun."

"Good." Edith reached into her coat pocket and took out another Luger. Throwing it to Francois, she grinned at him. "Now you are armed and a dangerous former waiter." Looking at the rest of her men, she motioned toward the door. "When I count 'One' I'll open the door. Rush in as fast as you can. Do not shoot either of them, just as I've instructed you. If you see any kind of a vial in Hitler's hands, grab it and strip it off him. He is a fanatic and fanatics often take cyanide to kill themselves."

Turning again to the door, Edith put both of her hands on the gleaming bronze handle. "One!"

When they all rushed in, Edith saw Hitler sitting on a couch with Eva Braun next to him. The woman was already half asleep probably due to the tranquiliser that her new husband had given to her.

"Stand up at once!" Francois shouted as he waved the black revolver at his old employer. "Stand up or I will shoot you in the face!"

"This is an outrage! *Das ist ein Skandal!*" the monster, Hitler, shouted as he took a Lugar out of the coffee table drawer in front of him and pointed it at the waiter. "Put down your gun or I will certainly kill you."

"Put down your own gun, you scum," Edith said as she smiled. Hitler looked around the room at Edith Piaf and the four men that were all pointing their weapons at him.

"I know you, don't I?" Hitler asked her. "You are the famous French singer that I saw only days ago when you tried to kill me."

"Yes I am, you toad. It's a pity that my boyfriend died in all that unnecessary arms fire. We only wanted to assassinate you and kill all of your Officers that were in my Theatre. But now, we are here to capture you and your wife, Eva Braun. What we do is an act of simple revenge."

"I will never be captured!" Hitler screamed at the top of his lungs. "I was about to kill myself and my new wife so that no Russian, American or Frenchman can torture us. But then you all come charging in here. What is the difference if I take my own life or you murder me? It's all the same thing."

As Hitler raised his weapon to his temple, the waiter took a steady aim and fired his Luger. Hitting Adolph Hitler's weapon in the barrel, it spun out of the crazy Nazi Leader's hand.

"Now, it is finished," Edith said to her new captive and her men. "Let's get him and that woman out of here. As to the others, we'll lock every door that we can find. If they kill themselves inside their new prison, what do we care? We will place Goebbels, Goering, and Hitler in handcuffs and, with their wives, march them outside. Then I'll call the Chief Inspector Mary Sweet on the new radio that she gave to me in Paris. They'll come down in their new Space Vehicle to take our captives into custody. Then, *mon amie*, we are finished with our Mission in Berlin."

When they all stood outside as Edith had ordered, she used the radio to call the Chief Inspector. As he looked up into the sky high above him, the captive Adolph Hitler started to laugh like a madman. "See that long flame in the night?" Hitler stated as he pointed a finger at the long tongue of bright white flame. "That is the new ballistic rocket that our Nazi engineers have been working on for so very long. It has come to free me and all those here and in the Bunker. Then, Edith Piaf and you French toads, I will have all of you lined up against that wall over there and shot!"

"You're wrong yet again," Edith stated in a lilting French accent. "That is a new Rocket that Scottish engineers have made. It is also a Time Machine."

"Time machine?" Hitler replied as he continued to point skyward. "No, my General from Russia and England, General Gusto Gatwick, is the pilot of that giant rocket above us."

"Wrong one last time, former Führer," Edith replied as she saluted him with a fist. "The time for justice is at hand. Have you heard of a Frenchman name Albert Pierrepoint? He is a very famous Hangman. He has carried out many executions for the past twenty years or more. If you are found Guilty of your crimes, a group of judges will sentence you to death. Be careful of this famous Hangman, Hitler. He is Jewish and he cannot and will not forget what you did to the Jews who were his relatives in all the camps you created with that bigot Goebbels. Pierrepoint will loosen your noose a little bit right before you fall through the trap door. Then, rather than snapping your neck for an easy death, you will die by strangulation."

"Enough! I command you to stay *Strummmm!*"

"Silent? Why should I stay silent? You have lost the War and so many battles. Now you will die not by your hand but the hand of a man who is much, much better than you."

When the Space Vehicle which was also a Time Machine landed in a large city Square near them, Edith commanded her prisoners to walk over to it. As the elevator descended, Ms Piaf could see Mary Sweet waving at her through the cubicle's open glass windows.

"*Mon amie*! Edith Piaf! Up here! I'm so delighted to find you safe."

"We are all safe, mon Chief Detective. I have many surprises for you today and they're all *bon*! Good! Here is Hitler and two crazy people who served under him. We also have Hitler and Goebbel's wives locked in a room and many more soldiers and Generals are locked in Hitler's Bunker."

"Then the War is over!" Mary shouted as the elevator door opened. "Edith, bring all the other prisoners out here while I descend to the ground to join you."

As Mary descended in the automated elevator, she watched as the other prisoners were marched out of the Bunker. Stepping onto the ground, she turned as the two Leaders of the Nazi Party joined Adolph Hitler.

"Adolph Hitler!" Mary yelled in passable German. "General Goering and you, you rat Goebbels! I command you to get onboard the U.S. Army truck that will be here shortly. No, we will not gas you or burn you alive. Instead, I will hand you over to General George S. Patton, my friend who is now invading Berlin like a storm. In the morning, he will take you to stand trial in Nuremburg. There, I am certain that you will be found guilty of high crimes against humanity. When you are, you will all hang by the neck until you are dead!"

The former Nazi's were so frightened by the German words that sprang from the strange woman who was dressed as a U.S. General that none of them uttered one single word. When a truck pulled up escorted by a U.S. Army Jeep, the Nazi's were forced to board at once. As the truck and Jeep pulled away, Mary smiled at Edith and the men who stood with her.

"That's it then. One more chore to do and then my Teams are going forward in time and back home to London. Edith, if I were you I'd take care of yourself better. Get more sleep and protect that voice of yours. Drink a glass of red wine every night. It will let you sleep better. If you do, then you'll live to be well over one hundred years old and I'll be able to see you again."

"Do you mean that I could die soon?" Edith asked. "But I feel so well!"

"You will die when you die!" Mary Sweet laughed. "So will we all. But just remember to be kind to yourself. Here's my Chief Inspector's business card with my address and phone number on it. I'll be back at this address in the year two-thousand and twenty-four and for twenty-something years before that. So whenever you get back to London do look me up. Go to any police station in the United Kingdom and tell them that we're friends. They'll give you my current address. You might have to sing for them!"

As Edith took the card and the two women began to laugh, McMouse peeked out of Mary's Uniform Jacket.

"So it's time to go to Moskva again and see if Putin is alive, Chief?"

"That's right, mouse friend. Mind you, with Hitler now held captive, that changes the course of history again! For all we know, Gusto Gatwick might never be born nor will his wife! And as for Putin? Perhaps the old Soviet Union will never survive! There could even be a new Czar in Mother Russia and that really would be transformational. Just think: no more Wars. Maybe not even in Korea or anywhere else on Earth. And China might even be our friend."

"That could also be true, Chief. We'll just have to wait until we get there to find out."

As they re-boarded the Space Time Machine, which had been renamed VICTORY by an American engineer who had worked on a new propulsion system, Mary waved again at Edith.

"Thank you, *mon cheri*!" Mary shouted to her French friend as the Space Vehicle's engines began to wind up. "Thank you, too, to everyone who has helped us win this War a year before it was supposed to be won!"

Edith waved back at her and smiled a huge big smile. "*Si vous plais!*" she shouted back. "Thank you too for everything you and your Teams have done for us."

When Mary and McMouse had taken their seats in the Command Unit, they looked out the window as dawn lit up the skies over Northern Europe.

"One more small Mission, mouse," Mary said to her friend. "Then it's home and I'm never leaving England again. Not on a Mission like this one."

"I hope you're right, Chief. But you never know. We could get another call or Telegram from the King and then…"

"Go to sleep, Senior Detective. Oh, and by the way. McMouse, you're out of Uniform. You're now a Chief Detective with the Mouse Squad of the London Police Force."

"Chief? I made Chief? Says who?"

"Says me, Winston Churchill, George Patton, Dwight Eisenhower and our current King in this time, King George the Sixth who some call King Edward."

"King George? But what about Edward the First? We're not going back in time to Scotland."

"Nope! That monster is dead and long gone. I mean the current King of this time. The one who is father to the Queen in modern times, Queen Elizabeth the Second."

"It's all so confusing, Chief Inspector. Way too confusing. I don't know about you, but I never want to fly in a Time Machine again. I'll leave that to Doctor Watson and Sherlock Holmes."

"That's right, mouse Chief. Leave it to the Ghosts who started it all.

When Mary and McMouse had reboarded the giant Rocket, the Officer on Duty ordered the VICTORY to blast off. The stars came out as they rocketed into a low altitude orbit around the Earth. Due to the advances in the propulsion system of the Starship, the space vehicle no longer had to go faster than the speed of light to move forward and back in time. Instead, a new Military Officer was sitting in the Captain's seat where Sarah Scots had always sat.

"Mary Sweet, this is Captain Johnson," Mary heard in her head. "Sarah Scots sends greetings to you. She's now a Commander with the Royal Marines and is based in Paris. She says that she'll meet you in Russia where she'll take charge of the VICTORY."

"Will she join us, Captain Johnson?" Mary thought back. "Tell her I'd appreciate it if she would."

"That's affirmative, General. Dwight Eisenhower knows all about your present and last Mission. He read everything there is to read about Twenty-First Century history that was given to him by the new President, Joe Biden. He ordered me to tell you that Putin is a lame duck and, if attacked, won't give anyone a command to fight back."

"Oh, thank God again!" Mary thought to the Captain. "Thank you, Sir. Now I'll have a good think about what I'll say to Putin if and when I scc him again."

Chapter 14

The Final Countdown

As Mary Sweet's highly advanced Space Vehicle moved forward in time, on a broad expanse of beach in 1944 Normandy, France, General Eisenhower climbed off a Landing Craft in front of his troops. He turned to a soldier next to him who was the General's personal radio operator and asked the exact date.

"Sir, I make it out to be June the Seventh, Nineteen-Forty-Four," the Army private replied as he waded through the light surf to what the American's had designated on their battle maps Omaha Beach.

"June the Seventh," his General said as he looked up at the cliffs towering over the beach and scanned them. "I can't see one German here, Private. And no enemy bombers or fighters. Looks to me like General Mary Sweet was right! Hitler must be dead, that bastard, or captured as was her plan. We're not going to lose a single soldier this day and I'd thought over ten thousand of our boys would have died, which doesn't include German soldiers or anyone injured or missing. If the German Command is as smart as General Sweet, they'll surrender ASAP and give back France, Poland, Italy and what they've captured in Russia."

"Sir, I have HQ on the line for you," the Private said as he pulled the phone from the sack on his back. "They say it's urgent, sir."

As the two men walked onto the golden beach, Eisenhower took the handset which the soldier held out to him, and listened intently.

"General Eisenhower, this is Winston Churchill," a deep rumbling voice stated from the small speaker. "I'm phoning you from Downing Street with some, ah, unbelievable news. I've had a message from our friend and Spy Edith Piaf who is now in Berlin. Hitler has been captured as well as many of his Officers and Political Nazi cronies. His Bunker has been overrun and we've taken captive an entire regiment. Herman Goering, who is the new Leader of that infamous Party, has been forced to surrender."

"Prime Minister, that truly is astonishing news," the American General replied. "I'm on Omaha Beach and can't see one damned German soldier here."

"Yes. That's the same report that I'm getting from General Montgomery. He's much further inland as you might know and has encountered not a single German soldier but *has* engaged with many French citizens who are welcoming him and the English Army."

"I just talked to General Patton, Sir," Eisenhower replied. "He's stormed Berlin with all of his tanks and troops. They've liberated the City and have freed many American, English and Russian soldiers who were held prisoner there. Speaking of the Russians…have you heard from Stalin?"

"Yes, I have. His Army is still bogged down near Moscow. The city is surrounded by thousands of German soldiers. He stipulates that the Allies including the French, Germans and Americans should wait until he destroys the German Army and then his Russian troops will join our Armies to take control of Berlin. Which, of course, is highly unlikely in the short-term."

Eisenhower looked at his private as he tried to think of an appropriate response. Grinning at the soldier, the General grunted as he looked toward the East. "Mister Churchill, we both know that all Stalin wants to do is divide the great city of Berlin. The madman is absolutely power mad! Sir, I talked to President Roosevelt this morning. He told me that out in a California desert, engineering teams are building a nuclear weapon powerful enough to destroy any city in Japan or any military compounds in Russia. Roosevelt is tasking General MacArthur, who was humiliated by the Japs when he was forced to leave the Philippines, to command a new Army not only to defeat the Japanese as quickly as we've defeated the German Nazis but also to push back Russian troops to their original borders should they be able to defeat the German Army forces surrounding Moscow. Roosevelt is convinced that Russia is the next global threat and, if they have their way and divide Berlin, they'll take over much of Europe."

"I agree with Roosevelt," the English Prime Minister replied. "General, congratulations. You can't be promoted, Dwight, because you already have your four stars, but I'm sure you'll serve your country in another significant role when this War is finally over."

Eisenhower gave the phone back to the private. Seeing a Sargent who was trudging across the beach toward him, he ordered the non-commissioned officer to erect a Command Centre on the beach, just above the high tide mark.

"This place is good enough for me and the rest of my men," General Eisenhower said to the private as the Sargent ran back to a Landing Craft to carry out the order. "Next stop Berlin but that can wait for a few days. I'll let General Patton have a great time in that City. Gosh, I wish I could see Patton's face when he sees the Nazi officers and meets Hitler. I wouldn't be at all surprised if that crazy General took out both of his special Colt 45's and executed the Nazi bastard with a single bullet through the head. Mind you, he'd let that Adolph say his prayers before he went to be judged by his Maker."

As he watched the Sargent lead a group of men back with a number of large tents, Eisenhower ordered a soldier who was carrying a small table to set it up so the General could use it. Getting a map of Europe and Asia out of his briefcase, the General spread it across the table and placed his sidearm on the paper to keep it from blowing off in the gentle wind.

"Right. Colonel, come over here."

A man in charge of the Omaha Beach landing walked to his General and saluted.

"You wanted me Sir?"

"Hell with official greetings, Colonel," Eisenhower stated dryly. "No saluting until we've fully secured this beach otherwise I could be shot by a German sharpshooter. Now look at this," Eisenhower said as he pointed to the map of Europe and Asia. "If, following the surrender of Germany, General's Montgomery and Patton sweep from Berlin toward Saint Petersburg and then on toward Moscow, they could be joined by General MacArthur and over five-hundred thousand American troops. What remains of the German Army will fight with us. They fear the Russians more than they fear God Himself. If that happens, and if we can topple the Stalin dictatorship, we'll control all of this." The General swept his hand over the entire map. "All that's left is China. Because they're communists, they'll be our next huge threat."

"If you say so, Sir, then I must agree," the Colonel replied. "But if the Allied Armies take over all of Europe and part of Asia, won't we be considered Imperialists by the rest of the world?"

Eisenhower grinned to his Colonel. "Yep, that's right. But remember, we have the Marshall Plan in place. We'll appease the entire world by rebuilding Germany, Russia and much of Europe.

We'll also rebuild Japan. By that, we'll demonstrate that our intentions are not Imperialistic but rather democratic and therefore sympathetic."

"Sir, I'm afraid I don't quite agree," the Colonel replied again. "General, I have a degree in History. And as you know, history often repeats itself. Power in the hands of the few and mighty can corrupt absolutely. If we force the American brand of democracy down the throats of the countries we've defeated, we'll create a force of Hatred that will be worse than the Nazi regime."

"Colonel, I must say that I agree with you. To be honest, I'm not sure that General MacArthur or Roosevelt will get the support of Congress to start another War against the Soviet Union following this God-awful one with Germany and Japan. The American public is tired of War. Hundreds of thousands of soldiers have died and many are still missing. While we've ended this War a year before we planned to, do we want another War now? Not even the President can make the American public believe that it's necessary."

"Sir, to that I fully agree with you," the Colonel said as he again looked down at the map. "History is a strange, strange thing. Hundreds of thousands of people can die and, unless you're affected directly, not many politicians give a Good Damn."

"I concur, Colonel. Those who served in this War have all been affected as have many throughout Europe. They alone understand what it's like to see so many people die or lose everything they've worked for all of their lives. If I've learned one thing during the past five years it's this: you can take a politician to the Garden of Eden. But rather than enjoying the fruits of victory all they'll want to do is eat a poisoned apple."

"Meaning, Sir?"

"Most politicians are really stupid, Colonel," Eisenhower said as he started to laugh. "Some are really smart like Roosevelt and

Churchill. But most? They don't give a damn about anyone. When the going gets rough all they want to do is save their own hides. And that includes Stalin. So they'll eat poisoned legislation just to get elected again."

"Yes Sir, General," the Colonel said as he also started laughing. "If nothing else, that Russian tyrant Stalin is a realist. When he hears that Berlin and all of Germany have now surrendered to our Army, he'll blow a gasket! He'll want another meeting in Yalta with the President and Churchill but those two reasonable men will certainly refuse it. So we'll just have to wait to see what happens. In my opinion, Russian communism is doomed and always has been. While our brand of democracy isn't perfect it's better than working under the thumb of a tyrant like Stalin."

` "Right you be, Colonel," Eisenhower replied. "Now, get a special team together. I want us out of her in two days at the latest. We march straight to Berlin."

"Yes, Sir." The Colonel walked away as the General looked to the sky.

'Mary Sweet, thank you so, so much and God Bless you,' the General prayed silently. 'Because of your stealth, courage and bravery, as well as the people who served with you, you saved many a life today.'

Ten days later, Eisenhower rode on top of a U.S. Army tank into central Berlin. There, he met his Generals Patton and Montgomery who had found little resistance by the German Army as they stormed into the centre of that bombed-out City. When the two Generals had met the new Nazi Leader, General Goering, they had forced him to sign an Unconditional Surrender of all of Germany. Goering, who's hand had been shaking as he signed that Treaty on a table in Hitler's Bunker, had taken a Luger from where it had been concealed beneath a chair and shot himself in the head before anyone could stop him. When Patton brushed the Nazi's blood off his face, he turned and grinned at General Montgomery.

"Monty, that's one dead Nazi General. Now all we have to do is get Hitler to kill himself. Where is he, anyway?"

"George, he's in a prisoner of war camp not far from here. We're treating him just like he treated our soldiers that were held prisoner by the Gestapo."

"Really? Monty, that means he's in solitary?"

The English General smiled which made his moustache stand up on both ends. "Solitary? Haha! My officers are making that son of a bitch clean all the latrines."

"A shit job for a real asshole," General Patton said as he watched a group of Nazi prisoners haul Goering's body up the stairs of the Bunker. "Let's go see Adolph, shall we? We'll see what he looks and smells like, the Nazi scum."

When the two Allied officers arrived at the POW camp which had been set up on the Western side of Berlin, they followed a private through a gate and then toward a long wooden structure that had just been built by the English Army. Standing on the steps near the front door, they could see a German Sargent on his knees scrubbing the wooden floor with a brush and a pail of water.

"Adolph Hitler, come to attention!" Patton's Adjutant ordered the prisoner. "Stand up, man, and salute."

When Hitler rose to his feet, the two Generals could see that his Nazi uniform was soaking.

"Adolph, it seems you've found your calling," General Patton said when the former Nazi Leader refused to salute him. "Your uniform is now perfect! And what's that I see sewn onto your jacket pocket? A gold-plated Nazi swastika? I think I'll have that as a keepsake."

Patton took out a small penknife. Opening it, he cut the Nazi emblem from Hitler's uniform.

"Now, I tell you what, Adolph. I'm giving you a choice to make. I know you don't understand English too damned well so I'm going to have Monty, here, translate my words for you. That okay with you, General Montgomery?"

"Right you are, General!" Montgomery replied. "Start talking and I'll translate."

"So here we go," Patton stated with a glint of ice in his two small eyes. "Option one. You can go to Nuremberg where you'll be tried, found guilty and be hanged like a pig. That's the choice of most of the English and American politicians that I've met. They'll have cameras there to record your every move and then, after they hang you, they'll bury you in an unmarked grave. But in that we're all historians, that's no way to treat the body of a former Nazi Leader, not even a murderer like you. All it will do is lead to long-term hatred. Look at what the Roman armies did to many captured leaders in Africa who were then killed by them. The bodies disappeared and hatred grew so much that Rome eventually fell which could happen to all of the Allied countries. The German people would hate us if they did not have time to mourn your death. So here's the other option that we're giving to you.

"Option two. General Montgomery and I will try you right here. You can choose any German you want to defend you. We'll have the entire trial recorded by a good stenographer in English and German. If, and I say if, you're found guilty, we'll then hang you right here. You're dead body can be collected by anyone you nominate and buried as you and your family see fit."

Patton could see Adolph Hitler thinking intently as he considered the two options. Then he smiled that very strange smile of his. He spoke one very small sentence then got back down on his knees and started washing the floor again.

"Monty, what did he say? Did he make his choice?"

"The man is adamant. He would rather be tried and hanged right here in his city of Berlin. General Eisenhower will be here tomorrow morning and he can be included as a judge in the trial."

"Oh, old Dwight wouldn't want to be concerned with any of this," Patton replied as he smiled. "Let the man be. He's gonna want to get off to Rooskie-land as soon as he can to take on that wise old chicken, Stalin."

Later that day, the trial for Adolph Hitler began in a room in the back of the prisoner's wooden structure. Hitler chose not to have a lawyer defend him but instead decided to defend himself. An English Army Colonel acted as the prosecuting attorney. In that there was no need for any testimony from the Allies or any witnesses, the former Nazi Leader took the stand first and last. As he spoke, a stenographer took comprehensive notes and a captive German officer translated Hitler's words.

"Mein Führer says that this trial is a sham!" the German Major said with words that rattled from his mouth. "He says that he is again the Leader of the Nazi Party since his friend Goering is dead. He says that he has won the War! He states that there never was any genocide of the Jewish People. That was a crime committed by the Politician Goebbels and his German General Himler."

Patton began to laugh and then Montgomery started, too.

"Major, old Adolph is saying that Himler and Goebbels weren't following his orders but their own orders?" Montgomery asked as he tried to stifle is laughter. "He had no idea that millions of Jews and other people were gassed in enormous ovens? But that's poppycock! George and I both saw them as we drove here. We saw the burned remains of bodies and the emaciated forms of the prisoners. *It is a matter of public record!*" Monty pointed at Hitler. "He is the Leader of the Nazi Party. He knew what everyone was doing. Millions and millions of men, women and children died at that coward's hand."

"Major, does the defendant have anything else to say in his defence?" Patton asked.

"Nein, General Patton. Mein Leader is finished with his defence."

"That's all he wants to say? Well then, let General Montgomery and I discuss this for a few minutes. In the meantime, and until we come back with a verdict, why not give the defendant a last meal?"

While Patton and Montgomery considered their verdict in another room, a German chef brought in two plates filled with Bratwurst, sauerkraut, potatoes and bread and two steins of beer. As the prisoner and his lawyer ate, Adolph looked out the single window at the blue skies of Germany.

"It is my fate to be a dead Leader of the Nazi people," Hitler said to the Major in German. "But I will be remembered for as long as people believe in a single, powerful leader of the entire world."

Thirty minutes later, Generals Montgomery and Patton came back into the room. As a U.S. Army soldier took photographs, Patton delivered the court's verdict.

"Guilty as charged, Adolph Hitler. Now, say your prayers to whatever God you might believe in, if you have a God. In two minutes, we'll hang you just outside the door and then your family can collect your body, as I promised."

"I do have a God," Hitler said in German. "The Major will translate as I speak. This court is a farce! And as to God, there is only one true God and that is Jesus Christ because I am and have always been Christian. That is a fact. I have already said my prayers. Hang me if you dare! I will scream as I die and all of my people who have gathered just outside this prisoner compound will know that I have been put to a cruel and unjust death. History will reveal that I, Adolph Hitler, is the true Emperor of the World! So it is written in my death, and so it shall be known forever."

Patton looked at Montgomery and smiled.

"The man has a point, Monty. We don't want him to wake the dead when he dies by hanging. We want this guy to have a rather peaceful death."

"You mean peaceful for us, our soldiers and the Germans who have gathered just outside the prison gates?"

"Yep, exactly." Patton looked Hitler in the eye. "Okay, joker. You've said your prayers? Then let me say a prayer, too." Looking up to Heaven, George Patton smiled and said, "Lord, I am a true believer in your great justice. We have found this man guilty. To keep the peace, I have only one option left. And that's this."

Using a pistol he took from the holster at his side, General George S. Patton took careful aim then let his grip slip. He fired once, hitting Hitler in the leg. He fired the weapon again, hitting him in the arm. He fired a third and fourth time, hitting the misfit leader in the groin and stomach. Firing two more times, Patton's bullets hit Adolph Hitler in both eyes.

"Well, Monty, that's that! The man was always blind to reason anyway, wasn't he? Now, he's truly blind."

"As well as blindly dead!" Monty replied. As the body was carried out of the room by two Germans who had said they were members of the deceased family, Patton took General Montgomery by his arm.

"General, it's time for dinner and a good bottle of German wine," Patton said to his new friend. "Let's celebrate a bit. Then we can figure out where to go from here."

"For me, George, it's back to London I go. I want to see Downing Street at peace for once in my life."

"A fine thing, too, Monty. So that's it. Victory at last and now I'm going to start thinking a little bit about writing my memoir."

"A memoir, George? You're not thinking of retiring, are you?"

"Me? Retire! Not on your life!"

As Mary Sweet and her tiny mouse were sitting in the Space Vehicle, a news broadcast from Berlin was transmitted directly to them over the Mouse Radio. The Report described the trial of Adolph Hitler and its outcome. It was only then that they both finally understood how much Hitler's execution had changed the course of history.

"McMouse, those two General's found Adolph Hitler guilty of Genocide and many other crimes against humanity. They had the foresight to execute him quietly so that the German people would not be haunted by hatred. After his death, Hitler's family and some German people buried him in a park near the old Reichstadt. Today, a very few people still honour him where he rests but for the most part, where he lies in a deep grave is now overgrown with grass and flowers. It can be deadly quiet except when the birds sing and, when the sun comes out, it's beautiful."

"That's what all the history book say now, isn't it Mary? Hitler wasn't killed by his own hand but was executed following the decision by the two Allied Generals who then went on to order his execution."

"Very true, McMouse," Mary replied. "The repercussions have been huge! Patton never died in a traffic accident following the end of that Godawful War but instead went on to become one of the best General's the U.S. Army ever had! He ended his career helping to defeat the Japanese then wrote a book on warfare that rivals the best such books ever published. And as for Mongomery? He became a champion scholar of History and ended his days as a professor teaching at Cambridge University."

"Isn't that amazing, Mary!" McMouse squeaked as he pulled out a history book from under his Space Vehicle's seat. "I brought this with me from the Global Mouse Library. It's already been updated to include all the history that has changed since we started this Mission. It's in English and it says, as I page on," the mouse said as he turned to a particular page and started to read, "that Stalin was defeated by the combined Armies of Germany, the United States, France, England and some members of the Russian Army who had survived the would-be invasion of Moscow. Stalin was imprisoned for life and the old Soviet Union collapsed."

"Which is now true, McMouse. Which might mean that when we arrive in Moscow on our Space Time Machine in the year Two-thousand and twenty-four, we may find that there is no Putin at all! In fact, we don't know what we'll find!"

"Which is a real hoot!" the mouse said as he began laughing. "It's very strange, isn't it? Change one single moment in history and, well, it's like a small pond. Drop a small rock into the centre, and the waves can change what's in it or the position of algae, small fish, or small frogs, or even the temperature. So it is with history."

"I agree," Mary replied. "Now sit back, my Mouse. Sara Scots has now come back to us as Captain. In a moment, she'll order this Space Time Machine to go immediately to the year she's targeted. I told her to take her time. I want at least a short nap and something to eat before we get to Moscow in modern times."

"I want the same things, Chief," the mouse replied as he sat down again on his tiny seat. "Good night for now and sleep well, too. Wake me when we're all there."

Which is exactly what she did. When Mary woke up, she saw that their Space Time Machine, VICTORY, had already landed in Moskva's Red Square. But when they disembarked, she was caught off-guard. Not only did the local residents of that Russian capitol city all speak English but the Square was no longer Red at all!

"Why, look, my Mouse Friend! Look at the flag over the tall Onion Domes! They're all Blue and White and a little bit of Yellow! Why, that's the Ukrainian flag, not the Russian flag!"

"Yes, Chief, that's exactly right!" the Mouse replied. "And look at the Red Eagle at the flag's very centre! It's as if the two countries have now combined as one single country."

"We'll have to find out what's going on," Mary said as they made their way toward what they thought would be Putin's old apartment if, of course, he had ever been born. "In ten minutes exactly, we'll know the new fate of the world."

Chapter 15

The Capture of Putin and the Death of General Gusto Gatwick

Entering what they thought would be the Russian Presidential Apartment through the front door, Mary and Senior Detective McMouse were met by a Royal Servant who spoke to them in both Russian and English.

"You are expected by the Czar and Czarina because of a note that was left to them by a man held hostage by Stalin after the end of the last giant War," the man dressed in Royal Livery said as he bowed to them. "The note states in fluent Russian that a Chief Inspector and General by the name of Mary Sweet should be expected in our Palace today at this precise moment. He knows this because before he was captured by Stalin, he worked as a Chef for General Dwight Eisenhower when he had his residence in this very room. My Mistress, Czarina Anastasia the Second asks for you to follow me up to her Highness's living area."

As Mary ascended the ornate marble stairway with McMouse on her shoulder, she realized just how much history had changed.

"McMouse, the last time we were near here this was Putin's apartment but we had no time to look around!" Mary whispered to her tiny friend. "Look at what he'd stolen from the Russian people!

The works of Art hanging from the walls. Is that a Renoir and next to it a Monet? The crystal chandeliers! The priceless jewelry resting in those amazingly lit display cases along with the Faberge ornate eggs. The man Putin is a thief as well as a liar and a murderer. If he's still alive somewhere we'll have to find him and arrest him"

"Chief, it really must be just what we'd all hoped," the Mouse whispered back. "Putin isn't alive! He was never born! The apartment is now a palace just as it was during the reign of Czar Nicholas the Second. Look around. Do you see any sign that Putin ever lived here?"

At the top of the stairway, a young woman with jet black hair and glinting green eyes, wearing a white gown with red, blue and embroidered flowers sewn onto the bodice, waited for them. When Mary and her Mouse friend climbed up the stairs to her, the Czarina extended a small and elegant hand.

"As you know, we've been expecting you. You are the English Chief Inspector Mary Sweet, are you not?" the young woman asked as Mary took her hand in a warm greeting. "My husband would also like to meet you. We have a great deal to discuss. You and I have never met but I am the great-grand-daughter of the only surviving family member of the late Russia Czar, Nicholas the Second. I am named after her. My name is Anastasia and when our joint Parliaments both here and in the Ukraine Republic asked me to serve, I agreed to do so for the rest of my life. When I was installed as the first Czarina in oh, how many hundreds of years, I chose this fine man to marry me. He is an ancestor of the great Czarina, Catherine the Great."

"So nice to meet you, Czarina Anastasia," Mary said as she curtsied before the Royal Russo-Ukrainian Queen. "And I have much to discuss with you, too. Just to get started, have you ever heard of a Russian man named Vladamir Putin? He is much older than you are and, though it might sound very confusing and I'm sure you won't understand, he is now, or might have been, the autocratic

President of Russia. In a time that is parallel to the time we're now in, there is no such thing as the Russo-Ukrainian Republic and never will be."

"Putin? Why yes, I've heard of him. When I became the Czarina of our new Russian Republic, our loyal Armies captured him. He is now imprisoned in a basement not too far from this apartment."

"Eureka!" Mary Sweet shouted. "That's it! He has been born but has now been captured and is being held prisoner by you."

"That is quite correct, Mrs. Sweet," a tall man said as he walked into the large living room to join them. "As my wife has just told you, the man is now a prisoner and will face trial soon for all the crimes he committed against the Russian people."

"What about the Ukrainian people?" Mary asked. "Isn't there a War in the Ukraine right now?"

"No," the Czar replied. "The Russian Army agreed to surrender when Putin was captured. They have helped our many Western Allies rebuild what was destroyed in the Ukraine."

"Good stuff!" Mary said, her eyes wide as saucers. "Sir, you are related to the Czarina Cathcrine the Great?"

"I am, Mrs Sweet. I am a distant ancestor of hers. My name is Czar Nicholas the Third. I am the great-great-grandson of the Czar who was captured and assassinated by that thug Lenin back when the Russian crown was overthrown."

"So, here we have two grown ancestors of former Russian Czars who have started a brand-new nation," Mary Sweet stated with a knowing look to her Mouse friend who still sat on her shoulder. "Czar and Czarina, I have a favour to ask. Would you mind if I visited Putin in his basement prison? I know exactly where it is because, a few years ago before you set up your new nation, I was trying to catch him."

Anastasia ordered a servant and a Russian army officer to escort the Chief Inspector to the basement prison of Vladamir Putin. As they crossed the Square that had been re-Christened the Red and Blue Square by the Russian people, McMouse crawled down Mary's arm and climbed back into her pocket. There, he found the Mouse Communications device that a Russian mouse relative had lent him. Dialling a telephone number, he heard the device make a noise like a clap of thunder then, when the signal had been established, he said,

"McMouse to all Animal and Human Teams. We're on our way to see President Vladimir Putin. History has changed more than we thought it would. That Putin is now in the hands of a new Russo-Ukrainian democratic government and I'm certain is due to stand trial in a Russian court soon. If any Human Team members are receiving this, can you contact the English Prime Minister and King Charles and ask us for new instructions. Over."

A hiss came from the secret phone and then a man he immediately recognised as the present King of Great Britain began talking.

"Senior Detective McMouse, this is me, your King Charles. By Royal degree, you are hereby commanded to take Putin into custody. Tell any Russian police or soldiers that you meet that this new instruction has been agreed with the Russian government. Too, if you see General Gusto Gatwick, you are instructed to capture him, wound him or kill him outright. That is all. This will not be followed by a signed instruction. Give my command to Mary Sweet as soon as possible."

When the signal immediately died, and the King had stopped talking, the mouse peeped out of his Chief's pocket. "Mary Sweet, the King commands us to take Putin into custody and to find that traitor General as soon as possible. With any luck, we'll be joined in our new Mission by our Animal and Human Teams."

"Good news, Mouse Chief" Mary said as she approached a single red and blue steel door. "We're almost to the prison. In a moment, we'll meet Putin again. Mouse, do you feel anything rather odd? Like tingling in your hands and feet?"

"As a matter of fact, Mary. All of my paws feel like they are full of pins and needles."

"Good. That's our Space Time Machine coming back here to join us. Soon, it will release another burst of energy but this time much stronger. Then, we'll all find that we've gone back in time, but not too far back. When that happens, we'll easily capture the General and Putin."

As the Russian soldier unlocked the prison door, Mary looked up to see a burst of light as bright as the sun fill the skies above the New Moskva. When the soldier saw the burst of light, and thinking that Moskva was under attack by a nuclear weapon, he opened the door and ran into the prison. As he did, the entire stone building began to shake. Light filled the large room lined with stone and, as Mary and McMouse watched, the Russian soldier disappeared. He was immediately replaced by a group of U.S. Army officers whom Mary and McMouse had seen before.

"See, mouse? History is now repeating itself!"

The room was filled with the sound of automatic gunfire. Two American officers led a platoon of soldiers across the room under a hail of Russian fire. Mary, knowing that one of the officers would be killed in moments, tackled him as a group of Russian soldiers led President Putin and Gusto Gatwick, again dressed as a Russian General, to the back of the dark, smoke-filled room. As Mary and the mouse watched, a woman appeared beside Putin's side. Seeing that it was his daughter, when he saw her point a gun at his head, the Russian President shot her in the stomach. As she fell over, Gusto Gatwick picked up the woman's weapon and pointed it at Putin.

"Now, my former President, get ready to die!" Mary and the mouse heard Gusto say in the sudden silence. Looking behind her, she could see that her Animal and Human Teams had entered the room and had helped the U.S. Army to kill or wound all of the Russian soldiers. "You remember who I am, do you not, Vladimir?"

"You are my General and servant, Gusto Gatwick. Where is your wife, Tully Gayle?"

"She is dead, you rat. You helped to kill her in a day not unlike today. Can't you feel the pins and needles in your hands and feet? History is repeating itself but it's different than it's supposed to be."

"I always thought you were crazy, General. You have defied me one time too many. Now, you will feel what it's like to have your belly filled with Russian lead."

Gusto Gatwick took one step back and as he did, Putin grabbed a Kalashnikov from a dead Russian soldier. Opening fire, he swept the weapon's bullets over the floor and toward the traitorous Russian. Gatwick returned fire but all that Putin did was duck. Aiming his weapon at Gatwick again, he emptied the automatic rifle over the entire length of the General's body. As Gusto Gatwick collapsed onto the floor, clutching his stomach with both hands, he looked up and saw Mary Sweet.

"You! You are my murderer! Mary Sweet, my dying wish is that you will someday die like I am right now. In a foreign country with no one around to take your hand and say that they love you."

As the Chief Inspector watched, the traitorous General closed his eyes and breathed his last breath.

"I'm free! I'm free at last!" Mary yelled to anyone who would listen. "With this single man at last dead, I can finally retire."

"What are you talking about," Putin hissed. "Beware, you English woman, or you will face the same fate as that Spy from England did."

Mary walked toward him and, as she did, Putin aimed his weapon at her head. "Attention!" he commanded. "Step away or I will kill you just as I have killed this General."

"Do you think he is a General, Vladamir?" Mary asked as she kicked a handgun away from Gatwick's dead body. "He was no Russian General. He's a British General and a Spy. He's impersonating a Russian officer and you fell for all of his lies. He told you that he would make you Emperor of the Earth, did he not?"

"He did," Putin sighed. "Not once but many times."

"And see where he's led you? To a Russo-Ukrainian prison." Mary looked down to see her tiny Mouse Friend crawl out of her pocket, up her arm, and take a standing position on top of her head. "Do mice speak English or Russian, Vladamir Putin?"

"Mice? Are you mad? No, they do not speak at all. This is no prison! This is my basement where I sometimes torture those that I hate."

"Wait one moment, Vladimir. In two-twitches of a mouse's ear we'll go forward in time again. Then, you will remember where you really are."

The hands and feet of everyone in the room began to tingle. There was a blast on white light and, when it went out, ex-President Vladimir Putin found himself standing in a small prisoner's cell with his hands and feet shackled together.

"What is going on! Where am I!" he shouted from behind the bars of his cell door. "A moment ago I had an automatic rifle in my hands. But now?"

"Nothing at all except some steel of your shackles, is that right?" Mary asked.

"I want out of here!"

"Oh, that will happen very, very soon, won't it mouse?" Then, clearing her throat, she looked through the bars and smiled. "Mice do speak Russian, you know that don't you? Which is why, as I speak the words that my dear King Charles ordered me to deliver, my Chief Inspector Mouse will translate for your benefit." Turning to the mouse that still stood on her shoulder, Mary asked, "Chief, are you ready to translate?"

"That I am, Chief!" the mouse replied. "Take it away!"

"Right. And now, by order of the King of Great Britain, I am taking you, Vladamir Putin, into custody. You will be brought back to London and then to the Hague and there you will be tried for murder and genocide. When you are found guilty, you will be kept in a Ukrainian prison for life."

"No, the King of England would never do that to Vladamir Putin," the prisoner screamed. "I am still the President of Russia which is far more powerful than Great Britain."

"Are you, now. Then who is living in your apartment. Answer me that."

"I remember," he said, spitting the names. "The so-called Royal Family. The ancestors of those who survived the purge made by Lenin on the former Czar of Mother Russia."

"That is so very true, Vladamir. It's odd, isn't it? You have the same first name as Lenin and you are also a threat to the world and to democracies anywhere. The Royal Couple in your apartment are the rightful heirs to the Ancient Russian throne and have been crowned Czar and Czarina by the Russian people when they were nominated for those positions by this countries new democratically elected Parliament."

"Impossible!" the former Russian leader yelled. "I will escape from this jail. This is, after all, my basement. I have hanged and tortured many guests of mine in here."

"You will escape? Really, Vladamir? Even when this room is filled with so many soldiers all of whom hate you passionately?"

Former President Putin looked through his prison bars to see a room full of Russian soldiers all holding automatic weapons. As he did, his face turned as red as any wild radish Mary Sweet had ever seen. Then, the prisoner smiled as wide as a carved Halloween pumpkin.

"Of course I will. Fortunately, no one had time or the thinking to search me."

The next thing that Mary saw through the prison cell bars was a handgun being pointed at her. "You think I will not shoot? Or that you'll be able to step aside and avoid the bullet? Think again, Sweet. There is only one metre separating us."

Seeing the danger to his Chief, the Mouse jumped off her shoulder and scampered to a Russian soldier who was holding the cell door keys. Whispering to him in Russian, the soldier nodded then stepped over to the steel door and opened it.

"Good," Putin said as he placed a hand on the soldier's shoulder. "You see? I still have friends. This weapon that I hold in my hand is a very good German handgun. It has twelve chambers and I have one round in the barrel. This means I have thirteen bullets and I will use them all to kill you and any soldier who gets in my way. I will take the elevator up to my apartment. There, I will ask my

Russian Army officers to help me escape to another country who would want me to help lead them, like China or North Korea."

Mary started to laugh as did her mouse friend. "What do you think of the plan that Putin has? Unfortunately, he doesn't know current history."

"Well, Mister Putin," the tiny mouse said to the Human Former President in Russian. "The world of today is at peace, unlike the world you helped to create. There is no North Korea anymore. There is only Korea. And as for China, they are now one of the most successful communist democracies in all of the world. As for the rest of your friends. India is now controlled by a democratic process that rebukes any other country that wants to force an autocracy on its people. You may be able to go to South Africa. After all, the people there are still mostly white skinned by are also ruled by a democracy. Or, you could simply kill yourself or allow yourself to be taken into custody. Those are the choices and they are very slim."

"You do speak Russian," Putin said with wide eyes. "Because you do, you are probably a Spy for Great Britain. Either that, or what I am hearing is crazy! Sorry, mouse and my great enemy Mary Sweet. Thank you but I'll take my chances and find a new country to rule."

As Putin moved toward his elevator that he knew would take him up to his Presidential rooms high in the apartment building above them, he pointed his sidearm at the soldiers who pointed back at him with many automatic weapons. Now striding to the silver door Putin pushed the UP button and, waiting, lowered his heavy revolver.

"You should never believe me, Mary Sweet. This weapon only has six cartridges in it. But I can still shoot you anytime I want to," Putin grinned as the elevator opened. "I will see you somewhere in Africa or South America. After all, Adolph Hitler is reputed to have lived out his days somewhere in Argentina."

"You really do look something like Hitler," Mary stated as she pointed an automatic weapon at Putin's head. "Hitler is dead, of course. Remember General George Patton, the man who helped win World War Two? He killed Hitler with any number of bullets, hitting him finally in both of his eyes. That will happen to you in a few moments. Now, Vlad-my-man, lay down that weapon before someone shoots you and takes you into custody again."

"I have always told you. You will never take me alive."

When the steel door opened, Putin stepped aboard the elevator, Mary looked at McMouse who had climbed up her body to stand on her shoulder again. "Mouse, why is it that dictators think that they're all invincible."

"Only the Good Lord of Mice knows, Chief Inspector," the tiny critter said as he began licking his furry paws. "Soon, that man will be in our custody as the King commanded or he'll be dead. That's D E A D. Dead."

"We'll have to wait and see what happens, Mouse." Looking to the soldiers and her Teams, Mary gave them all a single wink with her right eye. "Okay, all of you. Let's get upstairs. The Czar and Czarina don't know that Putin is coming up to see them but, when he gets there, I'd say that we'll all give him a big surprise. Sargent, you were on duty at the U.S. Embassy? Why are you here?"

A rotund U.S. Army Sargent stepped forward and saluted. "Name is Bilko, Ma'am, Sargent. I was coming home when I received an instruction from my Captain to high-tail it over here due to some shooting that the Royal Couple upstairs had heard. When I got here, I came down into the basement to look for the source of that gunfire. When I saw the Russian soldiers and your good self and that talking mouse, I just thought I'd hang around to see what happens."

"I'm so glad you stayed, Sargent! By the way, do you know anything about elevators?"

"As a matter of face yes, Ma'am, I do."

"Then please stop the elevator, Sargent. Turn off all the electricity down here or somehow jam the cables so that Putin is stuck between floors."

"That's easy, Chief. Before this blasted Mission I was an elevator technician for Otis."

"Good, Sargent. Very, very good! Carry out my request now, please."

Marching up to the elevator, the beefy Army Sargent opened the electronics door at the side of the elevator and, taking a screwdriver out of his jacket pocket, rammed it into the control panel as hard as he could. They all heard the screeching of the elevator's brakes as the car came to a stop.

"Completed as ordered," the Sargent said as he walked back to join the other soldiers. "That Putin has about thirty seconds to get out of the elevator car. Then the wires holding it in place will start to bust when the brakes fail."

"Oh, don't we all love it!" Mary said as she clapped her hands three times. "Now. Let's get upstairs to help the Czar and Czarina.

Above the basement prison and stuck in the elevator car, Putin pushed the UP button again and again but the car wouldn't move. He removed a small red phone from its box and, pushing a button, waited impatiently until he heard a woman's voice at the other end.

"To whom am I speaking, please?" the woman's voice asked.

"This is President Vladimir Putin!" the man roared down the phone. "The elevator is broken and I'm stuck! Get someone down here to get me out or fix this right now!"

"This is Czarina Anastasia the First, Mister Putin. Of course we will comply with your request. Wait there a few minutes, please."

When the line went dead, Putin threw down the phone at the sound of that haughty woman's voice and started beating on the steel elevator doors. When nothing happened, he placed his fingers into the gap and, using all of his immense strength, slowly opened them. Looking out the door, he saw an opening just above him. Reaching up, he grabbed the lip of that opening with both hands and, pulling himself out of the car, he dangled for a moment in the cold darkness of the elevator shaft.

"Oh, that there was a god above me," the former President whispered. Then, pulling as hard as he could, Putin pulled himself through a door. Finally standing on a hard floor that felt like wood, even in the total darkness he realised he was in a long hallway. "Good! This is the hallway that leads to my apartment. I know this place by heart so who needs any light. Fifty steps forward and my apartment door is right there. Open it and I'll be home and safe."

Walking forward in the darkness, Putin began to count. When he came to 'twenty-seven' he unexpectedly hit a hard cold wall. Using both hands, he tried to find the keypad that would open a door but found nothing, only an old-fashioned door knob.

"What happened to my keypad!" he whispered into the darkness. "Perhaps I'm on the wrong floor or made a wrong turn somehow."

Then the lights came on. Taking out his handgun from the coat pocket he'd pushed it into when he climbed onto the elevator, Putin saw a woman in a white gown striding down the hallway toward him.

"Mister Putin, you are very welcome to our home!" the woman stated with apparent delight. "I am Czarina Anastasia."

"Your home. This is mine! All of it is mine including the entire country of Russia. Soon, the Ukraine and the world will also be mine!"

"Oh, so you are Emperor Putin?" the woman said as she smiled. "Well, you're very welcome anyway. And may I present my husband, Czar Nicholas."

As a tall young man walked out of the shadows and up to the woman who said she was his wife, Putin couldn't help but start to chuckle as he raised his weapon. "It is a pleasure to meet you both! May I tell you that I have the same first name as Vladamir Lenin who took so much pleasure in having your Czar ancestor killed as well as most of your other ancestors. In three seconds, you both shall follow them into death and a dark unmarked grave."

"Before or after you burn us?" the Czar said as he smiled. "Mister Emperor, may I ask you a question?"

"One and only one. And then I will kill you both."

"I understand. But my question. Who are those men standing behind you?"

"Behind me?" Putin said without moving. Thinking that he was trying to be fooled the former Russian Leader simply smiled. "No one is behind me. You can fool a man one time but not twice. Mary Sweet tried to fool me down in the basement. She said that I was a prisoner but I'll never be taken prisoner. Who's behind me? Why nothing. Only a wall."

"Ah, but that's where you are wrong, Prisoner Putin," the Former Russian President heard from behind him. Turning around, he saw ten armed Russian soldiers and closest to him, a Russian officer who frowned deeply at the Former President. "I am General Constatine Karl Marx, head of the Russian Army that guards our Royal Couple. And yes, I do look much like my English and German ancestor who was the father of Communism. I have no beard but I resemble him very much. And yes, you were fooled into thinking you could find safety but, well, that will never happen. Drop that stupid weapon and put up your hands."

Looking at the armed General who did look rather like Karl Marx, Putin narrowed his small eyes and smiled. "General Marx, may I ask you one question?"

"No, you may not, Prisoner. Get down on your knees and put up your hands or you will be shot." Pointing his Ukrainian automatic weapon at the Former President, the General smiled. "Now we must all wait for Mary Sweet. My instructions are simple. Keep him here until she gets to us or, should he try to escape, wound him but do not kill him."

Putin smiled for what he thought would be his last time then put the gun to his head. "I told Mrs Sweet that I will never be taken alive, General, and I won't! Now, if you will excuse me, I go to join my ancestors."

But when Putin pulled the trigger once and then again and again, all he heard was a 'Click'. "This weapon is loaded!" he shouted as he opened the chambers. "I loaded it myself."

"Ah but you used old Russian bullets or duds, isn't that possible?" the General asked. "If you killed yourself, it would save the world a great deal of trouble. With any luck, you will be tried and hanged like the dog you are."

"I will never be hanged!" Putin shouted as he turned from the General. "I will join my family and my other ancestors right now!"

Running past the surprised figures of the Czar and Czarina, the General watched as Putin made his way down the dark hallway and toward the open elevator door. Pushing a button on the wall beside him, the General turned on the hallway lights. Now seeing the receding figure clearly, he hoisted the stock of his Ukrainian automatic weapon to his shoulder and, looking down the site, took careful aim. Using a single finger to place the weapon in single shot mode, he depressed the trigger. The bullet hit Putin in the back. The Czar and Czarina also watched as Putin roared like a wounded elephant and collapsed onto the hallway floor.

"Good shot, General Marx," he heard a voice say from behind him. Looking around, he saw a woman in a simple English Police uniform step toward him. "Just as I was hoping. The coward ran for it and was wounded." Turning toward the Czar and Czarina, Mary Sweet bowed then curtsied. "You know that my ultimate employer is the King of Great Britain. He has told me that you will have no problem if I take that man, who is wanted for murder and genocide across Great Britain and other parts of the world, into custody."

"Mary Sweet, that would be a great pleasure if you would," the Czar said as he smiled broadly. "If you did not, and I have discussed this with my wife, we would worry that mobs would descend on Moskva from all around the old Ukraine. They would take that murderer and roast him in a pit of fire then they would attach him to any rocket they might have left and, when it had blasted off and was a safe distance from any other human, explode it. But, and here's the thing, Mrs Sweet. If that had happened, Putin's remains would have been spread all over the Old Soviet Union. Which means, a death like that could have incited yet another revolution, one no one needs at this point in our new history of peace."

"Right you are, Czar Nicholas," the Chief Inspector said as she walked down the hallway toward her new Prisoner. "McMouse, where are you?"

"Right here, Chief," the mouse replied. Looking back, Mary saw the tiny mouse on the shoulder of the Czarina. Standing next to him was another small mouse. "Mary Sweet, meet my cousin the Czarina of the Russian Mouse Kingdom, Tina-Toy Tolstoy."

"Good God, mouse, how many cousins do you have?"

"At the last count done by my good wife, Betty, over one hundred and fifty-five, thousand three hundred and seven two."

"Stop mouse!" Mary laughed as she continued to walk toward Putin. "Call an ambulance, would you? Otherwise, this prisoner idiot will bleed out all over the floor! Tell all the members of our Human and Animal Teams that we're now done with our mission. Load the body of Gusto Gatwick onto our Space Time Machine and tell them to get onboard, too. You and I will follow in just a few minutes once we've managed to stabilize this Putin creep."

"Roger that, Mary Sweet," the mouse said as he took out the tiny communications device for one last time. Looking at the mouse who stood next to him, he smiled as he twitched his long whiskers. "Cousin Tina-Toy, do you want to come with us back to London for a few weeks? When you're done with your visit, I'll have our Space Team fly you back here."

"London! Why I would love to visit London," the mouse said in her Russian accent. "Perhaps I will meet the mouse man of my dreams in London. I've always wanted to marry an English mouse."

"Oh, I'm sure there's a mouse-fellow in London who might be interested," McMouse replied. "It seems like all of my female cousins are coming to London. Fortunately, our nest house has many, many bedrooms."

When the ambulance arrived, the Russian EMT experts placed the Prisoner Putin onto a wheeled gurney and took him down to the ground floor on the elevator that was now working again. Walking up to the Czarina, Mary Sweet stuck out a hand.

"Goodbye, Czarina Anastasia, and thank you so much for your Royal cooperation."

"It is no problem at all, my friend," the Czarina replied. Motioning to the servant who was walking toward her, the man servant held out a small box to Mary. "My husband and I would like to give you something for you to remember us by. Inside this box is a Faberge Egg that was given to Alexandra the wife of Czar Nicholas, by the English King who reigned his throne at that time. It is a very small egg but it is also very valuable. Do please keep this as a small memento of our time together."

Opening the box, Mary looked inside. Beneath the thin gold wrapping paper that protected the gift, Mary could make out the blue shell and the many diamonds that glittered in the bright lights of the hallway. "Oh, my God! Look at that! It's something that I will cherish for the rest of my life!"

Mary took the Czarina's hand again and, pulling her tight, kissed her three times on each cheek. "If you and your husband ever get to London, please come stay with me in my humble home. It is not a palace but it's a warm home, safe, and quite near the heart of London City."

"Someday, we will take you up on that," the Czar said as he bent over and kissed Mary on the cheek. "We will contact you when we make plans for the coming year. My wife is expecting her first child and, when we know when the child will be born, we will contact you by getting your phone number from my Royal distant cousin, King Charles."

"My thanks to both of you," Mary said. Motioning to her Mouse Chief, McMouse jumped from the floor and into Mary's Uniform pocket. "Goodbye to all of you," Mary continued, "and General Marx, thank you again for your accurate take down of the prisoner."

"It is no problem to serve my country and you," the General replied as he saluted her. "Mary Sweet, please be well. I salute you and the courageous Soldiers who have successfully captured this former President."

Finished with their very dangerous Mission, Mary and McMouse went outside to the Red and Blue Square and, looking up into the nighttime sky, saw a brilliant light streak once again across the Moskva sky.

"Mouse, when we went in to meet the Royal Couple, was it dawn or midday? I can't remember. Too much has happened."

"Chief, I don't remember either. I wonder what time of night it is now?"

A tiny Russian mouse pushing a brush looked up at Mary Sweet as the mouse cleaned the large Square.

"I know some English, my friend. It is almost seven o'clock in the morning and time for breakfast for most Russian citizens."

"Thank you, Russian mouse friend," Mary replied. "We'll have breakfast in London. Oh, I can't wait until I have a full English fry up again!"

"Me too, Mary Sweet," McMouse said as he crawled up her hair to sit on her head. "I'd like some fried cheese for breakfast. Betty McMouse makes fantastic fried cheese."

"Sounds great, mouse. Okay, in a minute or three we'll have our Space Vehicle here in the Square. When we board it, Sarah Scots will simply *think* the ship to be back in London. And we will!"

"Right you are, Chief," the mouse replied to her. "It will be so good to be home in only a few minutes."

Chapter 16

The Final Homecoming

"Which is exactly what happened, dear Human, Animal and Ghost friends," McMouse squeals to you as you read this final chapter.

Sitting by his home fire the night after the Mission had been won and the Scottish Advanced Space Vehicle had brought them across time and space and back to London, he takes a sip of whiskey from his small glass and winks at you.

"As Chief Mary promised, that immense Flying Dragon MacSweet met us above Loch Ness, flew into the large ship's cabin and came home with us. Sarah Scots has been promoted to Lieutenant Commander for her unbelievable bravery while all the other Team members received commendations from our new Scots/English Queen, Camilla, who is the wife of her Royal Consort, Charles, who stepped down from his Throne because he wants to protect all of the animals and nature in our world. Charles didn't mind giving up his Kingly status because Camilla is still much younger than he is. Someday, if medical science achieves all that it can, Charles will become much younger and he will accept a new Royal Crown and share the throne again with his good Queen.

"But you may ask, 'What became of the survivor's on the battlefield in Scotland between King Edward the First and Robert The Bruce, as well as the MacSquat Clan? I'll answer your question this way.

"The surviving English soldiers joined with the Scots to create one of the best countries in the known world. As you know, The Bruce married off his daughter Gloria to the son of the ancient, dead King Edward. They're children and their children's-children, who are part Human and part Flying Dragon, created the new technologies we have today. And, as was the promise, soon Dragons and Humans, together with Animals and Ghosts of all kinds, will be travelling again not across our Galaxy but into many new unknown Universes that have been created by All the Animal and Human Gods rolled into one. My mouse daughters and sons are now studying astrophysics and University and one day soon, they'll help to populate those new Universes with many, many mice and bring along their Human friends so that Humankind will always survive in a new kind of Eternal Peace.

"But what about everyone else in our various stories? Well…hold on and let me get another glass of Scotch Whisky."

As the husband of the large London nest poured his glass and set it on the small table, his good wife Betty McMouse came in with a glass of wine.

"Who are you squeaking to, husband of mine?"

"Oh, just a reader of this novel. See?" he said as he picked up a brand-new paperback from his table. "The person who is reading this."

"I've read it and enjoyed it truly," Betty replied as she pulled up a chair to sit beside her husband. "The problem, Tom-Jon, is that it's not finished yet. The last chapter is missing!"

"Betty, I'm dictating that last chapter right now to an unseen author who is transcribing my squeaky voice as we both sit here."

"Honestly?" she asked as she put on a pair of glasses and looked toward the far wall. "I don't see anyone."

"Oh, he's there, don't you know it. Right there. Hiding behind his Mouse Computer."

"If you say so, Tom-Jon, I have to believe you."

"So anyway, where was I?" McMouse takes a sip of whisky and clears his tiny throat. "So what happened to everyone else? Well, the entire Human Team is doing very well, thank our Mouse God. Francis McOuvre married the love of his life, Sally Orchid. They now have two sets of twins, all girls, and the last time I saw Francis he was taking golf lessons. He still swears that he'll never jump out of an airplane or go into any kind of Rocket again. Sally, of course, ended up joining the Royal Navy and very much enjoys her days as a Submarine Commander.

"As to everyone else? Well, Mary Sweet found out that she could afford to retire. She sold the Fabergé Egg that the Russian Royal Couple had given to her and made an absolute fortune! She saved it all in a number of Gilt Bonds and invested the rest in a wide variety of Scottish technology companies. Just like me, she is now back to walking the streets of our fair city as a London Police Officer."

"How is Mary anyway, husband," Betty asks as she cuts a piece of cheddar cheese from a big block that sits by the fire. "I haven't seen her since you all came back from Russia."

"I'm meeting her soon, darling. In fact, it's almost time for me to go to work."

Drinking the rest of his small glass of whisky, Betty helped the mouse on with his uniform coat.

"There! You look perfect, husband."

"Thank you, dearest. I'll see you and our children this evening."

As he made his way across the living room, someone pounded on the front door.

"I'll get it!" cried Betty. "If it's a Royal message I'll tell them you're still resting."

"No, my wife. I'll get it. If it's a Royal message I'll have to read it and send a copy to the Chief Inspector.

Opening the door, the mouse stepped into the rainswept street of London. As he did, Big Ben chimed 7AM. Looking down the wet cement path in front of his house, he saw a very small dog running toward him carrying an envelope in its tiny mouth.

"Oh, Dear God," the mouse sighed as he hunched his head against the rain and wind. "Another Royal letter? Today? But we just came home a few days ago!"

When the small dog padded up to the mouse, it bowed low before him.

"Honourable Sir. My name is China-chow-chow Dog. I am from Beijing, the capital city of the Republic of China. My good Emperor sends you Chinese Greetings!"

The tiny white dog gave the envelope to McMouse who promptly opened it. Inside, all he found was a card. The illustration on the front showed a small Chinese woman walking five dogs that looked just like China-chow-chow.

"Well, at least it's not a Top-Secret Letter from our Queen," McMouse said to his Dog visitor. "Lady China dog, why did your Emperor send this card?"

"To wish you a happy Chinese New Year! She asks you and your Chief Inspector to come visit her as soon as you can. There is an Emergency in our Chinese City that only you and your many Teams can solve. We need the kind of Help that only you and those that serve you can give. The Royal Russian Couple has highly recommended you to my Chinese owner. Please, please help us."

"Oh, Good Lord again! Another cry for help? Okay, China chow-chow, let me talk to my Chief. We'll give you a reply by this evening. Is that okay?"

"Oh, that would be wonderful," the white dog said as she pointed to the card with a very small paw. "If you look inside this card you will find a tiny, tiny Chinese communications device. It also has a recording on it that my Emperor now gives to you. If you agree to this Special Chinese Mission, all you have to do is say 'Yes' in any language at all. The device will then encode your answer and send it to a satellite above us. Thank you, our new Mouse Friend. We pay our respects to the Chief Inspector."

"Great," McMouse huffed as the small white dog padded back down the wet path and out into the street. "I really thought we'd never leave London or England again. Well, all I can do is ask Mary Sweet."

As the sun rose again over good Auld London Town, the mouse found the former Chief Inspector walking down the street. Standing by the park where she'd first met that fool and Spy Gusto Graves, now deceased, McMouse could hear his Human friend whistle a merry tune as he scampered closer to her.

"Good morning, Constable Sweet," the mouse said in Human language as he crawled up her leg. "Mary Sweet, I have a Chinese New Years card right here in my Uniform Pocket. You won't ever believe what's inside."

Mary looked down at him as he crawled up her jacket and sat on her shoulder.

"Mouse, is it a letter from…"

"No, no Top-Secret Letter from the Queen or even the former King!" the mouse squeaked in reply. "It's a letter that needs an answer to but we can do that later."

"Good!" Mary cried as she stepped down the path toward the Thames River. "Mouse, all I want to do is be a Constable for a year and walk the streets. Then I promise you, just as I promise everyone I meet, that I'm at last going to retire."

"Me too, Mary. I'm so very tired of it all. All the troubles in the world."

"And there will always be troubles, McMouse. But for once, let someone else solve them."

As the two walked toward London Bridge, Mary looked toward the French Restaurant where her husband, Hubert Sweet, and she always used to have lunch or dinner.

"Oh, my poor dead Hubert. I honestly thought he'd come back to me when he again met the Flying Dragon MacSweet."

"Maybe he will, Mary," the mouse replied. "In fact, I know he will."

As they continued along their London Beat, Mary looked down at the Gentle River Thames and then up at the London Eye. "By God above! Mouse, the Eye is here again and it's revolving! And look! A man in one of those glass carriages is waving at me with an umbrella!"

As they both looked at the London Eye, a flash of bright golden light blinded her as well as the mouse. When Mary found that she could see again, she looked beside her and saw a man that looked extremely familiar walking on her right-hand side.

"Hubert? Why it *is* you! I can't believe you're home in London again?"

"And see, dear wife? I'm really alive again."

When he reached out with a hand, Mary took it.

"You're so warm. Are you coming down with a flu again?"

"No flu," Hubert replied as he smiled broadly at her. "My hands are both warm because I'm so, so happy to see you again in the flesh this time, not as a Ghost."

Taking a clean white handkerchief from his tweed jacket pocket, Hubert brushed away the tears that were falling onto his wife's cheeks.

"But Hubert, I thought you'd be married by now to another Ghost."

"Married again. Me? Sweetheart, you're the only woman in the entire Universe that makes me happy. What would I be doing with two wives? And to be honest, I thought you would have remarried after I was murdered by that horrible creep, the Genera…"

"Hubert, forget him. The Mission is over now and we won by a mile and a half."

As Mary, the mouse and Hubert walked down the steps toward the River Thames, high above them Mary could see a small puff of smoke.

"Hubert, is that up there what I think he is?" she said, pointing to the smoke that was drifting away on the soft English winds.

"You mean the Flying Dragon McSweet?" Hubert replied as he started to laugh. "That's a relative of an ancient Uncle of mine. The Flying Englishman himself, McDonald McSweet."

"Hubert, I love it when you laugh. But except for McMouse, who is still standing on my shoulder, no more 'Mac's or 'Mc's for a while, okay? No more flying dragons. No more rockets. No more Generals. No more travel. No more…"

"No more nothing!" McMouse roared as he stood up on Mary's shoulder. "I told my good wife that I was staying home for good! And now, Mary and Hubert, do you know where we may have to go? To China, of all places."

"I've always wanted to go to China," Mary said softly as they all stepped down the concrete path leading to the French restaurant. "Maybe we should all take a fast airplane to see the Great Wall. Wouldn't that be lovely?"

"No, it would not be lovely," the mouse roared again. "If you want to go to see the Great Wall of China then do it with your husband. I'm going to stay on my beat. I'll find another Police Constable to ride on."

"Oh, mouse! Don't you know that I'm kidding? Now," she said as they climbed the steps toward the restaurant front door. "What shall we all have for an early lunch?"

As they all sat down at one of the small tables just inside the door, Mary looked at a larger table just beside them. There, a group of older people were having brunch. When an elderly woman ordered the waiter to open a bottle of very expensive champagne, Mary Sweet had a coughing fit and almost fell off her chair.

"Hubert, look at that woman!" Mary said as she sat up straight on her chair. "She sounds and looks just like…"

"Gertrude? No, darling," Hubert responded as he looked down at his menu. "That's my great-great Aunt Edwina. She's from Charlotte, North Carolina in America and has come over to stay with your neighbours for a few months."

"She's staying next door?"

"No, across the street. You see, *that* neighbour is a relation of mine. She's the daughter of my father or is she a niece? I can't remember. Anyway, Aunt Edwina Sweet is ninety-seven years old. She's very wealthy, you see, because she outlived all of the husbands she ever married."

"She outlived *all of them*? How many husbands did she have?"

"Eight or nine." Hubert looked across the room and called in a rather loud voice, "Waiter, here sir!"

The elderly woman at the table near them frowned. "Son, don't you *dare* shout in this here good old fashioned Francaise restaurant!" the woman shouted. "You may be a relation of mine, *but I won't have it*, hear now, boy!"

McMouse, who had crawled down to sit in Mary's pocket looked up at her. "I know, I know. It's time to go to China, right?"

"McMouse, anything but trying to deal with another old nag! I won't have it! Do you hear me, Hubert? That woman will drive me absolutely mad again!"

"Right, wife," Hubert said as the waiter walked toward their table. "Tomorrow, I'll book us all tickets to fly to China. Just tell me where and when and we'll go."

"Tomorrow, Hubert," Mary replied as she put her hand to her head. "I think I have another headache coming on."

"Which figures," McMouse said as he hopped down from the table and up onto the ledge of the window at the very front of the restaurant.

"Dear Reader, it seems to me that this is where we should end this novel. Poor Mary Sweet is facing even more trouble now that an Ancient Southern Bell will be living so near her. But, as I take my leave of you and anyone else reading this book, may I just say:

"I'LL BE DAMNED TO HELL IF I'M GOING TO CHINA! I NEED A HOLIDAY RIGHT NOW!"

And a final note from this author. As you can imagine, Mary is forced to take the next Mission so she'll be off to China rather too soon, if you ask me. Once again, she's going to need total bed rest for at least a month to allow her to get over the last Mission. But, as the old saying goes, 'What will be will be!' And that is so very true.

So until the next time in the next volume of the Mary Sweet Crime Series or until I see you either alive or as a Living Ghost,

This Mouse Author, or Human Author (I'm never quite sure what I am anymore. Perhaps a Flying Dragon named Mcrischeards?) bids you a fond *Adieu*!"

THE END
(or is it?)

Acknowledgements

As I write a few short paragraphs on this, my 69th Birthday, I take the opportunity to thank so many friends across the world who have made my life complete. Having just returned from my 50th High School Reunion (I went to Rolling Meadows High School, near Chicago Illinois, and graduated from there in 1974), I have finally made a decision that will positively affect the rest of my life: this mad Author is finally going home again. By 'home' I mean to the country and state where I was born in 1955. I'll be living in Crystal Lake, Illinois, about an hour from O'Hare Airport. So to those crazy 1974 Graduates from RMHS who made me feel so welcome and loved, I say THANK YOU for helping me finally make this huge leap of faith.

To fellow Graduates Carol Winkler, Michelle Lesley, Bill Arnold, Al Ahr, Mike Calabrese, Dave Lundahl (and his wife Shelly), Ann Debish Minor, Craig Dalquist, Brian Adamszyk, Patricia Callahan, Sandy Giese, John Gach, Steve Cage and all of the '74 Graduates that I've forgotten (what a Reunion, Dan Jordan! We'll never forget how hard you and the rest of the Reunion Committee worked);

To all the friends that I leave behind in Eyeries, County Cork especially my Mouse Friend Captain Frank McQuaid; to my children Kristin, Cathy and Jonathan for the love you give me;

And finally, to the Muse that is no longer here but – and I swear – she is standing just behind me, whispering into my ear about what I should write in conclusion:

To my loving Partner Carmel Pookey Murray (who should now have a surname Richards): Bless you and know that wherever this poor man roams you will always be at my side in spirit and in heart and mind.

Acknowledgements

    Bless you, Readers across the world. You make my Birthday Complete and Happy!

246

Tom Richards
Eyeries Village, County Cork, Ireland
Signing Off for Awhile but Not Forever!